Alfred Hudson Guernsey

Ralph Waldo Emerson: Philosopher and Poet

Alfred Hudson Guernsey

Ralph Waldo Emerson: Philosopher and Poet

ISBN/EAN: 9783743349285

Manufactured in Europe, USA, Canada, Australia, Japa

Cover: Foto ©Raphael Reischuk / pixelio.de

Manufactured and distributed by brebook publishing software (www.brebook.com)

Alfred Hudson Guernsey

Ralph Waldo Emerson: Philosopher and Poet

APPLETONS' NEW HANDY-VOLUME SERIES.

RALPH WALDO EMERSON:

PHILOSOPHER AND POET.

BY

ALFRED H. GUERNSEY,

AUTHOR OF " THOMAS CARLYLE—HIS LIFE, HIS BOOKS, HIS THEORIES."

NEW YORK:

D. APPLETON AND COMPANY,

1, 3, AND 5 BOND STREET.

1881.

CONTENTS.

EMERSON.

I.

INTRODUCTORY.

ABOUT twenty-five years ago Herman Grimm, a clever German writer, happened to be in the apartments of an American friend then sojourning in Germany. Upon the table lay a thin volume entitled "Essays by R. W. Emerson." He glanced hastily over the leaves, but could make nothing out of their contents, and declared that they seemed to him to be sheer nonsense. His friend assured him that this was by no means the judgment of competent persons in America, where Emerson had come to be regarded as one of the foremost thinkers of the age—a man whose utterances were worthy of all attention, and, even when they seemed to be obscure, of careful study and meditation.

Thus admonished, Grimm took up the book

again, read a little further, until flashes of light shone through the mist. He borrowed the book, took it home, and read still further ; then bought a copy, and set about the serious perusal of it. He found it no light labor. He had thought that he was well up in the vocabulary and grammar of the English tongue ; but he here found himself much at fault. He says that he was continuously embarrassed by the use of words new to him, or used in new meanings ; by the extraordinary construction of the sentences ; by the apparent absence of logical continuity, and the unexpected turns of thought, which met him everywhere. He was obliged to blast his way through the Essays by the aid of the dictionary.

We, to whom the language of Emerson is vernacular, can not well understand the kind of difficulty which the German found in comprehending him. Rarely do we find a word whose usual meaning we do not know, or which is used in an unusual sense. The sentences themselves are usually constructed in the simplest and most direct manner, going straight on from beginning to end, with rarely any involution or parenthetical clause. If the ordinary English reader finds any difficulty in getting at the meaning, it arises from the nature of the thought, not from the phrases in which it is expressed. The obscurity rests rather in the reader than in the writer. Grimm, having at last mastered the meaning of

Emerson, wrote an elaborate essay upon him, which was published in 1861, and republished a dozen years later, with additions and confirmations. He had, in the mean time, read and re-read the book; and now he says, "Every time I take it up, I seem to take it up for the first time." He continues thus:

GRIMM UPON EMERSON.

"As I read, all seems old and familiar, as if it was my old well-worn thought; all seems new, as if it had never occurred to me before. I found myself depending on the book, and was provoked with myself for it. How could I be so captured and enthralled, so fascinated and bewildered? The writer was but a man like any other; yet, upon taking up the volume again, the spell was renewed. I felt the pure air—the old weather-beaten motives recovered their tone. . . . Emerson regards the world with a fresh vision. The thing done or occurring before him opens the way to serene heights. The living have precedence of the dead; even the living of to-day of the Greeks of yesterday, nobly as the latter molded, chiseled, sang. For me was the breath of life; for me the rapture of spring; for me love and desire; for me the secret of wisdom and power.

"Emerson fills me with courage and confidence. He has read and observed, but he betrays no signs of toil. He presents familiar facts, but he presents them in new lights and combinations. From every object the lines of light run straight out, connecting it with the central point of life. What I had hardly dared to think—it was so bold—he brings forth as quietly as if it was the most familiar commonplace. He is a perfect swimmer on the ocean of modern existence. He dreads no tempest, for he is sure that calm will follow it. He does not hate, contradict, or dispute; for he understands men and loves them. I look on with wonder to see how the hurly-burly of modern life subsides, and the elements gently betake themselves to their allotted places. Had I found but a single passage in his writings that was an exception to this rule, I should begin to suspect my judgment, and should say no further word. But long acquaintance confirms my opinion. As I think of this man, I have understood the devotion of his pupils, who would share any fate with their master, because his genius banished doubt, and imparted life to all things."

Something like this has been the experience of nearly all of that slowly expanding but now wide circle who look up to Emerson as a master and guide. Few of them have come so to regard him from their own immediate intuition or perception. Most of them have read and studied him, because some one in whose judgment they had learned to confide had assured them that he was worth the reading or study. They have gradually grown up to Emerson, but have not outgrown him any more than they have outgrown the bards and prophets of the Old Testament or the Gospels and Epistles of the New Testament; Homer, and Æschylus, and Plato; Dante, and Shakespeare, and Milton. It is not well to speak with perfect confidence of the place which any man of our own age will hold in the judgment of after-ages. Yet we think that it will be long before the works of Emerson will die out from the record of human thought. Books of his, a thousand years hence, will stand on the same shelf with those of Plato, even though the English language, like the Greek, should have become what we foolishly call a dead tongue. We propose, in such brief space as is allotted to us, to present some estimate of the man and of his works.

II.

EARLY DAYS.

RALPH WALDO EMERSON was born in Boston, Massachusetts, May 25, 1803. He sprang on both sides from clerical stock. For eight generations there had been no time when one or more of his forefathers, on the paternal or maternal side, was not a minister of the gospel. Joseph Emerson was pastor at Malden a century and a half ago. His son, William, died as chaplain in the army of the Revolution. His son, likewise named William, graduated at Harvard in 1789, and ten years after became pastor of the First (Unitarian) Church in Boston. He was a noted pulpit orator, and several of his sermons were printed. He put

2

forth a "Selection of Psalms and Hymns," and wrote a "History of the First Church of Boston," which was published soon after his death. He died in 1811, in the forty-second year of his age, leaving a widow, a daughter, and four sons, of whom Ralph was the second.

It is worth while to trace something of the ancestral type, which was strongly impressed upon each of these four brothers. William, the eldest, graduated at Harvard in 1820, and soon after established a flourishing school for girls in Boston. Of him we are told that "although lacking the genius of the others, he was a natural idealist, a man whom it was a privilege to know."

Edward, the third brother, gave early promise of the rarest qualities. In 1832 he sailed for Porto Rico, where he died not long after. While the ship was sailing out of Boston Harbor, he wrote a tender farewell poem, which was published after his death in "The Dial," of which Ralph Waldo Emerson was then editor. Emerson gives this farewell a place in his own latest volume of poems, adding thereto some memorial verses to this "brother of the brief but blazing star; born for the noblest life; the loving champion of the right; who never wronged the poorest that drew breath." This memorial poem is among the best of its kind in our language, and is so characteristic of the author that portions of it may here find fitting place :

EARLY DAYS.

"IN MEMORIAM E. B. E.

" All inborn power that could
  Consist with homage to the good,
    Flamed from his martial eye.
He, who seemed a soldier born,
He should have the helmet worn,
    All friends to fend, all foes defy.
    Fronting the foes of God and man,
Frowning down the evil-doer,
Battling for the weak and poor,
    His from youth the leader's look,
    Gave the law which others took,
And never poor beseeching glance
Shamed that sculptured countenance. . . .

"There is no record left on earth,
    Save in tablets of the heart,
Of the rich inherent worth,
    Of the grace that on him shone
Of eloquent lips and joyful wit.
He could not frame a word unfit,
    An act unworthy to be done.
Honor prompted every glance,
Honor came and sat beside him,
    In lowly cot or painful road,
    And evermore the cruel god
Cried ' Onward ! ' and the palm-branch showed.

    Born for success he seemed,
    With grace to win, with heart to hold,
    With shining gifts that took all eyes,
      With budding power in college halls

As pledged in coming days to forge
Weapons to guard the State, or scourge
   Tyrants despite their guards or walls.
On his young promise Beauty smiled,
Drew his free homage unbeguiled,
And prosperous Age held out the hand,
And richly his large future planned;
And troops of friends enjoyed the tide:—
All, all, was given, and only health denied. . . .

"Fell the bolt on the branching oak,
The rainbow of his life was broke;
No craven cry, no secret tear:
He told no pang, he knew no fear;
Its peace sublime his features kept;
His purpose woke, his features slept;
And yet between the spasms of pain
His genius beamed with joy again.

" O'er thy rich dust the endless smile
Of Nature in thy Spanish isle
Hints never loss or cruel break,
And sacrifice for love's dear sake;
Nor mourn the unalterable days
That Genius goes and Folly stays.
What matters how or from what ground,
The freed soul its Creator found?
Alike thy memory embalms
That orange-grove, that isle of palms,
And these loved banks whose oak-boughs bold
Root in the blood of heroes old."

Of Charles Emerson, the youngest of the four
brothers, who died early, we are told that " he

combined the genius and saintliness of the others."
"The Dial" contains some papers written by
him entitled : "Notes from the Note-Book of a
Scholar," which one might suppose to be written
by Ralph Waldo Emerson. This for example :

THE UNITY OF HUMANITY.

"This afternoon we read Shakspeare. The verse so
sank into me that as I toiled my way home under the
cloud of night, with the gusty music of the storm around
and overhead, I doubted that it was all a remembered
scene; that humanity was indeed one—a spirit continu-
ally reproduced, accomplishing a vast orbit whilst individual men are but the points through which it passes.

" We each furnish to the angel who stands in the sun
a single observation. The reason why Homer is to me
like the dewy morning is because I too lived while Troy
was, and sailed in the hollow ships to sack the devoted
town. The rosy-fingered dawn, as it crimsoned the tops
of Ida, the broad sea-shore covered with tents, the Tro-
jan hosts in their painted armor, and the rushing char-
iots of Diomed and Idomeneus—all these too I saw.
My ghost animated the form of some ancient Argive.

" And Shakspeare, in 'King John,' does but recall to
me myself in the dress of another age, the sport of new
accidents. I who am Charles was sometime Romeo. In
Hamlet I pondered and doubted. We forget what we
have been, drugged by the sleepy bowl of the Present.
But when a lively chord in the soul is struck, when the
windows for a moment are unbarred, the long and varied
Past is recovered. We recognize it all; we are no brief
ignoble creatures; we seize our immortality, and bind
together the related parts of our being."

Or again this, which reads like a page dropped
out of Emerson's Essays :

INDIVIDUALITY.

"Let us not vail our bonnets to circumstances. If
we *act* so because we *are* so—if we sin from strong bias
of temper and constitution—at least we have in ourselves the measure and the curb of our aberration. But
if they who are around us sway us ; if we think ourselves
incapable of resisting the cords by which fathers and
mothers and a host of unsuitable expectations and duties,
falsely so called, seek to bind us—into what helpless dis-
cord shall we not fall. Do you remember, in the 'Ara-
bian Nights,' the princes who climbed the hill to bring
away the singing-tree—how the black pebbles clamored,
and the princes looked round, and became black pebbles
themselves?

"I hate whatever is imitative in states of mind as
well as in action. The moment I say to myself, 'I ought
to feel thus and so,' life loses its sweetness, the soul her
vigor and truth. I can only recover my genuine self by
stopping short, refraining from every effort to shape my
thought after a form, and giving it boundless freedom
and horizon. Then after the oscillation, more or less
protracted as the mind has been more or less forcibly
pushed from its place, I fall again into my orbit and
recognize myself, and find with gratitude that something
there is in the spirit which changes not neither is weary ;
but ever returns into itself, and partakes of the eternity
of God. Do not let persons and things come too near
you. They should be phenomenal. The soul should
keep the external world at a distance. Only in the

character of messengers charged with a mission from the Everlasting and the True, should we receive what befalls us or them who stand near us."

This, at first sight, would seem to set aside that great law of Duty, that "stern daughter of the voice of God," which is, as Wordsworth sings, in one of in his sublimest odes, "a light to guide, a rod to check the erring and reprove." But Charles Emerson nowise ignores the existence of this higher law; nor does his strong estimate of individuality lead him to make light of the obligation imposed upon every man, by the very constitution of his nature and by the environments in which he is placed, no less than by the command of God, to fulfill all the duties of social and civil life, in the completest manner, but in such manner as he best can with the endowments which have been vouchsafed to him. Following directly after the foregoing citation, he continues :

SELF AND SOCIETY.

"It is a miserable smallness of nature to be shut up within the small circle of a few personal relations, and to fret and fume whenever a claim is made on us from God's wide world without. If we are impatient of the dependence of man upon man, and grudge to take hold of hands in the ring, the spirit in us is either evil or infirm. If to need least is nighest to God, so also is it to impart most. There is no soundness in any philosophy short of that unlimited debt. As there is no man but is made up of the constitutions of God and the creatures of God, so there is no one who can reasonably deny himself to the calls which in the economy of the world he was provided with the means of satisfying. The true check of this principle is to be found in another general law— that each is to serve his fellow-men in that way he best can. The olive is not bound to leave yielding his fruit, and go and reign over the trees; neither is the astronomer, the artist, or the poet to quit his work that he may do the errands of Howard, or second the efforts of Wilberforce."

In this last citation from Charles Emerson's "Notes" we find the sum and substance of the practical philosophy of that brother of his with whom we have mainly to do. He has striven faithfully to serve his day and generation, and coming days and generations, in the way in which best he could. He has by no means stood aloof from taking part in the stirring questions of the time, and, in regard to them, has often taken the unpopular side, but always the right one. But his real life-work has been that of a thinker, dwelling in the severe realm of the ideal, and enunciating almost oracularly thoughts which he deemed it for the good of men that they should be aware of.

Something must now be said of the circumstances and influences by, through, or sometimes in spite of which Ralph Waldo Emerson came to be the manner of man which he is.

His father died when the boy was eight years

old, and the care of the household fell upon his excellent mother and her devoted daughter. He was trained in the public schools of Boston, where he made good progress, and was sometimes called upon to recite original poems at school exhibitions. In 1817, he being fourteen years of age, he entered Harvard College, where his elder brother had preceded him two or three years before. His college career, measured by ordinary academical rules, was not a very brilliant one. His renderings of the Greek and Latin classics were indeed quite above those of the majority of his classmates; of those who could go better through the declensions and conjugations, and give more accurately the rules of grammar and accidence. But we are told that "in philosophy he did very poorly, and mathematics were his utter despair." In certain other respects he stood well up in his class—ranking higher in the estimation of the students than upon the rolls of the Faculty. He made good use of the college library, which, although it then contained barely twenty-five thousand volumes, was the largest in the country. We are told that "he read and re-read the early English dramatists, and knew Shakspeare almost by heart." He also showed decided talent for composition and declamation, and in his junior year gained the first prize for an essay upon the "Character of Socrates," and in his senior year the second prize for an essay upon

"The Present State of Ethical Philosophy." These facts indicate that he must have really studied the higher forms of philosophy to good purpose, even though he received low marks for his formal recitations. He was also the poet of his class upon "Class-Day." Still, his general standing was little if any above the middle of his class. Of the sixty members, about half received places in the public Commencement exercises. The part assigned to Emerson was one in a "Conference on the Characters of John Knox, William Penn, and John Wesley," Emerson setting forth the paramount claims of the Scottish reformer. But his standing was not such as to gain for him an election to the Phi Beta Kappa Society, which admitted only those who were esteemed to be the best scholars of the successive classes.

He graduated in 1821, being seventeen years of age. His elder brother had in the mean while established a school in Boston, in which Ralph became a teacher for several years. He looked forward to the Christian ministry as his vocation in life, and set about the study of theology, without, however, entering the Cambridge Divinity School, the recognized avenue of approach to the Unitarian ministry. Notwithstanding this, he was in 1826 "approbated to preach" by the Middlesex Association. But, his health having become impaired, he passed a winter in the South. Returning to New England, his character and attainments must have come to be appreciated ; for, in 1829, he was called to the important position of colleague to Henry Ware in the pastorate of the Second Church (Unitarian) of Boston. A year after this Mr. Ware resigned in order to become Professor of Pulpit Eloquence and Pastor of Harvard College, and Emerson became sole minister of the Second Church of Boston. In 1830 he married Ellen Louisa Tucker, of Boston, who died within a year after their marriage.

III.

IN THE MINISTRY.

EMERSON'S career as a clergyman lasted about four years. That his duties were faithfully and acceptably performed is abundantly evinced by the circumstances which occasioned his resignation of the pastorate, and his virtual abandonment of the sacred office. Of his sermons only one, as far as we know, has ever been published, and that only four years ago as an appendix to Mr. Frothingham's "Transcendentalism in New England." It was his farewell discourse to the people of his charge, and the last sermon which he ever preached. It is worthy of somewhat ex-

tended mention, as indicating some important
modifications which had taken place in his theological views, and as marking the turning-point
in his career of life.

He had come to more than doubt the authority
and even the usefulness of the Christian rite of
the Lord's Supper. His objections to it did not
rest at all upon the mysterious doctrines of Tran-
substantiation and Consubstantiation, for which
so many men have been sent to the stake, and
have sent others to the stake. He was quite willing to let others understand in their own way the
meaning of the words, "This is my body," if so
be they could thereby gain any spiritual good.
His own objections to the present practice of the
ordinance lay far deeper than any mere question
as to the form of administering it. In his view
the rite was never instituted by Jesus as a permanent one for his followers through the ages ;
and whatever of usefulness it may have had in the
olden time, this had passed away ; and for him at
least, it was an outworn garment to be flung aside.
The sacerdotal blessing of the bread and wine was
a ceremony in which he could no longer take part.
He hoped, indeed, that some better form of commemoration of the death of Jesus might be de-
vised, in which he could conscientiously take
part. The congregation did not agree with him,
but decided unanimously that the rite should be
administered as it had always been with them.

Emerson thereupon formally resigned the pastorate, and preached this notable discourse.

THE FAREWELL SERMON.

The text and theme of the sermon was Romans xiv. 17, where Paul declares that "The kingdom of God is not meat and drink, but righteousness and peace and joy and peace in the Holy Ghost." The discourse began in a quiet way, touching first upon some of the disputes which have been waged in respect to the rite of the Lord's Supper. Some of the conclusions being that—

"There never has been any unanimity in the understanding of its nature, nor any uniformity in the mode of celebrating it. Without considering the frivolous questions as to the posture in which men should partake of it, whether mixed or unmixed wine should be served, whether leavened or unleavened bread should be broken, the questions have been settled differently in every church who should be admitted to the feast, and how often it should be prepared. In the Catholic Church infants were at one time permitted and then forbidden to partake; and since the ninth century the laity receive the bread only, the cup being reserved for the priesthood. . . . But more important controversies have arisen respecting its nature. The famous question of the Real Presence was the main controversy between the Church of England and the Church of Rome. The doctrine of Consubstantiation, taught by Luther, was denied by Calvin. In the Church of England, Archbishops Laud and Wake maintained that the elements

were an eucharist or sacrifice of thanksgiving to God;
Cudworth and Warburton that it was not a sacrifice, but
a sacrificial feast; and Bishop Hoadley that it was neither
a sacrifice nor a feast after a sacrifice, but a simple
commemoration. And finally it is now near two hundred years since the Society of Quakers denied the authority of the rite altogether, and gave good reasons for
disusing it."

Having premised that these facts were alluded
to "only to show that so far from the Supper
being a tradition in which men are fully agreed,
there has always been room for the widest difference of opinion upon this particular," Mr. Emerson goes on to define his own position, and the
essential grounds upon which it was based:

"Having recently given particular attention to this
subject, I was led to the conclusion that Jesus did not
intend to establish an institution for perpetual observance when he ate the Passover with his disciples; and
further, to the opinion that it is not expedient to celebrate it as we now do."

He then proceeds to discuss the question as to
the authority of the rite. An account of the Last
Supper, he says in substance, is given by the four
Evangelists: Matthew records the words of Jesus
in giving the bread and wine to his disciples on
that occasion; but there is nothing said which
indicates that the feast was hereafter to be com-
memorated. Mark gives the same words, still

with no intimation that the occasion was to be remembered. Luke, after relating the breaking of the bread, has these words, "This do in remembrance of me." In John, although the other transactions of the evening are related, this whole transaction is passed over without notice. The whole matter is thus summed up :

SCRIPTURAL AUTHORITY AS TO THE SUPPER.

"Now observe the facts. Two of the Evangelists, Matthew and John, were of the twelve disciples, and were present on the occasion. Neither of them drops the slightest intimation of any intention on the part of Jesus to set up anything permanent. John, especially, the beloved disciple, who has recorded with minuteness the conversation and the transactions of that memorable evening, has quite omitted such a notice. Neither does it appear to have come to the knowledge of Mark, who, though not an eye-witness, relates the other facts. This material fact, that the occasion was to be remembered, is found in Luke alone, who was not present. There is no reason, however, that we know, for rejecting the account of Luke. I doubt not the expression was used by Jesus. I shall presently consider its meaning. I have only brought these accounts together that you may judge whether it is likely that a solemn institution, to be continued to the end of time by all mankind, as they should come, nation after nation, within the influence of the Christian religion, would have been established in this slight manner—in a manner so slight that the intention of commemorating it should not appear, from their narrative, to have caught the ear, or dwelt in the mind, of

the only two among the twelve who wrote down what
had happened. But supposing that the expression, 'This
do in remembrance of me,' had come to the ear of Luke
from some disciple who was present, what does it really
signify?"

Mr. Emerson goes on to state what he supposes
lay in the mind of Jesus upon this memorable occasion : "He was a Jew, sitting with his countrymen, celebrating their national feast. He thinks
of his own impending death, and wishes the minds
of his disciples to be prepared for it. He says to
them : 'When hereafter you shall keep this Passover, it will have an altered aspect to your eyes.
It is now an historical covenant of God with the
Jewish nation. Hereafter it will remind you of
a new covenant, sealed with my blood. In years
to come, as long as your people shall come up to
Jerusalem to keep this feast, the connection which
has subsisted between us will give a new meaning
in your eyes to the national festival, as the anniversary of my death.'" And much more to the
same general purport ; the upshot of all being
that the supper was not a sequel to the Passover,
but was the Passover itself. "Jesus did with his
disciples exactly what every master of a family in
Jerusalem was doing at the same hour with his
household." He thus proceeds :

TEMPORARY DESIGN OF THE RITE.

"I see natural feeling and beauty in such language
from Jesus—a friend to his friends. I can readily im-

agine that he was willing and desirous, when his disciples met, that his memory should hallow their intercourse; but I cannot believe that in the use of such an
expression he looked beyond the living generation—beyond the abolition of the festival he was celebrating, and
the scattering of the nation, and meant to impose a memorial feast upon the whole world. He may have foreseen that his disciples would meet to remember him, and
that with good effect. It may have crossed his mind
that this would be easily continued a hundred or a thousand years—as men more easily retain a form than a virtue—and yet have been altogether out of his purpose to
fasten it upon men in all times and all countries."

Mr. Emerson admits that St. Paul presents a
view of the supper which accords in general with
the common view of its origin and nature. But
in this matter he gives little weight to the authority of Paul. To us, who regard the authority of
Paul as not inferior to any other, the argument
of Emerson and the conclusions based upon it
have no validity. Still, it is fitting that they
should be fairly presented :

THE AUTHORITY OF ST. PAUL QUESTIONED.

"I am of opinion that it is wholly upon the Epistle
to the Corinthians, and not upon the Gospels, that the
ordinance stands. But there is a material circumstance
which diminishes our confidence in the correctness of the
Apostle's view; and that is the observation that his
mind had not escaped the prevalent error of the primitive Church—the belief that the second coming of Christ

3

would shortly occur; until which time, he tells them that this feast was to be kept up. In this manner we may see clearly enough how this current ordinance got its footing among the early Christians; and this single expectation of the speedy reappearance of a temporal Messiah, which kept its influence even over so spiritual a man as St. Paul, would naturally tend to preserve the use of the rite when once established.

"We arrive, then, at this conclusion: First, that it does not appear, from a careful examination of the account of the Lord's Supper in the Evangelists, that it was designed by Jesus to be perpetual. Secondly, that it does not appear that the opinion of St. Paul, all things considered, ought to alter our opinion derived from the Evangelists."

Having, as he believes, set aside the historical argument for the perpetual observance of the rite of the Lord's Supper, Mr. Emerson proceeds to state at some length his own objections to its observance in its present form, or in any other in which its characteristic features should be essentially maintained. These objections resolve themselves into three, which are here presented, considerably abridged :

EMERSON'S OBJECTIONS TO THE RITE.

"(1.) If the view which I have taken of the history of the institution be correct, then the claim of authority should be dropped in administering it. You say every time that you celebrate the rite that Jesus enjoined it; but, if you read the New Testament as I do, you do not believe he did.

"(2.) It has seemed to me that the use of this ordinance tends to produce confusion in our views of the relation of the soul to God. It is the old objection to the doctrine of the Trinity—that the true worship was transferred from God to Christ, or that such confusion was introduced into the soul that an individual worship was given nowhere. The service does not stand upon the basis of a voluntary act, but is imposed by authority. It is an expression of gratitude to Christ, enjoined by Christ. Here is an endeavor to keep Jesus in mind, whilst yet the prayers are addressed to God. I fear it is the effect of this ordinance to clothe Jesus with an authority which he never claimed, and which distracts the mind of the worshipper. I believe that the human mind can admit but one God, and that every effort to pay religious homage to more than one Being goes to take away all right ideas.

"(3.) The use of the elements, however suitable to the peoples and modes of thought of the East, is foreign and unsuited to us. We are not accustomed to express our thoughts or emotions by symbolical actions. And men find the bread and wine no aid to devotion; and to some it is a painful impediment. To eat bread is one thing; to love the principles of Christ, and resolve to obey them, is quite another."

This last objection is the one most strenuously urged by Mr. Emerson. "I think," he says, "that this difficulty, wherever it is felt, is entitled to the greatest weight. It is alone a sufficient objection to the ordinance. It is my own objection." He adds emphatically:

AN APPROPRIATE COMMEMORATION.

"This mode of commemorating Christ is not suitable
to me. That is reason enough why I should abandon it.
If I believed that it was enjoined by Jesus on his disciples, and that he even contemplated making permanent
this mode of commemoration, every way agreeable to an
Eastern mind, and yet if on trial it was disagreeable to
me, I should not adopt it. I should choose other ways
which, as more effectual upon me, he would approve
more. For I choose that my remembrances of him should
be pleasing, affecting, religious. I will love him, as a
glorified friend, after the free ways of friendship, and
not pay him a stiff sign of respect, as men do to those
whom they fear. A passage read from his discourses, a
moving provocation to works like his, any act or meeting
which tends to awaken a pure thought, a flow of love, an
original design of virtue, I call a worthy, a true commem-
ation."

Impelled by these and such like considerations,
Emerson had proposed to the brethren of his congregation that the use of bread and wine, and all
claim by authority, should be dropped from the
administration of the ordinance. Not a man
would consent to this change—proof sufficient
that none of them were conscious of the difficul-
ties which pressed upon their pastor. Little
weight as any or all of these objections have upon
our mind, we cannot fail to honor the conscien-
tious and self-sacrificing spirit in which he carried
out his convictions, as thus set forth in the closing passage of this sermon :

THE FINAL RESOLVE.

"It is my desire, in the office of a Christian minister, to do nothing which I cannot do with my whole heart. Having said this, I have said all. I have no hostility to this institution ; I am only stating my want of sympathy with it. Neither should I have ever obtruded this opinion upon other people, had I not been called by my office to administer it. That is the end of my opposition, that I am not interested in it. I am content that it should stand to the end of the world, if it pleases men and pleases heaven, and I shall rejoice in all the good that it produces. . . .

"As it is the prevailing opinion and feeling in our religious community that it is an indispensable part of the pastoral office to administer this ordinance, I am about to resign into your hands the office which you have confided to me. It has many duties for which I am feebly qualified. It has some which it will always be my delight to discharge, according to my ability, wherever I exist. And whilst the recollection of its claims oppresses me with a sense of my unworthiness, I am consoled by the hope that no time and no change can deprive me of the satisfaction of pursuing and expressing its highest . functions."

Thus, for conscience's sake, early in September, 1832, Emerson, at the age of twenty-nine, virtually shut himself out from continuing in that career of life upon which he had so lately entered with such brilliant prospects of success. His resignation of the pastorate was accepted, but the " proprietors " voted that his salary should be continued. Most likely they hoped that the difficulty would somehow be got over, and he would resume his work. But he was broken in health and depressed in spirits, and meditated a trip to Europe. So, near the close of December, he relinquished his emoluments, and addressed a tender farewell letter to his congregation. Some portions of this letter are of special interest as setting forth his own religious status at this period of his life.

THE FAREWELL LETTER.

"Our connection has been very short. It is now to be brought to a sudden close; and I look back, I own, with a painful sense of weakness to the little service I have been able to render after so much expectation on my part, to the checkered space of time which domestic afflictions and personal infirmities have made still shorter and more unprofitable.

"As long as he remains in the same place, a man flatters himself, however keen may be his sense of his failures and unworthiness, that he shall yet accomplish much; that the future shall make amends for the past; that his very errors shall prove his instructors: and what limit is there to hope? But a separation from our place, the close of a particular career of duty, shuts the book, bereaves us of that hope, and leaves us only to lament how little has been done.

"Yet our faith in the great truths of the New Testament makes the change of place and circumstances of less account to us, by fixing our attention upon that which is unalterable. I find great consolation in the thought that the resignation of my present relations makes so little change to myself. I am no longer your minister, but am not the less engaged, I trust, to the love and service of the same eternal cause—the advancement, namely, of the kingdom of God in the hearts of men. The tie which binds each of us to that cause is not created by our connection, and cannot be hurt by our separation. To me, as one disciple, is the ministry of truth, as far as I can discern or declare it, committed; and I desire to live nowhere and no longer than that grace of God is imparted to me—the liberty to seek, and the liberty to utter it.

"I rejoice to believe that my ceasing to exercise the pastoral office among you does not make any real change in our spiritual relations to each other. Whatever is most desirable and excellent in it remains to us. If we have conspired from week to week in the sympathy and expression of devout sentiments; if we have received together the unspeakable gift of God's truth; if we have studied together any sense of the Divine Word, or striven together in any charity; above all, if we have shared in any habitual acknowledgment of that benignant God whose omnipotence raises and glorifies the meanest offices and the lowest ability, and opens heaven in every heart that worships him—then, indeed, are we united; we are mutually debtors to each other of faith and hope, engaged to confirm each other's hearts in obedience to the gospel. We shall not feel that the nominal changes and little separations of this world can release us from the strong courage of this spiritual bond. And I entreat you to consider how truly blessed will have been our connection if in this manner the memory of it shall serve to bind each one of us more strictly to the practice of our several duties. . . .

"I pray God that whatever seed of truth and virtue

we have sown and watered together may bear fruit unto
eternal life.   I commend you to the Divine Providence.
May he grant you in your ancient sanctuary the services
of able and faithful teachers ; and, whatever of discipline
may be appointed to you in this world, may the blessed
hope of the resurrection he has implanted in the constitution of the human soul, and confirmed and manifested
by Jesus Christ, be made good to you beyond the grave.
In this hope and faith I bid you farewell."

Immediately after sending this letter, Mr.
Emerson set out upon his first visit to Europe,
where he spent nearly a year, mainly in Italy and
Great Britain.

IV.

VISITS TO EUROPE.

Of his first visit Mr. Emerson has given only
a very brief account, extracted many years afterward from his note-books.   Of the places which
he visited, and the incidents of travel, he says
nothing, confining himself wholly to reports of
his interviews with a few notable men.   "As
they respect," he says, "parties quite too good
and too transparent to the whole world, there is
no need to affect any prudery of expression about
a few hints of these bright personalities."   These
personal sketches evince a phase of Emerson's ca-

pabilities of which there is elsewhere little trace except in what he has to say of Margaret Fuller, to whose biography by her brother and James Freeman Clarke he contributed some interesting chapters.

He went first to Italy. At Florence, where he made the longest stay, he was intimate with Horatio Greenough, the American sculptor, "whose face was so handsome, and his person so well formed, that he might be pardoned if, as was alleged, the face of his Medora and the figure of a colossal Achilles in clay were idealizations of his own."

HORATIO GREENOUGH.

"He was," says Emerson, "a superior man, ardent and eloquent, and all his opinions had elevation and magnanimity. He believed that the Greeks had wrought in schools or fraternities, the genius of the master imparting his design to his friends, and inflaming them with it; and, when his strength was spent, a new hand, with equal heat, continued the work, and so, by short relays, until it was finished in every part with equal fire. This was necessary in so refractory a material as stone; and he thought Art would never prosper until we left our shy, jealous ways, and worked in society as they. All his thoughts breathed the same noble generosity. He was an accurate and a deep man; a votary of the Greeks, and impatient of Gothic Art."

Through Greenough Mr. Emerson was introduced to Walter Savage Landor, then residing near Florence, to all appearance in the most happy manner. Landor was about sixty years old, and his character had not yet assumed those darker shades which it bore in his extreme old age. Emerson saw Landor only twice; but his representation of the man at his best is worthy of reproduction. We give his account of these two interviews :

WALTER SAVAGE LANDOR.

"On the 15th of May I dined with Mr. Landor. I found him noble and courteous, living in a cloud of pictures at his Villa Gherardesca, a fine house commanding a beautiful landscape. I had inferred from his book, or magnified from some anecdote, an impression of Achillean wrath, an untamable petulance. I do not know whether the imputation were just or not, but certainly on this May day his courtesy vailed that haughty mind, and he was the most patient and gentle of hosts. He admired Washington; talked of Wordsworth, Byron, Massinger, Beaumont and Fletcher. To be sure, he is decided in his opinions, likes to surprise, and is well content to impress, if possible, his English whim upon the immutable past. No great man, he said, ever had a great son, if Philip and Alexander be not an exception; and Philip he calls the greater man. In Art he loves the Greeks, and in sculpture them only. He prefers the Venus to everything else, and, after that, the head of Alexander, in the gallery here. He prefers John of Bologna to Michel Angelo; in painting, Raffaelle; and shares the growing taste for Perugino and the early masters. The Greek historians he thought the only good, and, after them, Voltaire. He pestered me with Southey, but who is Southey ?

"He invited me to breakfast on Friday, and I did not fail to go—this time with Greenough. He entertained us at once with reciting half a dozen hexameter lines of Julius Cæsar's. He glorified Lord Chesterfield more than was necessary; undervalued Burke, and undervalued Socrates; designated as the three greatest of men, Washington, Phocion, and Timoleon, and did not even omit to remark the similar termination of their names. 'A great man,' he said, 'should make great sacrifices, and kill his hundred oxen without knowing whether they would be consumed by gods and heroes, or whether the flies would eat them.' He despised entomology, yet in the same breath said, 'The sublime is in a grain of dust.' I suppose I teased him about recent writers; but he professed never to have heard of Herschel, not even by name. One room was full of pictures, which he likes to show, especially one piece, standing before which he said, 'I would give fifty guineas to the man who would swear that it was a Domenichino.' I was more curious to see his library, but was told by one of the guests that he gives away his books, and has never more than a dozen at a time in his house.

"Mr. Landor carries to its height the love of freak, which the British like to indulge, as if to signalize their commanding freedom. He has a wonderful brain, despotic, violent, and inexhaustible; meant for a soldier, by some chance converted to letters, in which there is not a style nor a tint not known to him; yet with an English appetite for action and heroes. 'The thing done avails, and not what is said about it; an original sentence, a step forward, is worth more than all the censures.' Landor is strangely undervalued in England, usually ignored, and sometimes savagely attacked in the Reviews. The criticism may be right or wrong, and is quickly forgotten, but year after year the scholar must still go back to Landor for a multitude of elegant sentences—for wisdom, wit, and indignation that are unforgetable."

From Italy Emerson proceeded to England by way of France. He tells almost cynically what were the motives which led him to visit Great Britain : "Like most young men of that time, I was much indebted to the men of Edinburgh and the 'Edinburgh Review'—to Jeffrey, Mackintosh, Hallam, and to Scott, Playfair, and De Quincey ; and my narrow and desultory reading had inspired the wish to see the faces of three or four writers : Coleridge, Wordsworth, Landor, De Quincey, and Carlyle, the latest and strongest contributor to the critical journals. I suppose, if I had sifted the reasons which led me to Europe, it was mainly the attraction of these persons. If Goethe had been still living, I might have wandered into Germany also. Besides those I have named (for Scott was dead) there was not the man living whom I cared to behold, unless it were the Duke of Wellington, whom I saw in Westminster Abbey at the funeral of Wilberforce." Of the men whom he saw in Great Britain, he gives sketches only of Coleridge, Wordsworth, and Carlyle. The account of the interview with Coleridge is of interest as presenting, as far as we

know, the latest word-picture which we have of
the man ; for Carlyle's characteristic mention of
him, in the "Life of Sterling," belongs to a period
some years earlier.

SAMUEL TAYLOR COLERIDGE.

"From London, on the 5th of August, 1833," says
Emerson, "I went to Highgate, and wrote a note to Mr.
Coleridge, requesting to pay my respects to him. It
was near noon. Mr. Coleridge sent a verbal message
that he was in bed, but if I would call after one o'clock,
he would see me. I returned at one, and he appeared—
a short, thick old man, with bright blue eyes, and fine,
clear complexion. He took snuff freely, which presently soiled his cravat and neat black suit.

"He asked whether I knew Allston, and spoke
warmly of his merits and doings when he knew him at
Rome [more than a quarter of a century before]. He
spoke of Dr. Channing: 'it was an unspeakable misfortune that he had turned out a Unitarian, after all.' On
this he broke out into a burst of declamation on the folly
and ignorance of Unitarianism—its high unreasonable-
ness ; and taking up Bishop Waterland's book, which
lay on the table, he read with vehemence two or three
pages written by himself on the fly-leaves—passages
which I believe are printed in his 'Aids to Reflection.'

"When he stopped to take breath, I interposed that,
'while I highly valued all his explanations, I was bound
to tell him that I was born and bred a Unitarian.'
'Yes,' he said, 'I supposed so,' and continued as before:
'It was a wonder that after so many ages of unquestion-

ing acquiescence in the doctrine of St. Paul—the doctrine of the Trinity, which was also, according to Philo Judæus, the doctrine of the Jews before Christ—this handful of Priestleians should take on themselves to deny it," etc., etc. He was sorry that Dr. Channing, 'a man to whom he looked up—no, to say that he looked *up* to him would be to speak falsely—but a man whom he looked *at* with so much interest—should embrace such views.' When he saw Dr. Channing, he had hinted to him that he was afraid he loved Christianity for what was lovely and excellent; he loved the good in it, and not the true; 'and I tell you, sir, that I have known ten persons who loved the good, for one person who loved the true; but it is a far greater virtue to love the true for itself alone, than to love the good for itself alone.' He himself knew all about Unitarianism perfectly well, because he had once been a Unitarian, and knew what quackery it was.

"He went on defining, or rather refining: 'The Trinitarian doctrine was realism; the idea of a God was not essential, but super-essential.' Talked of *trinism* and *tetrakism*, and much more, of which I only caught this: 'The will is that by which a person is a person; because if one should push me into the street, and so I should force the man next me into the kennel, I should at once exclaim, I did not do it, sir, meaning that it was not my will.' And this also, 'If you should insist on your faith here in England, and I on mine, mine would be the hotter side of the fagot.' "

It is not easy to understand what Coleridge meant to imply in this last sentence. The interview was not wholly made up of theological and theosophical declamation ; but Emerson contrived now and then to get in a word which for a moment interrupted the sing-song, snuffy flow of Coleridge's talk. Learning that his visitor had just been in Malta and Sicily, Coleridge said : " Sicily is an excellent school of political economy ; for it only needs to ask what Government has enacted, and reverse that, to know what ought to be done. It is the most felicitously opposite legislation to anything good and wise. There are only three things which the Government has brought into that garden of delights, namely, itch, pox [i. e. syphilis], and famine ; whereas, in Malta, the force of law and mind was seen in making that barren rock of semi-Saracenic inhabitants the seat of population and plenty." When Emerson rose to go, Coleridge said, " I do not know whether you care about poetry, but I will repeat some verses I lately made on my baptismal anniversary ;" and then, still standing, he recited with strong emphasis this poem, probably the last but one ever composed by him :

" God's child in Christ adopted, Christ my all,
     What that earth boasts were not lost cheaply, rather
Than forfeit that blest name by which I call
     The Holy One, the Almighty God, my Father ?
Father ! in Thee we live, and Christ in Thee—
Eternal Thou, and everlasting we.
The heir of heaven, henceforth I fear not death :
In Christ I live ! in Christ I draw the breath

Of the true life! Let, then, earth, sea, and sky
Make war against me! On my front I show
Their mighty Master's seal. In vain they try
To end my life, that can but end its woe.
Is that a deathbed where a Christian lies?
Yes! but not his—'tis death itself there dies."

Emerson thus concludes his account of the interview with Coleridge :

" I was in his company for about an hour, but find it impossible to recall the largest part of his discourse, which was often like so many printed paragraphs in his book—perhaps the same—so readily did he fall into certain commonplaces. As I might have foreseen, the visit was rather a spectacle than a conversation, of no use beyond the satisfaction of my curiosity. He was old and preoccupied, and could not bend to a new companion and think with him.

Not quite a year after this Coleridge passed from this earthly life. If his biography shall ever come to be fairly written, it would be one of the saddest books ever composed.

A fortnight after this interview with Coleridge, Emerson went to Rydal Mount to pay his respects to Wordsworth. The exterior aspect of the man, now sixty-three years old, belied the great philosophic poet. "He was," says Emerson, "a plain, elderly, white-haired man, not prepossessing, and disfigured by green goggles." We abridge the account of this interview :

WILLIAM WORDSWORTH.

" He had much to say of America, the more that it gave occasion for his favorite topic—that society is being enlightened by a superficial tuition out of all proportion to its being restrained by moral culture. 'Schools do no good. Tuition is not education.' He thinks more of the education of circumstances than of tuition. 'It is not a question whether there are offenses of which the law takes cognizance, but whether there are offenses of which the law does not take cognizance.' Sin is what he fears, and how society is to escape without gravest mischiefs from this source. He even said, what seemed a paradox, that they needed a civil war in America to teach the necessity of knitting the social ties stronger. 'There may be,' he said, 'in America some vulgarity in manner; but that's not important. That comes of the pioneer state of things. But I fear they are too much given to the making of money; and, secondly, to politics; that they make political distinction the end, and not the means. And I fear that they lack a class of men of leisure—in short, of gentlemen, to give a tone of honor to the community.' He was against taking off the tax on newspapers in England, which the reformers represent as a tax upon knowledge, for this reason, that they would be inundated with base prints. He wished to impress on me, and all good Americans, to cultivate the moral, the constructive, etc., and never to call into action the physical strength of the people, as had just now been done in England in the Reform Bill.

" The conversation turned upon books. Lucretius he esteems a far higher poet than Virgil; not in his system, which is nothing, but in his power of illustration. 'Faith is necessary to explain anything, and to reconcile the

4

foreknowledge of God with human evil.' Of Cousin, whose lectures we had all been reading in Boston, he knew only the name.

"I inquired if he had read Carlyle's critical articles and translations. He said he thought him sometimes insane. He proceeded to abuse Goethe's 'Wilhelm Meister' heartily. 'It was full of all manner of fornication. It was like the crossing of flies in the air.' He had never gone further than the first book; so disgusted was he that he threw the book across the room. I said what I could for the better parts of the book; and he courteously promised to look at it again. He said that Carlyle wrote most obscurely. He was clever and deep, but he defied the sympathies of everybody. Even Coleridge wrote more clearly, though he had always wished that Coleridge would write more to be understood.

"He led me out into his garden, and showed me the gravel walk in which thousands of his lines were composed. His eyes are much inflamed; this is no loss except for reading, as he never writes prose, and of poetry he carries hundreds of lines in his head before writing them. He had just returned from a visit to Staffa, and within three days had made three sonnets on Fingal's Cave. 'If you are interested in my verses,' he said, 'perhaps you will like to hear these lines.' I gladly assented; and he recollected himself for a few moments, and then stood forth and repeated, one after another the three entire sonnets with great animation. I fancied the second and third more beautiful than his poems are wont to be. This recitation was so unlooked-for and surprising—he, the old Wordsworth, standing apart and reciting to me in a garden-walk, like a school-boy declaiming—that I at first was near to laugh; but recollecting myself, that I had come thus far to see a poet, and that he was chanting poems to me, I saw that he was right and I was wrong, and gladly gave myself up to hear.

"I told him how much the few printed extracts had quickened the desire to possess his unpublished poems. He replied that he was never in haste to publish; partly because he corrected a good deal, and every alteration is ungraciously received after printing; but what he had written would be printed whether he lived or died. I said 'Tintern Abbey' appeared to be the favorite poem with the public, but more contemplative readers preferred the first books of the 'Excursion,' and the sonnets. He said, 'Yes, they are better.'"

This interview with Wordsworth took place in the summer of 1833. Fifteen years after, that is in 1848, Emerson again visited Europe, this time to deliver, by special invitation, a series of lectures in the principal places of England and Scotland. He was now no longer an unknown young American, but a man of mature years and established reputation, to whom the best doors in the land were open. Happening to be a guest of Harriet Martineau, a near neighbor of Wordsworth, the two paid a visit to the poet, now almost four score years of age. Emerson has preserved some interesting notes of the last visit, characteristic of the two men. A quarter of a century seems to have made little change in Wordsworth. "We found him," says Emerson, "asleep on the sofa. He was at first silent and indisposed, as an old man who had suddenly wakened up before he had ended his nap." But soon he became full of talk on the French news and various other topics. "His face sometimes lighted up, but his conversation was not marked by special force or elevation. He had a weather-beaten face; his features corrugated, especially the large nose. . . . He was nationally bitter on the French; bitter on the Scotchmen too. 'No Scotchman,' he said, 'can write English.' He detailed two models on one or other of which all the sentences of the historian Robertson are framed. Nor could Jeffrey or the Edinburgh Reviewers write English; nor could Carlyle, who was 'a pest to the English tongue.' He added incidentally, 'Gibbon cannot write English.'" Of Tennyson he spoke in terms of rather reluctant approval. In fact, Wordsworth had long wrapped himself up in the belief that there was very little poetry worth reading except his own. Personally, though one of the best of men, he was one of the most ungenial.

One would have supposed that, of all English poets, Wordsworth would have been the prime favorite with Emerson. He does indeed speak highly of him, but usually with a kind of constraint, as though he was half sorry to be obliged to praise him. But, in the end, at the close of the account of this last interview, he gives this fair and just estimate of the poet:

"Who that reads him well will know that in following the strong bent of his genius he was careless of the many, careless also of the few, self-assured that he should 'create the taste by which he was to be enjoyed.' He lived long enough to witness the revolution he had wrought, and 'to see what he foresaw.' There are torpid places in his mind; there is something hard and sterile in his poetry; want of grace, want of variety, want of due catholic and cosmopolitan scope. He had conformities to English politics and traditions; he had egotistical peculiarities in the choice and treatment of his subjects. But let us say of him that, alone of his time, he treated the human mind well, and with absolute truth. His adherence to his poetic creed rested on real inspirations. The Ode on 'Immortality' is the high-water mark which the intellect has reached in this age. New means were employed, and new realms added to the empire of the muse by his courage."

THOMAS CARLYLE.

To see Carlyle was one of the main motives which led Emerson, after a six months' sojourn in Italy, to visit Great Britain. Carlyle was now thirty-eight years old, eight years the senior of Emerson. Destined for the ministry of the Kirk of Scotland, he had at the age of twenty-two found that he did not believe in the doctrines of the Church of his fathers, and could not honestly enter upon its ministry. He engaged in literary task-work with stubborn industry and fair suc-

cess. He translated Legendre's Geometry from
the French, prefixing a valuable Introduction;
translated Goethe's "Wilhelm Meister," and several volumes of tales from the German; and wrote
for Encyclopædias, Reviews, and Magazines. At
thirty he married Jane Welch, whose moderate
fortune relieved him from the necessity of doing
task-work for his daily bread. In 1828 he took
up his abode at Craigenputtoch, a lonely estate
among the granite hills and black morasses which
stretch westward through Galloway almost to the
Irish Sea. In a letter to Goethe he describes the
reasons which led him to take up his abode in
this solitary spot, and his mode of life there:

"In this wilderness of heath and rock our estate
stands forth a green oasis, a tract of plowed, partly inclosed and planted ground, where corn ripens and trees
afford a shade, although surrounded by sea-mews and
rough-wooled sheep. Here, with no small effort, have
we built and furnished a neat and substantial dwelling;
here, in the absence of professional or other office, we live
to cultivate literature according to our strength, and in
our own peculiar way. We wish a joyful growth to the
roses and flowers of our garden; we hope for health
and peaceful thoughts to further our aims. This nook
of ours is the loneliest in Britain, six miles removed from
any one who would be likely to visit me. But I came
with the design to simplify my way of life, and to secure
the independence through which I could be enabled to
remain true to myself. Nor is the solitude of so great
importance, for a stage-coach takes me speedily to Edin-

burgh. And have I not too, at this moment, piled up upon the table of my little library, a whole cart-load of French, German, American, and English periodicals— whatever may be their worth!"

At Craigenputtoch, during the six years preceding Emerson's visit, were written the greater part and certainly the best of those critical and biographical essays which showed him to be "the latest and strongest contributor to the critical journals." Unlike Coleridge and Wordsworth, the aspect and bearing of the man more than confirmed the high estimate which Emerson had formed of the writer. He describes this first meeting :

CARLYLE AT CRAIGENPUTTOCH.

"From Edinburgh I went to the Highlands. On my return I came from Glasgow, to Dumfries, intent on delivering a letter which I had brought from Rome, and inquired for Craigenputtoch. It was a farm in Nithsdale, in the parish of Dunscore, sixteen miles distant. No public coach passed near it, so I took a private carriage from the inn. I found the lonely house amid desolate heathery hills, where the lonely scholar nourished his mighty heart. Carlyle was a man from his youth; an author who did not need to hide from his readers; and as absolute a man of the world, unknown and exiled on that hill-farm, as if holding on his own terms what was best in London.

"He was tall and gaunt, with a cliff-like brow; holding his extraordinary powers in easy control; clinging to his northern accent with evident relish; full of lively

anecdote, and with a streaming humor which floated
everything he looked upon. His talk, playfully exalting
the familiar objects, put the companion at once into acquaintance with his Lares and Lemurs, and it was very
pleasant to learn what was destined to be a pretty mythology.

"Few were the objects, and lonely the man; 'not a
person to speak to except the minister of Dunscore'; so
that books universally made his topics. He had names
of his own for all the matters familiar to his discourse.
Blackwood's was the 'Sand Magazine'; Fraser's, a
nearer approach to possibility of life, was the 'Mud
Magazine.' A piece of road near by, that marked some
failed enterprise, was the 'Grave of the Last Sixpence.'
When too much praise of any genius annoyed him, he
professed hugely to admire the genius of his pig. He
had spent much time and contrivance in confining the
poor beast to one enclosure of the pen; but pig, by a
great stroke of judgment, had found out how to let a
board down, and had foiled him. For all that, he still
thought man 'the most plastic little fellow on the planet.'
He liked Nero's death ('*Qualis artifex pereo*—What an
artist do I die) better than most history. He worships
a man that will manifest any truth to him. At one time
he had inquired and read much about America, whither
he had thoughts of emigrating. Landor's principle was
mere rebellion, and that, he feared, was the American
principle. The best thing he knew of the country was
that in it a man can have meat for his labor. He had
read in Stewart's book that, when he inquired in a New
York hotel for 'Boots,' he had been shown across the
street, and had found Mungo in his own house, dining on
roast turkey.

"He talked of books. Plato he does not read, and he despised Socrates; and, when pressed, persisted in making Mirabeau a hero. Gibbon he called 'the splendid bridge from the old world to the new.' His own reading had been multifarious. 'Tristram Shandy' was one of his first books after 'Robinson Crusoe,' and Robertson's 'America' an early favorite. Rousseau's 'Confessions' had discovered to him that he was not a dunce. It was now ten years since he had learned German, by the advice of a man who told him that in that language he would find what he wanted. He took despairing or satirical views of literature at this moment; recounted the great sums paid in one year by the great booksellers for puffing. 'Hence it comes that no newspaper is trusted now; no books are bought, and the booksellers are on the verge of bankruptcy.'

"He still returned to English pauperism; the crowded state of the country, and the selfish abdication by public men of all that public persons should perform. 'Government,' he said, 'should direct poor men what to do. Poor Irish folk come wandering over these moors. My dame makes it a rule to give to every son of Adam bread to eat, and supplies his wants to the next house. But here are thousands of acres which might give them all meat; and nobody to bid these poor Irish to go to the moor and till it. They burned the stacks, and so found a way to force the rich people to attend to them.'

"We went to walk over the long hills, and looked at Criffel—then without his cap—and down into Wordsworth's country. There we sat down, and talked of the immortality of the soul. It was not Carlyle's fault that we talked on that topic; for he had the natural disinclination of every nimble spirit to bruise himself against

walls, and did not like to place himself where no step
can be taken. But he was honest and true, and cogni-
zant of the subtle links that bind ages together; and saw
how every event affects the future. 'Christ,' he said,
'died on the tree; that built Dunscore yonder; that
brought you and me together. Time has only relative
existence.'

"He was already turning his eye toward London,
with a scholar's appreciation. 'London,' he said, 'is the
heart of the world, wonderful only from the mass of
human beings. I like the huge machine. Each keeps its
own round. The baker's boy brings muffins to the window at a fixed hour every day; and that is all that the
Londoner knows or wishes to know of the subject. But
it turns out good men.' He named certain individuals,
especially one man of letters, his friend, the best man he
knew, whom London had well served."

This first meeting with Carlyle, in 1833, brief
as it was, resulted in a warm personal friendship
which was never broken until Carlyle was laid in
his grave four-and-forty years after. Emerson,
by his collection of the "Sartor Resartus" papers,
a few years later, was the first to fairly make Carlyle known, upon this side of the Atlantic. Carlyle had vainly ransacked London to find a pub-
lisher who would print them in a book. The best
that any bookseller's "reader" could say of it
was, that "The author is a person of talent. His
work displays, here and there, some felicity of
thought and expression, considerable fancy and
knowledge; but whether it would take with the

public is doubtful. The author has no great tact;
his wit is frequently heavy." And when at length
" Sartor Resartus " began to appear piecemeal in
" Fraser's Magazine," whatever remark it occasioned in England was of a no wise flattering
character. The newspaper critics fell upon it in
their most flippant manner. One pronounced it
" a mass of clotted nonsense, mixed, however, here
and there, with passages marked by thought and
striking poetic vigor." There were sentences
which might " be read backward or forward, for
they are equally intelligible either way. Indeed,
by beginning at the tail, and so working up to
the head, we think the reader will stand the fair-
est chance of getting at the meaning." Emerson
himself, warned perhaps by the slight favor which
has been shown to his own " Nature," did not
expect for the book any immediate popularity.
In an almost apologetic preface, he says :

" SARTOR RESARTUS."

" The editors would not undertake, as there was no
need, to justify the gay costume in which the author delights to dress his thoughts, or the German idioms with
which he has sportively sprinkled his pages. It is his
humor to advance the gravest speculations in a quaint
and burlesque style. If his masquerade offend any of his
audience to that degree that they will not hear what he
has to say, it may chance to draw others to listen to his
wisdom. But we will venture to remark that the distaste
excited by these peculiarities, in some readers, is greatest

at first, and is soon forgotten. The author makes ample amends for the occasional eccentricity of his genius, not only by frequent bursts of pure splendor, but by the wit and sense which never fail him."

After those few hours of genial discourse at Craigenputtoch, Carlyle and Emerson never saw each other again until 1848. During the intervening almost twenty years the position of the two men had materially changed. Both had passed the noonday of life, but both were in full possession of their rare powers. Both had fought the battle of life, and both had come out victors. Emerson had, by his " Nature," Lectures, and Essays, won a high place in the domain of thought in his own country, and his reputation had crossed the ocean, so that he had been invited to lecture in all the principal towns in England and Scotland ; and the door of every house which he could care to enter was open to him. Carlyle had written the " French Revolution," " Chartism," " Past and Present," and had gathered together the " Letters and Speeches of Cromwell," " gathered them from far and near ; fished them up from foul Lethean quagmires where they lay buried ; washed them clean from foreign stupidities," and accompanied them with a running commentary which comes near to being a life of the great Lord Protector, or at least furnishes abundant material for such a life. Now, at the age of two-and-fifty, he stood the foremost figure in English literature. Emerson saw much of Carlyle in his modest London home; and years after, in his "English Traits," he gave some account of this intercourse; especially of a summer trip which they made together to see the ancient Druidical structure of Stonehenge. Of this trip he gives a full account. We present it here, out of its chronological order, as furnishing some striking characteristics of the two men, who acted and interacted so largely upon each other; men so like in a few respects, so unlike in many respects.

To Emerson, as he says, this trip had a double attraction: of the monument, which neither had seen, and of the companion. "It seemed a bringing together of extreme points to visit the oldest religious monument of Britain in company of her latest thinker, one whose influence may be traced in every contemporary book. I was glad to sum up a little of my experiences, and to exchange a few reasonable words on the aspects of England with a man on whose genius I set a high value. We took the railway to Salisbury, where we found a carriage to convey us to Amesbury, passing by Old Sarum, a bare, treeless hill, once containing the town which sent two members to Parliament —now, not a hut." The fine weather and Carlyle's local knowledge of Hampshire, where he was wont to spend a part of every summer, made the journey short. Of the conversation by the way

Emerson gives a few characteristic bits, treasured up in note-book and memory :

TALK ON THE ROAD.

" There was much to say of the traveling Americans, and their usual objects in London. I thought it natural that they should give some time to works of art collected here, which they can not find at home ; and a little to scientific clubs and museums, which make London very attractive. But my philosopher was not contented. ' Art,' and ' High Art,' is a favorite object of his wit. ' Yes,' he said, ' *Kunst* is a great delusion ; and Goethe and Schiller wasted a great deal of time on it.' And he thinks he discovers that old Goethe found this out, and in his later writings changed his tone. He said, ' As soon as a man begins to talk of art, architecture, and antiquities, nothing good comes of it.' He wishes to go through the British Museum in silence, and thinks a sincere man will see something and say nothing. In these days he thought it became an architect to consult only the grim necessity, and say, ' I can build you a coffin for such persons as you are, and for such dead purposes as you have ; but you shall have no ornament.' For the sciences he had, if possible, even less tolerance ; and compared the savants of Somerset House to the boy who asked Confucius, ' How many stars in the sky ? ' Confucius answered that he minded things near him. ' How many hairs in your eyebrows ? ' Confucius said he didn't know and didn't care. Of the Americans, Carlyle complained that they dislike the coldness and exclusiveness of the English, and run away to France, and go with their countrymen, and are amused, instead of manfully staying in London, confronting Englishmen, and acquiring their culture, who have really so much to teach them."

If we may put faith in a tithe of what Carlyle was wont to say and write in those days, Englishmen, or at least the London species of Englishmen, had very little to teach which it was worth anybody's while to take the trouble to learn. He seems to have spoken, as was often the case with him, the things which lay nearest the tip of his tongue, without taking much heed as to whether it was truth or caricature. Emerson responded with that earnestness and sincerity of which he never lost sight.

"I told Carlyle that I was easily dazzled, and was accustomed to concede readily all that an Englishman would ask. I see everywhere in this country proofs of sense and spirit, and success of every sort. I like the people. They are as good as they are handsome. They have everything, and can do everything. But meantime I surely know that, as soon as I return to Massachusetts, I shall lapse into the feeling, which the geography of America inevitably inspires, that we play the game with immense advantage; that there, and not here, is the seat and center of the English race; and that no skill or activity can long compete with the prodigious natural advantages of that country, in the hands of the same race; and that England, an old and exhausted country, must be contented, like other parents, to be strong only in her children."

"This," says Emerson, "is a proposition

which no Englishman, of whatever condition, can easily entertain."

It is seldom that Emerson undertakes any detailed description of particular natural scenery. Indeed, the general scope of his prose works precludes such. But scattered everywhere are detached sentences which evince that he looked upon nature with open eyes ; and his account of Stonehenge and their visit shows that he had within him capacities for picturesque description which would have enabled him to write a brilliant book of travel—say another " Eöthen."

THE VISIT TO STONEHENGE.

" After dinner we walked to Salisbury Plain. On the broad downs, under the gray sky, not a house was visible; nothing but Stonehenge, which looked like a group of brown dwarfs in the wide expanse—Stonehenge, and the barrows which rise like green bosses about the plain, and a few hayricks. On the top of a mountain the old temple would not be more impressive. Far and wide, a few shepherds with their flocks sprinkled the plain, and a bagman drove along the road. It looked as if the wide margin given in this crowded isle to this primeval temple were accorded by the British race to the old egg out of which all their ecclesiastical structures and history had proceeded.

" Stonehenge is a circular colonnade with the diameter of a hundred feet, and inclosing a second and a third colonnade within. We walked round the stones, and clambered over them, to wont ourselves with their strange associations and groupings. We found a nook, sheltered from the wind, among them, where Carlyle lighted his cigar. It was pleasant to see that just this simplest of all simple structures—two upright stones, and a lintel laid across—has long outstood all later churches, and all history, and is like what is most permanent on the face of the planet. These, and the barrows—mere mounds—of which there are one hundred and sixty within a circle of three miles about Stonehenge—like the same mound on the plain of Troy, which still makes good to the passing mariner on the Hellespont the vaunt of Homer and the fame of Achilles. Within the inclosure grow buttercups and nettles, and all around wild thyme, meadow-sweet, golden-rod, thistles, and the sheltering grass. Over us larks were soaring and singing: as Carlyle said, 'the larks which were hatched last year, and the wind which was hatched many thousand years ago.'

"We counted and measured by paces the biggest stones, and soon knew as much as any man can suddenly know of the inscrutable temple. There are ninety-four stones, and there were once probably one hundred and sixty. The temple is circular and uncovered, and the situation fixed astronomically; the grand entrance, here and at Abury, being placed exactly northeast, as all the gates of the old cavern temples are. How came the stones here? for these *Sarcens*, or Druidical sandstones, are not found in this neighborhood. The 'Sacrificial Stone,' as it is called, is the only one of all these blocks that can resist the action of fire; and, as I read in books, must have been brought a hundred and fifty miles. I, who had just come from Professor Sedgwick's Cambridge Museum of Megatheria and Mastodons, was ready to maintain that some cleverer elephants or mylodonta had borne off and laid these rocks on one another: only the

5

good beasts must have known how to cut a well-wrought
tenon and mortise, and to smooth the surface of some of
the stones.

"The chief mystery is that any mystery should have
been allowed to settle on so remarkable a monument, in
a country on which all the Muses have kept their eyes
now for eighteen hundred years. We are not yet too
late to learn much more than is known of this structure.
Some diligent Layard or Fellowes will arrive, stone by
stone, at the whole history, by that exhaustive British
sense and perseverance, so whimsical in its choice of subjects, which leaves its own Stonehenge or Choir Gaur to
the rabbits, while it opens pyramids and uncovers Nine-
veh. Stonehenge, in virtue of the simplicity of its plan,
and its good preservation, is as if new and recent; and a
thousand years hence men will thank this age for the accurate history which it will eliminate."

Stonehenge furnished Emerson with topics for
characteristic reflection, and Carlyle with a theme
for some of his weird utterances. Emerson continues :

"We walked in and out, and took again and again a
fresh look at the uncaring stones. The old Sphinx put
our petty differences of nationality out of sight. To
these conscious stones we two pilgrims were alike near
and dear. We could equally well revere their old British
meaning. Carlyle was subdued and gentle. 'In this
great House of Destiny,' he said, 'I plant cypresses
wherever I go ; and, if I am in search of pain, I cannot
go wrong.' The spot, the gray blocks, and their rude
order, which refuses to be disposed of, suggested to him
the flight of ages and the succession of religions. The

old times of England impress him much. He reads but little, he says, in these last years, but the 'Acta Sanctorum,' the fifty-two volumes of which are in the London Library. He can see, as he reads, the old Saint of Iona, sitting there and writing—a man to men. 'The " Acta Sanctorum " shows plainly that the men of those times believed in God and in the immortality of the soul, as their abbeys and cathedrals testify. Now, even Puritanism is gone. London is Pagan.' He fancied that greater men had lived in England than any of her writers; and, in fact, about the time when those writers appeared, the last of these great men had gone."

We suppose that Carlyle would have named William of Wykeham as about the last of those great men who appeared in England about the time of Chaucer. During this whole trip Carlyle was in his most genial mood. There is hardly a trace of his almost chronic cynicism. Emerson gives a few characteristic incidents which occurred. At Salisbury Cathedral they loitered outside the choir while the service was going on ; they listened to the organ, and Carlyle remarked : " The music is good ; but somewhat as if a monk were panting to some fine Queen of Heaven." Near Winchester they stopped at the quaint old Church of St. Cross, and demanded a piece of bread and a draught of beer, which Henry de Blois, who founded the church in 1136, ordered should be given to every one who should ask for it at the gate. This was doled out to them by the old couple who take care of the church. Some twenty people a day, they said, made the same demand. "This hospitality of seven hundred years' standing did not hinder Carlyle from pronouncing a malediction on the priest who receives two thousand pounds a year that were meant for the poor, and spends a pittance on this small beer and crumbs." They went to Winchester Cathedral, the largest in the country, the length of the nave being 556 feet, and the breadth of the transept 250 feet, and which Emerson preferred to any church which he had seen in England except Westminster and York. Here Canute was buried; here Alfred the Great was crowned and buried; here the Saxon kings were buried; and here, also, in his own church, was buried the great Bishop William of Wykeham. "William of Wykeham's shrine-tomb was unlocked for us," says Emerson, and Carlyle took hold of the marble hands of the recumbent statue and patted them affectionately; for he values the brave man who built Windsor, this cathedral, and the school here, and New College at Oxford."

Once again, after a lapse of twenty years, Emerson made a third visit to England, where he must have had some solemn interviews with Carlyle, now verging upon fourscore, bent and infirm, his life's work altogether done, and looking wearily for the impending end of all earthly things. But of these interviews we have no record.

V.

LECTURES AND ADDRESSES.

AFTER an absence of nearly a year, Emerson returned to America, late in 1833, with health restored and spirits reinvigorated. The system of popular lectures, somewhat pedantically denominated the "Lyceum," had begun to develop itself. It gave scope for any one to discourse upon any topic respecting which he had, or thought he had, anything to say. Emerson at once availed himself of the opening. His first lecture, delivered before the Boston Mechanics' Association, was upon "Water"; then followed three others describing his recent visit to Italy, and another upon the "Relations of Man to the Globe." In 1834 he delivered a series of five lectures upon Michel Angelo, Milton, Luther, George Fox, and Edmund Burke, the first two of which were published in the "North American Review," and appear to have been his first appearances in print.

In 1835 he married Lidian Jackson, of Plymouth, and took up his residence in the quiet little village of Concord, twenty miles from Boston, where his home has been ever since. From this period he fairly devoted himself to the new career of a lecturer, delivering from time to time courses in all the principal places from Maine to California. For forty successive years he lectured

before the Lyceum at Salem, Massachusetts. His
principal courses are these : In 1835, ten lectures
upon "English History"; in 1836, twelve upon
"The Philosophy of History"; in 1837, ten upon
"Human Culture"; in 1838, ten upon "Human
Life"; in 1839, ten upon "The Present Age";
in 1841, seven upon "The Times." Many of
these were frequently redelivered. Besides these
are several others, the gist of which is embodied
in his printed works.

His first book was "Nature," a thin volume
which appeared in 1836, of which more will be
said hereafter. In the mean while there had been
gradually gathering in Boston and its vicinity a
small group of thinkers who had come to be dis-
satisfied with the prevalent material and formal
modes of thought, and sought to introduce something fresh. Small as this circle was, it included
persons of almost every shade of thought and culture. Some were profoundly mystical ; some were
full of projects of practical effort ; but they were
popularly grouped together under the vague name
of Transcendentalists. Among these persons were
Ralph Waldo Emerson, Margaret Fuller, William
H. Channing, Theodore Parker, Henry D. Tho-
reau, George Ripley, and Charles A. Dana.

In 1840 these set up a quarterly magazine entitled "The Dial," which was continued for four
years, Margaret Fuller being editor during the
first two years, and Emerson during the last two.

Upon the whole, "The Dial" deserved to be a failure, although from its pages might be collected a goodly volume of prose and verse worthy of preservation in permanent shape. From the first Emerson contributed largely to "The Dial," both in prose and verse ; sometimes anonymously and sometimes over his own signature. Many of these contributions have been brought together by himself in his collected works.

Most of the prose papers had been recently delivered as addresses before college societies and literary associations. They are all quite above the ordinary run of such productions, being thoughtful and marked by the strong individuality of the man. One of them, an "Address to the Senior Class in Divinity College, Cambridge," delivered on Sunday evening, July 15, 1838, is notable in many ways. Of this address, Theodore Parker, then fresh in the ministry, writes to various correspondents. To one he says :

"In this Emerson surpassed himself as much as he surpasses others in a general way. I shall give no abstract, so beautiful, so just, and terribly sublime was his picture of the Church in its present condition. My soul is roused; and this week I shall write the long-meditated sermon on the state of the Church and the status of the times."

To another, Parker writes :

"It was the noblest of all his performances. A little exaggerated, with some philosophical untruths, it seemed

to me; but the noblest, the most inspiring strain, I ever
listened to. It caused a great outcry; one shouting,
'The Philistines be upon us!' another, 'We be all dead
men!' while the majority called out, 'Atheism!' The
Dean said, 'That part of it which was not folly was
downright atheism.' . . . Some seem to think that the
Christianity which has stood some storms will not be
able to weather this gale; and that truth, after all my
Lord Bacon has said, will have to give it up now. For
my part, I see the sun still shines, the rain rains, and the
dogs bark; and I have great doubts whether Emerson
will overthrow Christianity this time."

And again:

"The other day we discussed the question, in the
Association, whether Emerson was a Christian. One
said he was not; another maintained that he was an
atheist; but nobody doubted that he was a virtuous, devout man—one who would enter heaven when they
were shut out. Of course, they were in a queer predica-
ment. Either they must acknowledge that a man may
be virtuous, and yet no Christian (which most of them
thought a great heresy to suppose); and religious, yet
an atheist (which is a contradiction—to be without God,
and yet united with God); or else affirm that Emerson
was not virtuous nor religious—which they could not
prove. Others thought he should be called a Christian,
if he desired the name."

THE DIVINITY COLLEGE ADDRESS.

The position offered to and accepted by Emerson was, indeed, a peculiar one for a conscien-
tious man to assume. Upon such occasions, it is

taken for granted that the speaker is in the main
in accord with his hearers ; or, at least, if he differs from them upon any important points, those
points shall be kept in abeyance. Here was a
man who had not yet reached middle life, who had
deliberately set aside much that was held vital to
the exercise of the Christian ministry, and who
had yet by formal request to speak upon the duties
of that ministry to young men who were on the
point of entering upon that career which he could
no longer tread. From the very constitution of
his nature he must, upon such an occasion, speak
from his very heart of hearts. It was for him no
time for commonplace generalities. Quite pos-
sibly, he thought that the things which he had
come to hold as true had come to have lodgment
in the minds of these divinity students. At all
events, if he had any misgivings, he betrayed no
token of their existence. He spoke as though he
were a seer and prophet, whose utterances needed
no external authority to enforce their validity,
but needed only to be heard to be accepted. They
were chapters of that Divine Law, not engraved
upon tables of stone, or written down upon parch-
ment, in human speech, but inwrought into the
very constitution of our nature. For ourselves,
we see nothing in this address which looks at all
like Atheism or Pantheism. On the contrary, it
is full of Theism and Monotheism, expressed in
terms far more explicit than he would have been

likely to use a few years later, when his ideas,
or at least his forms of expressing them, had
come to be more or less influenced by Hindoo
theosophy.

The opening passages are calm and quiet, as
though they had been inspired by that summer
Sabbath day whose sun had just set. After
speaking of the perception of beauty and perfection awakened in us by the observation of the
laws of the physical universe, he passes to the
consideration of the higher laws of moral beauty.

THE SENTIMENT OF VIRTUE.

"A more sweet and overpowering beauty appears to
man when his heart opens to the sentiment of Virtue.
Then he is instructed in what is above him. He learns
that his being is without bound; that to the good, the
perfect, he is born—low as he now lies in evil and weakness. That which he venerates is still his own, though
he has not realized it yet. He *ought*—he knows the
sense of that grand word, though his analysis fails to
render account of it. When, in innocency, or when by
intellectual perception, he attains to say, 'I love the
Right; Truth is beautiful within and without for evermore. Virtue, I am thine; save me; use me; thee will I
serve day and night, in great, in small, that I may not be
virtuous, but Virtue '—then is the end of the Creator
answered, and God is well pleased.

"The sentiment of Virtue is a reverence and delight
in the presence of certain divine laws. It perceives that
this homely game of life we play covers, under what
seem foolish details, principles that astonish. These laws

refuse to be adequately stated. They will not be written out on paper or spoken by the tongue. They elude our persevering thought; yet we read them hourly in each other's faces, in each other's actions, in our own remorse. This sentiment is the essence of all religion. . . . If a man is at heart just, then, in so far, is he God. The safety of God, the majesty of God, do enter into that mind with justice. . . . See, again, the perfection of the law, as it applies itself to the affections, and becomes the law of society. As we are, so we associate. The good, by affinity, seek the good; the vile, by affinity, seek the vile. Thus, of their own volition, souls proceed into heaven, into hell."

This passage is most likely one of those which the estimable Dean of the Divinity School judged to be "folly." Knowing the quality of brain with which some men are endowed, and how apt it is to get dried up in the process of the manufacture of its possessor into a doctor of divinity, we can comprehend how the Dean should thus judge utterances like these, so different from those which he was wont to propound to his pupils.

"Atheist" is a very convenient term of reproach to be hurled at any one whose finite conceptions of the nature and attributes of the Infinite Being differ from our own finite ones. To the Athenians, Socrates was an atheist because he could not conceive of Zeus as they did. In one or two of his poems, and here and there in his later writings, Emerson speaks with apparent approval of the Hindoo theosophy, which represents Bráhma,

"the Adorable," as a being to whom all things
are indifferent ; who is himself all and in all ; to
whom past and present, shadow and sunlight,
shame and fame, the better and the worse, are all
alike. This theosophy he styles "the best gymnastics of the mind." We are not fully assured
as to how far Emerson really holds to any such
view. In this address there is no trace of any
such thing. There is certainly nothing that looks
like atheism ; but much to the direct contrary—
as in this passage, which follows immediately the
one last cited :

THE ONE SUPREME BEING.

"These facts have always suggested to man the sublime creed that the world is not the product of manifold
power, but of one Will, of one Mind ; and that one Mind
is everywhere active, in each ray of the star, in each
wavelet of the pool ; and whatever opposes that Will is
everywhere balked and baffled, because things are as
they are and not otherwise. Good is positive. Evil is
merely privative, not absolute ; it is like cold, which is
the privation of heat. Benevolence is absolute and real.
So much benevolence as a man hath, so much life has he.
For all things proceed out of this same Spirit, which is
differently named Love, Justice, Temperance, in its different applications, just as the ocean receives different
names on the several shores which it washes. All
things proceed out of the same Spirit, and all things
conspire with it."

It is hard to conceive how this teaching differs
essentially from the most orthodox conception of

a universal Providence which has directed the creation of all things, and presides over and controls all things—those which to a finite mind seem the smallest, as well as those which seem the greatest ; and that Providence is only one name for the actual manifestation of the will of the one Mind, the one Infinite Being.   People, if they choose, may designate Emerson's mode of presentation as Pantheism.   He has been styled a Pantheist, and has never taken special pains to disown the appellation.   We can understand how Trinitarians could consistently set aside any claim made by or for Emerson to be recognized as a Christian.   In their view, the belief that Christ, the Son, is God —"very God of very God"—is a fundamental article of the Christian creed ; and whosoever did not hold to that could not properly be called a Christian, whatever else he might be.   But we fail to see how such could be the case with any member of the Middlesex Unitarian Association. Emerson speaks of Jesus, from their own avowed standpoint, not merely as *a* man sent from God, as John the Baptist and many another was, but emphatically as *the* man sent of God.   As thus :

THE MAN JESUS.

"Jesus Christ belonged to the true race of the prophets.   He saw with open eye the mystery of the soul. Drawn by its serene harmony, ravished by its beauty, he lived in it, and had his being there.   Alone of all humanity, he estimated the greatness of man.   He saw that God incarnates himself in man, and evermore goeth forth to take possession of his world. He said, in the jubilee of this sublime emotion, ' I am divine. Through me God acts; through me, speaks. Would you see God, see me, or see thee when thou thinkest as I now think.' . . . He felt respect for the prophets; but no unfit tenderness to postponing their initial revelations to the hour and the man that now is: to the eternal revelation in the heart. Thus was he a true man. Having seen that the Law in us is commanding, he would not suffer it to be commanded. Boldly, with hand and heart and life, he declared it was God. Thus is he, as I think, the only soul in history who has appreciated the worth of a man."

Mr. Emerson has some sharp things to say against the prevailing idea of the Christian world in regard to the character of Jesus. This was to have been expected from him when speaking to a company of prospective preachers, who by their denominational affiliations were pledged to a very different view. He then proceeds to those passages which, we suppose, were the ones which Theodore Parker pronounced to be so terribly sublime, setting forth the faults of the Church in its present condition ; closing with what was the ultimate theme of the address, that for which mainly it was meditated. This is preaching, and the office of the preacher, in the present age.

THE OFFICE OF THE PREACHER.

" This office is coeval with the world. But observe the conditions, the spiritual limitations, of the office. The spirit only can teach. Not any profane man, not any sensual, not any liar, not any slave; but only he can give who has. The man on whom the soul descends, through whom the soul speaks, alone can teach. Courage, piety, love, wisdom, can teach; and every man can open his door to these angels, and they shall bring him the gift of tongues. But the man who aims to speak as books enable, as synods use, as fashion guides, as interest commands, babbles. Let him hush.

"To this holy office you propose to devote yourselves. I wish you may feel your call in the throbs of desire and hope. The office is the first in the world. It is of that reality that it can not suffer the deduction of any falsehood. And it is my duty to say to you that the need was never greater of a new revelation than now. From the views I have already expressed you will infer the sad conviction which I share, I believe, with numbers, of the universal decay and almost universal death of faith in society. The Soul is not preached. The Church seems to totter to its fall, almost all life extinct. On this occasion any complaisance would be criminal which told you, whose hope and commission it is to preach the faith of Christ, that the faith of Christ is preached."

FORMALITY IN PREACHING.

"It is time that this ill-suppressed murmur of all thoughtful men against the famine of our churches—this moaning of the heart because it is bereaved of the consolations of hope, the grandeur that comes alone out of the culture of the moral nature, should be heard through the sleep of indolence, and over the din of routine. This great and perpetual office of the preacher is not discharged. Preaching is the expression of moral sentiment in application to the duties of life. In how many churches, by how many prophets, tell me, is man made sensible that he is a living soul? Where shall I hear words such as in elder ages drew men to leave all and follow—leave father and mother, house and land, wife and child? Where shall I hear those august laws of moral being so pronounced as to fill my ear, and I feel ennobled by the offer of my uttermost action and passion?

"Wherever the pulpit is usurped by a formalist, there is the worshiper defrauded and disconsolate. We shrink as soon as the prayers begin which do not uplift, but smite and offend us. We are fain to wrap our cloaks around us, and secure as best we can a solitude that hears not.

"I once heard a preacher who sorely tempted me to say I would go to church no more. A snowstorm was falling around us. The snow was real, the preacher merely spectral; and the eye felt the sad contrast in looking at him, and then out of the window behind him into the beautiful meteor of the snow. He had lived in vain. He had not one word intimating that he had laughed or wept, was married or in love, had been commended or cheated. If he had ever lived or acted, we were none the wiser for it. The capital secret of his profession, namely, to convert life into truth, he had not learned. Not one fact in all his experience had he converted into doctrine. The true preacher can be known by this, that he deals out to his people his life—life passed through the fire of thought."

There are in this connection some passages which read as though they might have been written by Carlyle ; not from their form of expression, but from the sad pessimist tone of thought. As this :

DECAY OF FAITH.

"Certainly, there have been periods when a greater faith was possible. The Puritans in England and America found in the Christ of the Catholic Church, and in the dogmas inherited from Rome, scope for their austere piety, and their longings for civil freedom. But their creed is passing away, and none comes in its room. I think no man can go into one of our churches without feeling that what hold the public worship had on men is gone or going. It has lost its grasp on the affection of the good, and on the fear of the bad. It is already beginning to indicate character and religion to withdraw from the religious meetings. I have heard a devout person, who prized the Sabbath, say in bitterness of heart, 'On Sundays it seems wicked to go to church.' And the motive that holds the best there is now only a hope and a waiting. And what greater calamity can fall upon a nation than the loss of worship? Then all things go to decay. Genius leaves the temple, to haunt the senate or the market. Literature becomes frivolous. Science is cold. The eye of youth is not lighted by the hope of other worlds, and age is without honor. Society lives to trifles, and, when men die, we do not mention them."

Yet Emerson does not believe that this dark state of things is to be perpetual. In the future, nay in the near present, a remedy will be found. And this remedy, he thinks, will be found within the Church itself ; a church reformed, not in

6

external rites and ordinances—not perhaps largely even in creeds—but by having breathed into it the breath of a new life, and that through the voice of the living preacher. And to this high function he earnestly exhorts the young aspirants to the sacred office :

THE COMING CHURCH.

"And now let us do what we can to rekindle the smoldering wellnigh quenched fire on the altar. The evils of the Church that now is are manifest. The question returns, 'What shall we do?' I confess that all attempts to project and establish a cultus with new rites and forms seem to me vain. Faith makes us, and not we it, and Faith makes its own forms. All attempts to construct a system are as cold as the new worship introduced by the French to the Goddess of Reason. Rather let the breath of new life be breathed by you through the forms already existing, for, if once you are alive, you shall find that they shall become plastic and new. A whole popedom of forms one pulsation of virtue can uplift and vivify."

THE SABBATH AND PREACHING.

"Two inestimable advantages Christianity has given us : First, the institution of the Sabbath—the jubilee of the whole world—whose light dawns welcome alike into the dark closet of the philosopher, into the garret of toil, and into prison cells, and everywhere suggests, even to the vile, the dignity of spiritual being. Let it stand for evermore, a temple which new love, new faith, new sight, shall restore to more than its first splendor to mankind. And, secondly, to the institution of preaching—

the speech of man to man—essentially the most flexible
of forms. What hinders that now, everywhere, in pul-
pits, in lecture-rooms, in houses, in fields—wherever the
invitation of men or your own occasions lead you, you
speak the very truth, as your life and conscience lead
you—you speak the very truth as your life and conscience teach it, and cheer the waiting, fainting hearts of
men with new hope and new revelation?"

The address closes in a strain prophetically
hopeful :

THE COMING TEACHER.

"I look for the hour when that supreme beauty
which ravished the souls of those Eastern men—and
chiefly of those Hebrews—and through their lips spoke
oracles to all time, shall speak in the West also. The
Hebrew and Greek Scriptures contain immortal sentences that have been the bread of life to millions. But
they have no special integrity; are fragmentary; are not
shown in their order to the intellect. I look for a
Teacher that shall follow so far these shining laws, that
he shall see them come full circle; shall see the World
to be the mirror of the Soul; shall see the identity of
the law of gravitation with purity of heart; and shall
show that the Ought, that Duty, is one thing with Beauty, with Science, with Joy."

More than forty years have passed since these
brave words were uttered. Most of those upon
whose ears they fell have passed away from the
here to the hereafter. The ardent young man who
spoke them is now verging upon fourscore; his
life-work—whatever it was ordained to be—is

done. His lofty anticipations have not been realized. No Teacher like the one for whom he looked, who should follow the shining laws of the universe beyond the point visible in the Hebrew and Greek Scriptures—follow them until he should see them come full circle—has appeared to Emerson. For such a Teacher we look in vain to him. He has seen but a few points of that mighty circle whose infinite center is the will of the Eternal Mind, whose radii are the immensities, and whose circumference holds the universe ; or, as one of old phrased it, " whose center is everywhere, and whose circumference is nowhere." Of Emerson we must say, what he said of the Hebrew and Greek Scriptures : " His utterances have no special integrity, and are not shown in their order to the intellect." Perhaps he himself came to a conclusion not unlike this ; for, in one of his later works, he says : " Every surmise and vaticination of the mind is entitled to a certain respect. A wise writer will feel that the ends of study and composition are best answered by announcing undiscovered regions of thought, and so communicating, through hope, new activity to the torpid spirit." This, indeed, Emerson has done ; and his undigested theories may well, to use his own phrase, " be preferred to digested systems which have no one valuable suggestion."

VI.

CRITICAL AND BIBLIOGRAPHICAL.

EMERSON's whole mature life has been that of a Thinker and a Teacher. For the utterance of his thoughts he has found two mediums : oral discourse and written books. It is with the latter that we shall have to do ; for the mere spoken word dies almost as soon as it has been uttered, unless it has such vitality as to enter into the life of some auditor, or has so sunk into his memory that, perhaps, years after, he is enabled to write out at least the substance of it, and so the discourse becomes substantially permanent. Such is the case with some of the discourses of Socrates, as preserved by Plato. Such is the case with a few of the discourses of Jesus. Some of these—as the Sermon on the Mount, as recorded by Matthew, the last discourse to the disciples on Passover-eve, as recorded by John, and many of the parables—seem to be full reports, giving the very words of our Saviour. Oral discourse has one advantage over that which is written : if a man speaks from the fullness of his heart, the interaction between speaker and auditors gives a new life to the words. The flashing eye, the impassioned utterance, the spontaneous action, impart a force to thoughts and words which, when read, move us but little.

The sermons of Whitefield or the orations of Edward Irving, when read, seem cold, and hardly worth printing ; but when delivered they thrilled the hearts of thousands. Of Emerson's Lectures, we know that they took strong hold upon those who heard them ; but, as a whole, he has never thought them adapted for publication. They were clearly designed to be heard, not to be read. Perhaps the best parts of them have been substantially embodied in his books. Sometimes he seems to have condensed a lecture, or a number of lectures, into an essay or a chapter ; sometimes to have expanded a chapter into a lecture. But the written book possesses this great advantage over the spoken word : it preserves the very thought of the author, and in the very form in which he wished to express it. And if the book comes to be printed—as most books worthy of preservation do, sooner or later—it remains a possession for evermore. A good book is the most imperishable of all man's works. Herodotus will live when the Pyramids shall have crumbled into dust. Thucydides has outlived the Parthenon. Shakespeare and Milton will be as fresh as they are to-day when London shall have come to be what Memphis is. Some of the Hebrew Scriptures have outlived more than three millenniums, and all the kingdoms and empires which have grown up and fallen into decay ; and they and the New Testament Scriptures can never cease to sway man's heart so long as man shall exist here or in the hereafter. Many good books have, indeed, been apparently lost to after-ages. Some of these have been from time to time recovered. The manuscripts had been stored away in closets, piled over with dusty archives, or scrawled over with worthless stuff in palimpsests, but have been unearthed, cleaned off, and deciphered ; so that we now have them as perfect as they were when they came from the hands of their authors. The process of discovery is still going on ; and it is by no means impossible, not even perhaps improbable, that the lost " Decades " of Livy and the missing dramas of Æschylus and Sophocles will yet be brought to light. What need is there to speak of the clay-inscribed tablets and cylinders of Assyria, which, after lying utterly unknown beneath heaps of ruins of temple and palace for five-and-twenty long centuries, have, within our own generation, been exhumed and deciphered, shedding a flood of light upon the darkness which had gathered over and around the history and legends of preceding ages ?

Still another advantage of the written book over oral discourse is that the reader can always recur to it. The spoken discourse impresses us mainly in the mass. Many of the most vital points may fail to strike us ; or they may be misunderstood or not understood at all ; and we have no means of correcting the errors into which

we shall have fallen.   But we can go back to the
printed volume, can study it over and over again
until we are assured that we understand it, or
that we cannot understand it.   Let, then, the
preacher or the orator commit his best thoughts
to the press ; not that all or a tithe of what he
has said should be presented just as he spoke it,
but that the cream and marrow of his thoughts
should be set forth in their due order and in the
best form at his command.   This, we think, has
been done by Emerson.

Of the leading characteristics of Emerson's
course of thought and mode of expression, we
can not better express our own estimate than by
citing a portion of Mr. Whipple's thoughtful article in Appletons' "Cyclopædia" :

WHIPPLE UPON EMERSON.

" As a writer, Emerson is distinguished for a singular union of poetical imagination with practical acuteness.   His vision takes a wide sweep in the realms of
the ideal, but is no less firm and penetrating in the
sphere of facts. His observations on society, on manners, on character, on institutions, are stamped with
sagacity, and indicate a familiar knowledge of the homely
phases of life, which are seldom viewed in their poetical
relations.   One side of his wisdom is worldly wisdom.
The brilliant Transcendentalist is evidently a man not to
be easily deceived in matters pertaining to the ordinary
course of human affairs. His common-sense shrewdness
is vivified by a pervasive wit. With him, however, wit

is not an end, but a means, and usually employed for the detection of pretense and imposture.

" His practical understanding is sometimes underrated from the fact that he never groups his thoughts by the methods of logic. He gives few reasons, even when he is most reasonable. He does not prove, but announces, aiming directly at the intelligence of his readers, without striving to extract a reluctant assent by force of argument. Insight, not reasoning, is his process. The bent of his mind is to ideal laws, which are beyond the province of dialectics. Equally conspicuous is his tendency to embody ideas in the forms of imagination. No spiritual abstraction is so evanescent but he thus transforms it into a concrete reality. He seldom indulges in the expression of sentiment, and in his nature emotion seems to be less the product of the heart than of the brain.

" His style is in the nicest harmony with the character of his thought. It is condensed almost to abruptness. Occasionally he purchases compression at the expense of clearness, and his merits as a writer consist rather in a choice of words than in the connection of sentences, though his diction is vitalized by the presence of a powerful creative element. The singular beauty and intense life and significance of his language demonstrate that he not only has something to say, but knows exactly how to say it. Fluency, however, is out of the question in a style which combines such austere economy of words with the determination to load every word with vital meaning.

" But the great characteristic of Emerson's intellect is the perception and sentiment of beauty. So strong is this, that he accepts nothing in life that is uncomely, haggard, or ghastly. The fact that an opinion depresses,

instead of invigorating, is with him a sufficient reason
for its rejection. His observation, his wit, his reason,
his imagination, his style, all obey the controlling sense
of beauty which is at the heart of his nature, and in-
stinctively avoid the ugly and the base.

"Those portions of Emerson's writings which relate
to philosophy and religion may be considered as fragmentary contributions to the 'Philosophy of the Infinite.'
He has no system ; and, indeed, system in his mind is
associated with charlatanism. His largest generalization
is 'Existence.' On this inscrutable theme his conceptions vary with his moods and experience. Sometimes
it seems to be man who parts with his personality in
being united to God ; sometimes it seems to be God
who is impersonal, and who comes to personality only
in man ; and the real obscurity or vacillation of his metaphysical ideas is increased by the vivid and positive
concrete forms in which they are successively clothed."

Mr. Frothingham, in his "New England
Transcendentalism," while affirming that Emerson cannot be clearly designated as a Transcendentalist, in the technical sense of the term,
styles him "the Seer," and under that title devotes to him an elaborate chapter, from which
we make some excerpts, not always preserving
the order in which they were written :

FROTHINGHAM UPON EMERSON.

"Emerson has been called 'the prince of Transcendentalists.' It is nearer the truth to call him the prince
of Idealists. Certainly he can not be reckoned a disciple

of Kant, or Jacobi, or Fichte, or Schelling. He calls no
man master; he receives no teaching on authority. It
is not certain that he ever made a study of the Transcendental philosophy in the works of its chief exponents.
In his lecture on 'The Transcendentalist,' delivered in
1842, and embodied by him in his collected works, he
conveys the impression that it is Idealism, active and
protesting, an excited reaction against formalism, against
tradition, and conventionalism in every sphere. As such,
he describes it with great vividness and beauty. But as
such, merely, it was not apprehended by metaphysicians
like James Walker, theologians like Theodore Parker,
or preachers like William Henry Channing.

"Emerson does not claim for the soul a special faculty, like faith or intuition, by which the truths of the
spiritual order are perceived, as objects are perceived by
the senses. He contends for no doctrines, whether of
God, or the hereafter, or the moral law, on the credit
of such interior revelation. He neither dogmatizes nor
defines. On the contrary, his chief anxiety seems to be
to avoid committing himself to opinions, to keep all
questions open, to close no avenue in any direction to
the free ingress of the mind. He gives no description of
God that will class him as Theist or Pantheist, no definition of immortality that justifies his readers in imputing
to him any form of the popular belief in regard to it.
Does he believe in personal immortality? It is imper-
tinent to ask. He will not be questioned; not because
he doubts, but because his beliefs are so rich, so various
and many-sided, that he is unwilling, by laying emphasis
on any one of them, to do an apparent injustice to the
others.

"He will be held to no definitions; he will be reduced

to no final statements. The mind must have free range. Critics complain of the tantalizing fragmentariness of his writing; it is evidence of the shyness and modesty of his mind. He dwells in principles, and will not be cabined in beliefs. He needs the full expanse of the Eternal Reason."

While affirming that "Emerson's place is among poetic, not among philosophic minds," and in effect that he has nothing which can be fairly denominated a system, or the approach to a system of philosophy, Mr. Frothingham, in the end, attempts to set forth what that philosophy really is. We do not attempt to reconcile these two ideas respecting Emerson, but simply cite the somewhat brief exposition of the latter one. He says:

" We now stand at the center of Emerson's philosophy. His thoughts are few and pregnant; capable of infinite expansion, illustration, and application. They crop out on almost every page of his characteristic writings; are iterated and reiterated in every form of speech, and put into gems of expression that may be worn on any part of the person. His prose and poetry are aglow with them; they make his essays oracular, and his verse prophetic. By virtue of them his best books belong to the sacred literature of the race; by virtue of them, but for the lack of artistic finish of rhythm and rhyme, he would be the chief of American poets."

The summation of Emerson's beliefs and teachings is brief, and to us not altogether satisfactory. It runs thus :

" The first article in Emerson's faith is the primacy of mind.   That mind is supreme, eternal, absolute, one, subtile, living, immanent in all things, permanent, flowing, self-manifesting ; that the universe is the result of mind ; that nature is the symbol of mind ; that finite minds live and act through concurrence with infinite mind.   His second article is the connection of the individual mind with the primal mind, and its ability to draw thence wisdom, will, virtue, prudence, heroism—all active and passive qualities."

Mr. Frothingham proceeds to give some further insight into his views of the special religious bearing of Emerson's teachings.   He says :

" Emerson is never concerned to defend himself against the charge of Pantheism, or the warning to beware lest he unsettle the foundation of morality, annihilate the freedom of the will, abolish the distinction between right and wrong, and reduce personality to a mask. He never explains ; he trusts to affirmations pure and simple.   By dint of affirming all the facts as they appear, he makes his contribution to the problem of solving all ; and, by laying incessant emphasis on the cardinal virtues of humility, fidelity, sincerity, obedience, aspiration, simple acquiescence in the will of the Supreme Power, he not only guards himself against vulgar misconception, but sustains the mind at an elevation that makes the highest hill-tops of the accepted morality disappear in the dead level of the plain.   He takes the primary thoughts of his philosophy—if such it may be termed—with him wherever he goes.   Does he study history, history is the autobiography of the Eternal Mind."

The key to all this Mr. Frothingham finds in the opening sentences of Emerson's essay on " History."

EMERSON UPON HISTORY.

" There is one mind common to all individual minds. He that is once admitted to the right of reason is made a freeman of the whole estate. What Plato has thought, he may think; what a saint has felt, he may feel; what at any time has befallen any man, he can understand. Who hath access to this universal mind is a party to all that is or can be done; for *that* is the only and sovereign agent. Of the universal mind each individual man is one more incarnation. . . .

" What is the use of telegraphy? What of newspapers? To know in each social crisis how men feel in Kansas or California, the wise man waits for no mails, reads no telegrams. He asks his own heart. If they are made as he is, if they breathe the same air, eat of the same wheat, have wives and children, he knows that their joy or resentment rises to the same point as his own. The inviolate soul is in perpetual telegraphic communication with the source of events; has earlier information, a private dispatch, which relieves him of the terror which presses on the rest of the community. . . . . We are always coming up with the emphatic facts of history in our private experience, and verifying them here. All history becomes subjective. In other words, there is properly no history—only biography. Every mind must know the whole lesson for itself—must go over the whole ground. What it does not see, what it does not live, it does not know."

Surely no thoughtful man can accept this without making great allowances for the idiosyncrasies of Emerson, and his ever-present wont of expressing the varying moods of his own mental experiences. His practical philosophy descends to lower flights. We have no doubt that in times of great crisis he read the newspapers and telegrams to learn what men in Kansas and California, in Vermont and South Carolina, were feeling, never having received from the source of events any private dispatch which relieved him of the terror which was pressing on the rest of the community. His joy or resentment did not rise to the same point nor in the same direction as many of theirs. He rejoiced in many things over which the people of Carolina grieved, and grieved in many things over which they rejoiced.

For science, in the ordinary use of the term, Emerson cares little, and appears to know little. His reading, we are told, is very extensive in range, but most especially in the department of the higher imagination. "He is at home with the seers, Swedenborg, Plotinus, Plato, the books of the Hindoos, the Greek mythology, Plutarch, Chaucer, Shakespeare, Henry More, Hafiz; the books called sacred by the religious world; and books of natural science, especially those written by the ancients," which may be fairly put down as to a great extent imaginative. Oddly enough, Montaigne is a prime favorite with him. Upon this point Mr. Frothingham says:

"Emerson, by his principle, is delivered from the alarm of the religious man, who has a creed to defend, and from the defiance of the scientific man, who has creeds to assail. For the scientific *method* he professes no deep respect; for the scientific *assumption* none whatever. He begins with the opposite end. They start with matter; he starts with mind. They feel their way up; he feels his way down. They observe phenomena; he watches thoughts. They fancy themselves to be gradually pushing away as illusions the so-called entities of the soul; he dwells serenely with those entities, rejoicing to see men paying jubilant honor to what they mean to overturn. The facts they bring in—chemical, physiological, biological: Huxley's facts, Helmholtz's, Darwin's, Tyndall's, Spencer's, the ugly facts which theologians dispute—he accepts with eager hands, and uses to demonstrate the force and harmony of the spiritual laws."

All this seems to us to be a partial and one-sided view of Emerson's philosophy, which to us is in its main aspects most essentially practical. Using the word in a good sense, it is wholly a "this world" philosophy. Of the future life, as future, he takes little account. He finds the universe thus and so. Nature is what it is; man is what he is. All are but parts of one mighty whole; and it is man's place to know nature and to put himself into harmony with it. In his view, the life that now is, and each day of it, is a part of the eternal *now;* not merely a preparation for some unknown future. Youth exists for itself, manhood for itself, age for itself. There never will be a day longer than the one which is now passing ; there will never be a moment more full of duty and obligation than the one in which we are drawing our present breath. To be at this moment, and at all future moments, what he ought to be ; that is, in other words, to live in perpetual harmony with the immutable laws of nature—laws which are, because they could not be otherwise, being the outgrowth of the inmost being of the Divine Mind—this, in our view, is not only the central core but the sum and substance of Emerson's entire philosophy, no matter in what varying forms it may clothe itself, or how it may be tinged with hues reflected from Buddha or Plato, from Swedenborg or Confucius, from Zoroaster or Jesus. We shall try to elucidate still further our idea of the man and his teachings by passing in review over his successive works.

Considering that an interval of fully forty years elapsed between the composition of the earliest and the latest of Emerson's books, he is by no means a voluminous writer. His prose works as finally collected by himself are now issued in several shapes. In their most compact form they are comprised in three moderate volumes, each containing about as much matter as one of Dickens's large novels. The poems would make another volume somewhat smaller. The prose works are here arranged in the order of their

7

publication, which is not always coincident with that of their composition.

"Nature" (1836) ; "Miscellanies," consisting of nine collegiate addresses and public lectures, most of which had already been printed in "The Dial," and were in 1849 gathered into a volume which also included "Nature" ; "Essays," in two volumes (1841 and 1847). These, revised and corrected, constitute the first volume of his prose works, brought together in 1869.

"Representative Men" (1850), "English Traits" (1856), "Conduct of Life" (1860). These constitute the second volume of his prose works, brought together in 1869.

"Society and Solitude" (1870), "Letters and Social Aims" (1875). These, with the addition of some minor pieces, constitute the third volume of the prose works. Besides these, he furnished, in 1852, several valuable chapters for the "Memoirs of Margaret Fuller Ossoli," which are not contained in the collection of his works.

His poetical works are "Poems by R. W. Emerson" (1846), and "May-day, and Other Pieces" (1867). These poems were mostly written at intervals between 1840 and 1867. Most of them are short. The longest are "Woodnotes," of about five hundred lines ; "May-day," of about six hundred, "Monadnock," of about five hundred, and "The Adirondacks," of about four hundred lines.   In all, there are about one hundred and forty pieces, ranging from four lines upward, few of them exceeding fifty lines.

VII.

NATURE.

"NATURE," the earliest of Emerson's books, was published in 1836.   It was a small volume of some two hundred pages, openly printed, and containing less than half as much matter as this little book.   While, perhaps, not the greatest of his works, it is to us the most delightful.   Mr. Whipple has said that "Emerson seldom indulges in sentiment, and in his nature emotion seems to be less the product of the heart than of the brain."   This remark does not hold good in respect to "Nature," which is replete with the deepest sentiment and the liveliest emotion.   In it the heart predominates over the brain.   The style is glowing rather than austere, rising not unfrequently to a lofty pitch of eloquence.   It is inspired throughout by a glad spirit born of recovered health, a happy new-found home, and pleasant domestic and social surroundings.   Than Concord no more fitting residence could be found for a man like him.   The place itself was, and still is, of the quietest. A half-hour's walk would place him in complete solitude; but there were within sight of his door the abodes of men and women of culture, enough to furnish congenial society, while a ride of a couple of hours would bring him to the doors of his literary friends in Boston and Cambridge, and to the alcoves of the great libraries there. But the book, created under such happy auspices, fell almost still-born from the press. We are told that it took twelve years to dispose of an edition of five hundred copies. Like Wordsworth, he had to bide his time, and "create the taste by which he was to be enjoyed"; and, like Wordsworth, he has not waited in vain.

We shall speak at some length of this book— the first fruits of his genius, the "first crushings" of the grapes of his intellectual vineyard— for the reason that in it he more or less developed the germs of most of his speculations and theories. We shall also bring together passages from his later writings bearing upon the same or kindred topics, which explain, confirm, and in some degree modify the views therein propounded. In a brief Introduction, he sets forth the general design and aim of the book.

THE END OF NATURE.

"Our age is retrospective. It builds the sepulchres of the fathers; it writes biographies, histories, and criticism. The foregoing generations beheld God and Nature face to face; we through their eyes. Why should not we also enjoy an original relation to the universe? Why should not we have a poetry and philosophy of insight and not of tradition, and religion by revelation to us, and not the history of theirs? Imbosomed for a season in Nature, whose floods of life stream around and through us, and invite us by the powers they supply to action proportioned to Nature, why should we grope among the dry bones of the past, or put the living generation to masquerade out of its faded wardrobe? There is more wool and flax in the fields. There are new lands, new men, new thoughts. Let us demand our own work and laws and worship.

" Undoubtedly we have no questions to ask which are unanswerable. We must trust the perfection of the creation so far as to believe whatever curiosity the order of things has awakened in our minds the order of things can satisfy. Every man's condition is a solution in hieroglyphic of those inquiries he would put. He acts it as life before he apprehends it as truth. In like manner, Nature is already, in its forms and tendencies, describing its own design. Let us interrogate the great apparition that shines so peacefully around us. Let us inquire, To what end is Nature? "

We will not here pause to call in question the accuracy of the foregoing proem further than to say that, in our judgment, the generalization is far too broad. If by " generations " we are to understand the mass of mankind living at any one time, or even any considerable portion of them, we do not find in all our reading any generation

who "beheld God and Nature face to face." Here
and there indeed, scattered through the ages,
there have been men to whom God and Nature
seem to have manifested themselves partially in
an original manner. Of such men, in our view,
were the prophets and bards of the Old Testament,
the evangelists and apostles of the New Testament, and, above all—speaking only humanly of
him, and without touching the point of his divinity—the "man Jesus." If Mr. Emerson, or any
one else, chooses to put Buddha and Zoroaster,
Menu and Plato, Milton and Swedenborg, into the
category, we will not dispute them. Did not all
of them claim, in some way or other, to have
talked face to face with God ? And yet they all
looked at the universe, and the great laws of the
universe, more or less, and very largely, through
the eyes of others. Did not Jesus look through
the eyes of Moses and David and Isaiah ? Did
not Buddha and Plato draw from wells digged by
wise men who had gone before them ? Does not
Emerson look through partially the eyes of all
these men, and those of many another ? All ages
have been retrospective ; and we believe that all
ages—our own included—are also prospective.

Every age dresses itself more or less in the garments woven by preceding ones. Some of these
are indeed faded and worn out ; others are fading
and decaying ; some, we believe—and we suppose
Emerson believes—will never be outworn through

all human generations. Thus, in a passage already cited from his " Divinity Address," he inculcates the thought that the Christian cultus, with two at least of its distinguishing features, the Seventh-day rest, " the jubilee of the whole world," and the institution of preaching, will stand to the end of time. A revelation is not the less a revelation to us because it comes to us through Moses or Paul, through Plato or Confucius. The thing which we see and feel is none the less our sight and feeling because Swedenborg or Emerson has told us where to look for it ; and has told us, moreover, how the view of it affected him. If only I see and feel it, it is mine, as really and truly as though no man had ever before felt or thought it. I myself might never have thought out that sublime law of gravitation which binds the entire physical universe into one whole, that law in virtue of which the stars in their courses are kept from wrong, and by which the most ancient heavens are as strong as they were at the dawn of creation. Yet, when Newton has discovered this universal law, and taught it to me, it is mine as much as it was his. It is no more his, the possession of his generation, than it is the possession of all future generations of men.

The trouble with most earnest men, when they compare the present with the past, is that they overlook the immensity of the past ; they put ages at one beam of the scale and years at the

other. The good in the one scale is but dust when
weighed against that in the other. Half unconsciously, they overlook the fact that the good of
the past is the net sum and residue of all that
countless generations have achieved; while the
good in the other scale is just that which has been
achieved by the men of a single generation. And
still again, the folly of past generations, their
manifold stupidities and unbeliefs, have all gone
the way to dusty death; they offend us no more,
and we only know that they ever existed when
we grope amid the dead ashes in their sepulchres;
while, on the other hand, the follies and stupidities of our own day confront us at every turn;
like the frogs of Egypt they come up into our bed-
chambers and our kneading-troughs; like the locusts, they seem to be devouring every green thing.
But the frogs die, the locusts are driven away, and
Nature retains no token that they ever were. To
the widest observation all evil is transient and
perishable; the good only survives, and is immortal. To the thinking man of no age has his own
generation seemed an heroic one. Most turn to
the far past for the Golden Age; some look for it
in the far or near future; few in the immediate
present. But if there be an all-wise, an all-good,
an all-powerful Creator and Ruler of the universe,
then it follows as a matter of certainty that the
course of things must be ever tending toward the
better, not toward the worse. Rather than be-

lieve otherwise, I would be an atheist. If we read history with open eyes, we shall see that such is the case. The world does move, and moves in the right direction. Doubtless there are periods when the movement seems checked, or even apparently reversed. Trace the Mississippi from its sources downward, and here and there it seems to the voyager that its course is checked or reversed, and that the current is flowing back to its fountains. But all the while the waters are circling around some obstacle which they will in the end either elude or sweep away. Could one mount high enough, and with sure vision survey the whole course, all these petty divergencies would vanish from the view, and he would perceive that the whole mighty flood is all the while moving onward to the ocean.

So it is with the general history of human generations. Doubtless there have been dark ages, miserable ages, ages seemingly altogether barren of good and unprofitable in every way. But yet the human race is growing better. How many of the best of the Hebrew patriarchs would be out of the penitentiary in any modern civilized community? Yet, beyond doubt, they were the best men of their times. The rear of the present good men of civilized races is farther on in morals than the vanguard of them was two, three, or four thousand years ago, and the bad are no worse. The advance is seen also in even savages races.

Do not the Esquimaux and the Zulus rank higher
in the scale of being than did the cave-dwellers
and men of the Stone Age, traces of whom every
now and then crop up ?   Or, to sum up the whole
in a sentence, is the world of to-day such as it was
at the time of the Deluge, good for nothing in
fact or in prospect, and fit only to be swept away
to the last individual, saving only the eight souls
who entered into the ark and were saved ?

Whether this generation of ours is really one
of the decadent generations is a matter which
we are not called upon to discuss, only—Carlyle
often, and Emerson sometimes to the contrary—
we think it is not.   Nay, more, we believe it to
be very distinctively an age of progress and even
of faith.   We believe that to-day there are more
men who look upon God and Nature face to face
than there ever were before at one time upon
earth.   Indeed, notwithstanding Emerson's apparent pessimism, the whole tone of his writings
is essentially optimist ; and in none of them more
so than in this book upon " Nature."

He does not always, if we understand him,
use the term " Nature " in exactly the same
sense.   Sometimes he appears to mean by it the
Supreme Mind from which all things proceed ;
sometimes apparently the phenomena of the outward world ; sometimes the laws in virtue of
which these phenomena manifest themselves to the
individual man.   But in this book he gives a for-

mal definition of Nature wide enough to include everything saving the inmost consciousness of each individual man and the Supreme Being. His definition stands thus:

WHAT NATURE IS.

" Philosophically considered, the universe is composed of Nature and the Soul. Strictly speaking, therefore, all that is separate from us, all which philosophy distinguishes from the *Not Me*—that is, both Nature and Art, and all other men, and my own body—must be ranked under this name 'NATURE.' In enumerating the values of Nature and casting up their sum, I shall use the word in both senses—in its common and in its philosophical import. In inquiries so general as our present one, the inaccuracy is not material; no confusion of thought will occur. *Nature*, in the common sense, refers to essences unchanged by man: space, the air, the river, the leaf. *Art* is applied to the mixture of his will with the same things, as in a house, a canal, a picture, a statue. But his operations, taken together, are so insignificant —a little chipping, baking, patching, and washing—that in an impression so grand as that of the world on the human mind they do not vary the result."

He proceeds to lay down the end and purpose of all study, thought, and speculation.

THEORIES AND PHENOMENA.

" All science has one aim, namely, to find a theory of Nature. We have theories of races and of functions, but scarcely yet a remote approach to an idea of creation. We are now so far from the road to truth that

religious teachers dispute and hate each other, and speculative men are esteemed unsound and frivolous. But
to a sound judgment the most abstract truth is the most
practical. Whenever a true theory appears, it will be
its own evidence. Its test is that it will explain all phenomena. Now, many are thought not only unexplained
but inexplicable: language, sleep, madness, dreams,
beasts, sex."

We do not believe that Mr. Emerson would
claim that he has in any good degree arrived at
such a general theory—one which explains all
phenomena. We do not think that any finite
mind can frame such a theory ; or that, if framed
by a higher power, that any finite mind could
grasp it in anything like its full extent. But
what Mr. Emerson has done in this book of his
is to set forth many aspects in which Nature
works for the weal of man. These varying aspects are presented in picturesque forms. Thus :

THE STARS.

"To go into solitude a man needs to retire as much
from his chamber as from society. I am not solitary
while I read and write, though nobody is with me. But,
if a man would be alone, let him look at the stars. The
rays that come from those heavenly worlds will separate
between him and what he touches. One might think
the atmosphere was made transparent with this design to
give man in the heavenly bodies the perpetual presence
of the sublime. Seen in the streets of cities, how great
they are! If the stars should appear only one night in a

thousand years, how would men believe and adore, and preserve for many generations the remembrance of the city of God which had been shown! But every night come out these envoys of beauty, and light the universe with their admonishing smile."

Most persons "do not see the sun; at least they have a very superficial seeing." We may add, that which the most thoughtful seer beholds —say in a star—is by no means the picture painted upon the retina of the eye. All that is there pictured is only a minute bright point. The gas-light far up a church steeple outshines the morning and the evening star, outshines Sirius and Orion. To the eye alone the lighted street of a city is brighter than all the galaxies. To the eye alone the illuminated dome of St. Peter's is more magnificent than the star-lit firmament. It is only when science comes in and tells us that these minute points of light are worlds, that man begins to see the starry heavens. What he then really sees is indeed not the stars themselves, but the stars as he has come to know them to be. The eye of your dog sees the same stars that your eye sees. Yet he never stops to gaze upon them, although he will go frantic at the blaze of an exploding fire-rocket. To him this is a phenomenon more imposing than any meteoric shower. And when science goes further, and tells of the immensity of space which separates us from the stars, we gain a still higher idea of their magnificence.

Yet to the mere eye this immensity of space is invisible. For aught the eye can tell us, the pole-star is no farther off than the candle which shines from a cottage window on the top of a hill a few furlongs away; and that candle is to the physical eye by far the brighter of the two. And when science goes still further, and tells us that all the stars which we see, all those which the telescope reveals to us, and even those which the telescope refuses to distinguish separately, but gathers together into a faint cloud the accumulated light from untold myriads of them; and, still further, when it tells us that all these innumerable stars are but parts of one great system, bound together by one eternal and immutable law; that as the moon revolves around the earth, and the earth and all her sister planets around the sun, so all these starry suns are but satellites or sub-satellites of a still mightier sun, which mortal eye has never seen—when his intellect has fairly grasped these and such-like facts, and just so far as he has grasped them, then man begins to see the stars. But he sees them with the inward, not with the outward eye. To be a lover of Nature, a man must be an understander of Nature. Or, as Emerson phrases it, "The lover of Nature is he whose inward and outward senses are truly adjusted to each other. Then his intercourse with heaven and earth becomes part of his daily food. In the presence of Nature a wild delight runs through him, in spite of real sorrows." To such a one only apply such passages as this :

DELIGHT IN NATURE.

"Not the sun or the summer alone, but every hour and season yields its tribute of delight; for every hour and change corresponds to and authorizes a different state of the mind, from breathless noon to grimmest midnight. Nature is a setting that fits equally well a comic or a mourning piece. In good health the air is a cordial of incredible value. Crossing a bare common, in snow puddles, at twilight, under a clouded sky, without having in my thoughts any occurrence of special good fortune, I have enjoyed a perfect exhilaration. In the woods, too, a man casts off his years, as the snake his slough. In the woods is perpetual youth. Within these plantations of God, a decorum and sanctity reign, a perennial festival is dressed, and the guest sees not how he should tire of them in a thousand years.

"In the woods we return to reason and faith. There I feel that nothing can befall me in life—no disgrace, no calamity (leaving me my eyes), which Nature can not repair. I become a transparent eyeball; I am nothing; I see all; the currents of the Universal Being circulate through me; I am part and particle of God. In the tranquil landscape, and especially in the distant line of the horizon, man beholds somewhat as beautiful as his own nature. The greatest delight which the fields and woods minister is the suggestion of an occult relation between man and the vegetable. I am not alone and unacknowledged. They nod to me, and I to them. The waving of the boughs in the storm is new to me and old. It takes me by surprise, and yet is not unknown. Its effect on me is like that of a higher thought or a better emotion coming over me, when I deemed I was thinking justly or doing right."

Some of this is true to a certain extent of most men, perhaps at times to all men ; and to none at all times. There is a certain mere physical delight in Nature even to the beasts. Some rejoice in sunlight and warmth ; the Arctic bear delights in snow and ice. But to how many men is there ever anything which answers to this glowing description of the delights of Nature? Has the woodsman who sees in the tree at best only so much fuel or timber, or perhaps a thing to be got rid of so that he may plant his corn or potatoes, any such delight in the woods? Emerson is in no wise oblivious of the fact that all this does not belong wholly to Nature itself, but comes greatly out of our imminent relations to it. Thus he follows the foregoing by this pregnant limitation :

NATURE AND OUR MOODS.

"Yet it is certain that the power to produce this delight does not reside in Nature, but in man, or in a harmony of both. It is necessary to use these pleasures with great temperance. For Nature is not always tricked in holiday attire ; but the same scene which yesterday breathed perfume and glittered as for the frolic of the nymphs is overspread with melancholy to-day. Nature always wears the colors of the spirit. To a man laboring under calamity, the heat of his own fire hath sadness in it. Then there is a kind of contempt of the landscape felt by him who has just lost a dear friend by death. The sky is less grand as it shuts down over less worth in the population."

That is, though the real aspect of Nature may not have changed, its aspect to us is but the counterpart of our own present mood. Does one wish to cast a gloom over the brightest summer day, he need only put on a pair of sad-colored glasses. As Coleridge has well said :

> " We receive but what we give,
> And in our life alone does nature live. . . .
> The rill is tuneless to his ear who feels
> No harmony within ; the south wind steals
> As silent as unseen among the leaves.
> Who hath no inward beauty none perceives,
> Though all around is beautiful."

Passing from the material to the spiritual aspect of nature, Emerson proceeds to say that " whoever considers the final cause of the world will discern a multitude of uses that enter as parts into that result. They all admit of being thrown into one of the following classes : Commodity, Beauty, Language, and Discipline," and he treats of these uses in that order.

COMMODITY.

" Under the general name of ' Commodity ' I rank all those advantages which our senses owe to Nature. This of course is a benefit which is temporary and mediate, not ultimate, like its service to the soul. Yet, although

8

low, it is perfect in its kind, and is the only use of Nature
which all men apprehend. The misery of man appears
like childish petulance when we explore the steady and
prodigal provision that has been made for his support
and delight on this green ball which floats him through
the heavens. What angels invented those splendid ornaments, those rich conveniences; this ocean of air above,
this ocean of water beneath, this firmament of earth between; this zodiac of lights, this tent of dropping clouds,
this striped coat of climates, this four-fold year? Beasts,
fire, water, stones, and corn serve him. The field is at
once his floor, his workshop, his playground, his garden,
his bed."

He goes on to say that "Nature, in its ministry to man, is not only the material, but is also
the process and the result. The wind sows the
seed; the sun evaporates the sea; the ice on the
other side of the planet condenses rain on this;
the rain feeds the plant; the plant feeds the animal. And thus the endless circulations of the
divine charity nourish man." The useful arts,
moreover, are reproductions or new combinations
by the wit of man of the same natural benefactors. Such are the steam-engine and the railroad.
"The private man hath cities, ships, canals,
bridges, built for him. He goes to the post-office,
and the human race run on his errands; to the
bookshop, and the human race read and write
of all that happens to him; to the court-house,
and nations repair his wrongs." But he adds,
pregnantly, "This mercenary benefit is one which

has respect to a further good. A man is fed, not that he may be fed, but that he may work."

BEAUTY.

"But Nature serves a much nobler want of man than any or all of these which are served by "Commodity." This nobler end is the love of Beauty, that orderly arrangement which led the Greeks to call the world '*Kosmos*,' 'Beauty.' All the primary forms of Nature are capable of giving delight in and for themselves. This is partly owing to the eye itself; for the eye is the best of artists; and so, too, light is the best of painters. There is no object so foul that intense light will not make beautiful; and the stimulus which it affords to the sense, and a sort of infinitude which it hath, like space and time, make all matter gay. And besides this general grace diffused over Nature, almost all the individual forms are agreeable to the eye, as is proved by our endless imitations of them."

He goes on to distribute the aspects of Beauty into three categories. First, the simple perception of natural forms is a delight, "although in its lowest functions this seems to lie on the confines of Commodity and Beauty. To the body and the mind which have been cramped by noxious work or company, Nature is medicinal, and restores their tone. The tradesman, the attorney, comes out of the din and craft of the street, and sees the sky and the woods, and is a man again. In their eternal calm he finds himself. The health of the eye seems to demand a horizon.

We are never tired so long as we can see far enough." But he continues:

BEAUTY FOR ITSELF.

"In other hours Nature satisfies by its loveliness, without any mixture of corporeal benefit. I see the spectacle of morning from the hilltop over my house, from daybreak to sunrise, with emotions which an angel might share. The long slender bars of cloud float like fishes in the sea of crimson light. From the earth, as a shore, I look into that silent sea. I seem to partake of its rapid transformations; the active enchantment reaches my dust, and I dilate and conspire with the morning wind. How does Nature deify us with a few and cheap elements! Give me health and a day, and I will make the pomp of emperors ridiculous. The dawn is my Assyria; the sunset and moonrise my Paphos and unimaginable realms of faerie; broad noon shall be my England of the senses and the understanding; the night shall be my Germany of mystic philosophy and dreams. . . .

"But this beauty of Nature, which is seen and felt as beauty, is the least part. The shows of day, the dewy morning, the rainbow, mountains, orchards in blossom, stars, moonlight, shadows in still water, and the like, become shows merely, if too eagerly hunted, and mock us with their unreality. Go out of the house to see the moon, and it is mere tinsel; it will not please as when its light shines upon your necessary journeys. The beauty that shimmers in the yellow afternoons of October, who could ever clutch it? Go forth to find it, and it is gone. It is only a mirage as you look from the windows of diligence."

But in the mere matter of Beauty, Nature has a far higher function for the soul than that which it has for its own sake. This is its spiritual aspect.

THE SPIRITUAL ASPECTS OF BEAUTY.

"The presence of a higher, namely, of the spiritual, element is essential to its perfection. The high and divine beauty, which can be loved without effeminacy, is that which is found in combination with the human will. Beauty is the mark which God sets upon virtue. Every natural action is graceful. Every heroic act is also decent, and causes the place and bystanders to shine. We are taught by great actions that the universe is the property of every individual in it. Every rational creature has all Nature for his dowry and estate. He may divest himself of it; he may creep into a corner, and abdicate his kingdom, as most men do, but he is entitled to the world by his constitution. In proportion to the energy of his thought and will, he takes up the world into himself. 'All those things for which men plow, build, or sail, obey virtue,' said Sallust. 'The winds and waves,' said Gibbon, 'are always on the side of the ablest navigators.' So are the moon and all the stars of heaven."

It will be borne in mind that Emerson, here and almost always elsewhere, uses the term "virtue," as Paul did the corresponding Greek word, in its primary etymological signification, equivalent to our word "manliness"; not as in its ordinary and more extended sense, as the summation of all good qualities and affections. Pursuing the same line of thought, he continues:

THE BEAUTY OF NOBLE ACTS.

" When a noble act is done—perhaps in a scene of
great natural beauty; when Leonidas and his three hundred martyrs consume one day in dying, and the sun and
moon come each and look at them once in the steep de-
file of Thermopylæ; when Arnold Winkelreid, in the
high Alps, under the shadow of the avalanche, gathers
in his side a sheaf of Austrian spears to break the line for
his comrades: are not these heroes entitled to the beauty of the scene, to the beauty of the deed? When the
bark of Columbus nears the shore of America—before it
the beach lined with savages, fleeing out of all their huts
of cane, the sea behind, and the purple mountains of the
Indian archipelago around—can we separate the man
from the living picture? Does not the New World
clothe his form with her palm-groves and savannas, as
fit drapery? Ever does natural beauty steal in like air,
and envelope great actions."

BEAUTY IN ASSOCIATION.

"Nature stretcheth out her arms to embrace man,
only let his thoughts be of equal greatness. Willingly
does she follow his steps with the rose and the violet,
and bend her lines of grandeur and grace to the decora-
tion of her darling child. Only let his thoughts be of
equal scope, and the frame will suit the picture. A virtuous man is in unison with her works, and makes the
central figure of the whole visible sphere. Homer, Pindar, Socrates, Phocion, associate themselves fitly with
the geography and climate of Greece. The visible heavens and earth sympathize with Jesus. And in common
life, whosoever has seen a person of powerful character
and happy genius, will remark how easily he took all

things with him. The persons, the opinions, and the day, and Nature became ancillary to a man."

The third and last of the general aspects under which Beauty is considered is its relation to the intellect. "Besides the relation of things to virtue, they have a relation to thought."

INTELLECTUAL BEAUTY.

"The intellect searches out the absolute order of things as they stand in the mind of God, and without the colors of affection. The intellectual and the active powers seem to succeed each other, and the exclusive activity of the one generates the exclusive activity of the other. There is something unfriendly in each to the other; but they are like the alternate periods of feeding and working in animals: each prepares and will be followed by the other. Therefore does Beauty, which in relation to actions, as we have seen, comes unsought, and comes because it is unsought, remain for the apprehension and pursuit of the intellect; and then again, in its turn, of the active power. Nothing divine dies. All good is eternally reproductive. The beauty of Nature re-forms itself in the mind; and not for barren contemplation, but for new creation."

Emerson here devotes a few sentences to a rapid survey of the relations between Beauty and Art.

BEAUTY AND ART.

"All men are in some degree impressed by the face of the world—some men even to delight. This love of Beauty is *taste*. Others have the same love in such excess that, not content with admiring, they seek to embody it in new forms. The creation of Beauty is *Art*. The production of a work of art throws a light upon the mystery of humanity. A work of art is an abstract or epitome of the world. It is the result or expression of Nature in miniature. For, although the works of Nature are innumerable, and all different, the result or expression of them all is similar and single. Nature is a sea of forms radically alike and even unique. A leaf, a sunbeam, a landscape, the ocean, make an analogous impression on the mind. What is common to them all—that perfectness and harmony is *Beauty*. The standard of Beauty is the entire circuit of natural forms—the totality of Nature which the Italians expressed by defining Beauty as '*Il piu nell' uno.*' Nothing is quite beautiful alone ; nothing but is beautiful in the whole. A single object is only so far beautiful as it suggests this universal grace. The poet, the painter, the sculptor, the musician, the architect, seek each to concentrate this radiance of the world on one point; and each in his several work to satisfy the love of Beauty which stimulates him to produce. Thus is Art a Nature passed through the alembic of man. Thus in Art does Nature work through the will of a man filled with the beauty of her first works."

In closing this chapter on Beauty, Mr. Emerson gives the keynote to all his philosophy of the universe—in fact, almost a summation of it, embracing, as it does, his view of the ultimate reason of the world, in so far, at least, as we can in any good degree apprehend it :

BEAUTY NOT THE ULTIMATE END.

" The world thus exists to the soul to satisfy the desire of Beauty. This I call an ultimate end. No reason can be asked or given why the soul seeks Beauty. Beauty, in its largest and profoundest sense, is one expression for the universe. God is the All-Fair. Truth and Goodness and Beauty are but different faces of the same All. But Beauty in Nature is not ultimate. It is the herald of inward and internal Beauty, and is not alone a solid and satisfactory good. It must stand as a part, and not as yet the last or highest expression of Nature."

Language in Emerson's classification is the third of the uses which Nature subserves to man. A few sentences, much disjointed in our condensation, but yet, as they stand, serving to show the high estimate which he puts upon this use. "Words are signs of natural facts. The use of natural history is to give us aid in supernatural history; the use of the outer creation is to give us language for the beings and changes of the inward creation. Every word which is used to express a moral or intellectual fact, if traced to its root, is found to be borrowed from some material appearance." Thus, "right" means *straight;* "wrong" means *twisted;* "spirit" primarily means *wind;* "transgression" the *crossing of a line.* We say the "heart" to express *emotion,* the "head" to denote *thought,* and so on. "And 'thought' and 'emotion' are words borrowed from sensible things, and now appropriated to spiritual nature. Most of the process by which this transformation is made is hidden from us in the remote time when language was framed ; but the same tendency may be daily observed in children. Children and savages use only nouns, or names of things, which they convert into verbs, and apply to analogous mental acts." But, continues Emerson, in phrases that might have been written by Swedenborg :

NATURAL SYMBOLISM.

" This origin of all words that convey a spiritual import—so conspicuous a fact in the history of language—is our least debt to Nature. It is not only words that are emblematic; it is things which are emblematic. Every natural fact is a symbol of some spiritual fact. Every appearance in Nature corresponds to some state of the mind; and that state of the mind can only be described by presenting that natural appearance as a picture. An enraged man is a lion; a cunning man is a fox; a firm man is a rock; a learned man is a torch. A lamb is innocence; a snake is subtle spite; flowers express to us the delicate affections. Light and darkness are our familiar expressions for knowledge and ignorance; and heat for love. Visible distance, behind and before us, is respectively our image for memory and hope."

This idea of universal symbolism is followed still farther into the realms of the spiritual and the ideal, up to the very dwelling-place of the Supreme Being :

FACTS AS TYPICAL.

" Who looks upon a river, in a meditative hour, and is not reminded of the flux of all things? Throw a

stone into the stream, and the circles that propagate
themselves are the beautiful type of all influence. Man
is conscious of a universal soul within or behind his individual life, wherein, as in a firmament, the natures of
justice, truth, love, freedom, arise and shine. This universal soul he calls Reason. It is not mine or thine
or his; but we are its. We are its property and men.
And the blue sky in which the private earth is buried,
the sky with its eternal calm, and full of everlasting
orbs, is the type of reason. That which, intellectually
considered, we call reason, we call Spirit when considered in relation to Nature. Spirit is the Creator.
Spirit hath life in itself. And man, in all ages and
countries, embodies it in his language as the FATHER.

"There is nothing lucky or capricious in these analogies; but they are constant, and pervade Nature. These
are not the dreams of a few poets here and there; but
man is an analogist, and studies relations in all objects.
He is placed in the center of beings, and a ray of relation passes from every other being to him. And neither
can man be understood without these objects, nor these
objects without man.

"All the facts in natural history, taken by themselves, have no value, but are barren like a single sex.
But marry it to human history, and it is full of life.
Whole Floras, all Linnæus's and Buffon's volumes, are
dry catalogues of facts; but the most trivial of these
facts—the habit of a plant, the organs or work or noise
of an insect, applied to the illustration of a fact in intellectual philosophy, or in any way associated with human
nature, affects us in the most lively and agreeable manner. The seed of a plant—to what affecting analogies in
the nature of man is that little fruit made use of in all

discourse up to the voice of Paul, who calls the human
corpse a seed: 'It is sown a natural body; it is raised
a spiritual body.' This immediate dependence of language upon Nature—this conversion of an outward phenomenon into a type of somewhat in human life, never
loses its power to affect us. It is this which gives that
piquancy to the conversation of a strong-natured farmer
or backwoodsman, which all men relish."

But there are many conditions requisite to anything like the adequate use of language as the
vehicle of thought and emotion. First and foremost, as presented by Emerson, is sincerity on the
part of the speaker. By this we understand him
to mean that, at least for the time being, the man
who speaks well must be himself in earnest.
The thing which he says must be subjectively
true. The moment his auditors fairly suspect
that he is merely talking for effect, his most eloquent words are to them like idle wind.

VERITY IN LANGUAGE.

"A man's power to connect his thought with the
proper symbol, and so to utter it, depends on the simplicity of his character; that is, upon his love of truth,
and his desire to communicate it without loss. The corruption of man is followed by the corruption of language.
When simplicity of character and the sovereignty of ideas
are broken up by the prevalence of secondary desires—
the desire of riches, of pleasure, of power, and of praise,
duplicity and falsehood take the place of simplicity and
truth; the power of Nature as an interpreter of the will

is lost. New imagery ceases to be created, and old words
are perverted to stand for things which are not ; a paper
currency is employed when there is no bullion in the
bank. In due time the fraud is manifest, and words lose
all power to stimulate the understanding or the affections.
Hundreds of writers may be found in every long-civilized
nation who for a time believe, and make others believe,
that they see and utter truths, who do not of themselves
clothe one thought in its natural garment, but who feed
unconsciously on the language created by the primary
writers of the country—those, namely, who hold primarily on Nature."

WORDS AND THINGS.

"But wise men pierce this rotten diction, and fasten
words again to visible things; so that picturesque language is at once a commanding certificate that he who
employs it is a man in alliance with truth and God.
The moment our discourse rises above the ground-line of
familiar facts, and is inflamed with passion or exalted by
thought, it clothes itself in images. A man conversing
in earnest, if he watches his intellectual processes, will
find that a material image, more or less luminous, arises
in his mind contemporaneous with every word which
furnishes the vestment of the thought. Hence, good
writing and brilliant discourse are perpetual allegories.
This imagery is spontaneous; it is the blending of experience with the present action of the mind; it is its
proper creation ; it is the working of the original cause
through the instruments he has already made."

A few paragraphs like these are to our minds
worth more than all the volumes of rhetoric which
clutter up the shelves of our libraries, and are a

perpetual weariness to the student, who wishes
somehow to gain the secret of getting men to
think and feel as he thinks and feels, or perhaps
as he dimly imagines that he thinks and feels.
Everywhere does Emerson insist upon this loving
intercourse with Nature in her visible forms as
the primal necessity for the adequate presentation
of thought.   As in this noble passage :

NATURE AND THE ORATOR.

"These facts may suggest the advantage which the
country life possesses for a powerful mind over the artificial and curtailed life of cities. We know from Nature
more than we can at will communicate. Its light flows
into the mind for evermore, and we forget its presence.
The poet, the orator, bred in the woods, whose senses
have been nourished by their fair and appeasing changes,
year after year, without design and without heed, shall
not lose their lesson altogether in the roar of cities or
the broil of politics. Long hereafter, amidst agitation
and terror in national councils—in the hour of revolution—these solid images shall reappear in their morning
luster, as fit symbols and words of the thoughts which
the passing events shall awaken. At the call of a noble
sentiment, again the woods wave, the pines murmur, the
river rolls and shines, and the cattle low upon the mountains, as he saw and heard them in his infancy. And
with these forms the keys of persuasion, the keys of
power, are put into his hands."

In this special passage stress is mainly laid
upon the influence of physical nature upon the
formation of language—this and its intimate rela-

tions to the growth of the individual soul. But nature, in Emerson's view, also includes human beings; and the influence of all men upon each man is elsewhere fully insisted upon. In considering the mighty uses of nature in the forming, or rather in enabling man to form, a language, while admitting the value of its use for our daily needs, he speaks almost scornfully of applying such an implement to ordinary affairs of daily life. This, of course, must be taken with very much of limitation; for if man, standing as he does in the universe, must needs have his kitchen and common council, he can not well avoid talking about them. Emerson's purpose is not to actually underrate this lower use to which language is put, but rather, by contrast, to exalt the higher use.

PARTICULAR MEANINGS.

"We are thus assisted by natural objects in the expression of particular meanings. But how great a language to convey such pepper-corn informations! Did it need such noble races of creatures, this profusion of forms, this host of orbs in heaven, to furnish man with the dictionary and grammar of his municipal speech? Whilst we use this grand cipher to expedite the affairs of our pot and kettle, we feel we have not yet put it to its use, neither are able. We are like travelers using the ashes of a volcano to roast their eggs."

The chapter on Language thus concludes, iterating and reiterating much that had been said before, and bringing all to a single point:

THE MYSTERY OF THE UNIVERSE.

"The relation between mind and Nature is not fancied by some poet, but stands in the will of God, and so is free to be known by all men. It appears to men, or it does not appear. When in fortunate hours we ponder over this miracle, the wiser man doubts, if at all other times he is not blind and deaf. For the universe becomes transparent, and the light of higher laws than its own shines through it. It is the standing problem which has exercised the wonder and the study of every fine genius since the world began; from the era of the Egyptians and Brahmans to that of Pythagoras and Plato, of Bacon, of Leibnitz, of Swedenborg. There sits the Sphinx at the roadside, and from age to age, as each prophet comes by, he tries his fortune at reading her riddle. There seems to be a necessity in spirit to manifest itself in material forms; and day and night, river and storm, beast and bird, acid and alkali, preëxist in necessary ideas in the mind of God, and are what they are by virtue of preceding affections in the world of spirit. A fact is the end or last issue of spirit. The visible creation is the termination or the circumference of the invisible world. 'Material objects,' said a French philosopher, 'are necessary kinds of *scoriæ* of the substantial thoughts of the Creator, which must always preserve an exact relation to their first origin; in other words, visible nature must have a spiritual and moral side.'"

It would be curious, were it worth the while, to compare this view of the relation between the Creator and the created with that wrought out with such infinite speculation by the Gnostics, a millennium and a half ago, and by Hindoo

sages who lived and thought a thousand years
before. They argue and refine; build theories
one upon another, as the old astronomers piled
epicycles upon cycle and epicycle, as each new
discovery in relation to the movements of the
stars and planets demanded a new law to account
for each new fact. Copernicus swept all these
away by stating the one central law which gov-
erns our solar system, that the earth revolves
upon its own axis, and also circles around the sun;
and so that the apparent movements of the stars
are imaginary, not real. Emerson affirms, in substance, that there is such a law in the universe of
existence. The foregoing is the nearest approach
which we can find to a statement of what that
law is, so far as relates to material and spiritual
facts. To us, we acknowledge that we have not
been able to attain to any clear conception of the
teaching, and await some expositor to elucidate
it. None such has shown himself to us. It is a
Sphinx riddle. Emerson so styles it. He says:

THE SPHINX RIDDLE.

" This doctrine is abstruse, and though the images of
'garment,' 'scoriæ,' 'mirror,' etc., may stimulate the
fancy, we must summon the aid of subtler and more vital
expositors to make it plain. 'Every scripture is to be
interpreted by the same spirit which gave it forth,' is
the fundamental law of criticism. A life in harmony
with Nature, the love of truth and of virtue, will purge
the eyes to understand her text. By degrees we may

come to know the primitive sense of the permanent objects of Nature, so that the world shall be to us an open book, and every form significant of its hidden life and final cause."

Forty years passed between the appearance of this book and the date of the last of Emerson's writings; and yet we do not find that he has come any nearer to the explication of this Sphinx riddle. We read his address before the Phi Beta Kappa Society at Cambridge, delivered in 1867. It is as eloquent as anything which he ever wrote or spoke. The old doctrine is repeated with added emphasis and new wealth of illustration. He really seems to have reached in his own consciousness to a definite apprehension upon the matter in question. Yet to us the whole stands just as before. Thus, he says:

THE UNITY OF ALL THINGS.

"Shall we study the mathematics of the sphere, and not its causal essence also? Nature is a fable whose moral blazes through it. There is no use in Copernicus if the robust periodicity of the solar system does not show its equal perfection in the mental sphere: the periodicity, the compensating errors, the grand reactions. I shall never believe that centrifugence and centripetence balance unless mind heats and meliorates as well the surface and soil of the globe. On this power, this all dissolving unity, the emphasis of heaven and earth is laid. Nature is brute but as the soul quickens it; Nature always the effect, Mind the flowing cause. Mind carries the law; history is the slow and atomic unfolding.

"Every inch of the mountains is scarred by unimaginable convulsions, yet the new day is purple with the bloom of youth and love. Look out into the July night, and see the broad belt of silver flame which flashes up the half of heaven, fresh and delicate as the bonfires of the meadow flies. Yet the powers of numbers can not compute its enormous age; lasting as time and space— imbosomed in time and space. And time and space, what are they? Our first problems, which we ponder all our lives through, and leave where we found them; whose outrunning immensity, as the old Greeks believed, astonished the gods themselves; of whose dizzy vastitudes all the worlds of God are a mere dot on the margin : impossible to deny, impossible to believe. Yet the moral element in man counterpoises this dismaying immensity, and bereaves it of terror."

This is certainly nowise in contravention of the sublime truth with which the Hebrew Scriptures open : "In the beginning, God created the heavens and the earth." But it seems to us to be intended to convey far more than is implied in that terse phrase. Fail as we may to at all assure ourselves that we have reached the center core of Emerson's philosophy, we are at least prepared to say with him : "A new interest surprises us, whilst, under the view now suggested, we contemplate the fearful extent and multitude of objects, since every object, rightly seen, unlocks a new faculty of the soul. That which was unconscious truth becomes, when interpreted and defined in an object, a part of the domain of knowledge—a new weapon in the magazine of power." And truths not a few, which had lain, as it were, dormant in our consciousness, have by him come to be so alive that, as with Grimm, they are as new to us as though we had never heard them before, and as old as though they had always been parts of our intellectual being.

In the chapter on "Discipline" are grouped together a series of suggestions touching closely upon what has before been said under the title of "Commodity." Still, there is valid reason for thus grouping them.

DISCIPLINE.

"In view of the significance of Nature, we arrive at once at a new fact, that Nature is a 'discipline.' This use of the word includes the preceding uses as parts of itself. Space, time, society, labor, climate, food, locomotion, the animals, the mechanical forces, give us sincerest lessons day by day, whose meaning is unlimited. They educate both the understanding and the reason. Every property of matter is a school for the understanding, its stolidity, or resistance, its inertia, its extension, its figure, its divisibility. The understanding adds, divides, combines, measures, and finds nutriment and room for its activity in these worthy scenes. Meanwhile, reason transfers its own lessons into its own world of thought by perceiving the analogy that marries matter and mind."

A few isolated sentences will, in some fair degree, set forth the general aim and scope of this chapter on "Discipline."

DISCIPLINE OF THE UNDERSTANDING.

"Nature is a discipline of the understanding in intellectual truths. Our dealing with sensible objects is a constant exercise in the necessary lessons of difference, of likeness, of order, of being and seeming, of progressive arrangement, of ascent from particular to general, of combination to one end of manifold purposes. Proportioned to the importance of the organ, is the extreme care with which its tuition is provided. What tedious training, day after day, year after year, never ending, to form the common sense, what continual reproduction of annoyances, inconveniences, dilemmas, what rejoicings over little men, what disputing of prices, what reckonings of interest! and all to form the hand of the mind, to instruct us that 'good thoughts are no better than good dreams unless they be executed.''

DISCIPLINE BY PROPERTY.

"The same good office is performed by property, and its filial systems of debt and credit. Debt, grinding debt, which consumes so much time, which so cripples and disheartens a great spirit with cares that seem so base, is a preceptor whose lessons can not be foregone, and is needed most by those who suffer from it most. Moreover, property, which has been well compared to snow—'if it fall level to-day, it will be blown into drifts to-morrow '—is the surface action of internal machinery, like the index on the face of the clock. Whilst now it is the gymnastics of the understanding, it is hiving in the foresight of tho spirit-experience in profounder laws."

DISCIPLINE BY DIFFERENCES.

"The whole character and fortune of the individual are affected by the least inequalities of the understanding. For example, in the perception of differences. A bell and a plow have each their use, and neither can do the office of the other. Water is good to drink, coal to burn, wool to wear; but wool can not be drank, nor water spun, nor coal eaten. The wise man shows his wisdom in separation, in gradation; and his scale of creatures and of merits is as wide as Nature. The foolish have no range in their scale. What is not good they call the worst, and what is not hateful they call the best."

DISCIPLINE OF THE WILL.

"The exercise of the will is perpetually taught in every event. From the child's successive possession of his several senses, up to the hour when he saith 'Thy will be done,' he is learning the secret that he can reduce under his will not only particular events but great classes; nay, the whole series of events, and so conform all facts to his character. Nature is thoroughly mediate. It is made to serve; it receives the dominion of man as meekly as the ass on which our Saviour rode. It offers all its kingdoms to man as the raw materials which he may mold into what is useful; and he is never weary in working it up. He forges the delicate and subtile air into wise and melodious words, and gives them wings as angels of persuasion and command. One after another, his victorious thought comes up with and reduces all things, until the world becomes, at last, only a realized Will—the double of man."

DISCIPLINE OF THE REASON.

"Sensible objects conform to the premonitions of reason and reflect the conscience. All things are moral, and in their boundless changes have an unceasing reference to spiritual nature. . . . Therefore is Nature ever the ally of religion—lends all her pomp and riches to the religious sentiment. Prophet and priest—David Isaiah, Jesus—have drawn deeply from this source. This ethical character so penetrates the bone and marrow of Nature as to seem the end for which it was made. Whatever private purpose is answered by any member or its part, this is its public and universal function, and is never omitted. Nothing in Nature is exhausted by its first use. In God everything is converted into a new means. Every natural process is a version of a moral sentence. The moral law lies at the center of Nature, and radiates to its circumference. All things with which we deal preach to us. What is a farm but a mute gospel? Nor can it be doubted that this moral sentiment which thus scents the air grows in the grain, and impregnates the waters of the world, is caught by man and sinks into his soul. The moral influence of Nature upon every individual is that amount of truth which it illustrates to him. Who can estimate this? Who can guess how much firmness the sea-beaten rock has taught the fisherman? how much tranquillity has been reflected to man from the azure sky? how much industry and providence and affection we have caught from the pantomime of brutes? What a searching preacher of self-command is the varying phenomenon of health!"

"Herein is especially apprehended the unity of Nature—the unity in variety which meets us everywhere. The fable of Proteus has a cordial truth. A leaf, a drop, a crystal, a moment of time, is related to the whole. Each particle is a microcosm, and faithfully renders the likeness of the world."

This idea of unity in variety is illustrated under various forms. "Not only resemblances exist in things whose analogy is obvious, as when we detect the type of the human hand in the flipper of the fossil saurus, but also in objects wherein there is great superficial unlikeness." Thus, architecture is styled "frozen music" by De Staël and Goethe. Coleridge said that a Gothic church is a "petrified religion." Michel Angelo maintained that to an architect a knowledge of anatomy is essential. And, says Emerson: "In Haydn's oratorios the notes present to the imagination not only motions, as of the snake, the stag, or the elephant, but colors also, as of the green grass. The law of harmonic sounds reappears in the harmonic colors. The granite is differenced, in its laws, only by the more or less of heat, from the river which it wears away. The river, as it flows, resembles the air that flows over it; the air resembles the light which traverses it with more subtile currents; the light resembles the heat which rides with it through space. Each creature is only a modification of the other; the likeness in them is more than the difference, and their radical law is one and the same. A rule of one art or a law of one organization holds true throughout Nature."

UNITY OF THOUGHT AND OF ACTION.

"So intimate is this unity that it lies under the undermost garment of Nature, and betrays its source in universal spirit. For it pervades Thought also. Every universal truth which we express in words implies or supposes every other truth: '*Omne verum vero consonant.*' It is like a great circle on a sphere, comprising all possible circles, which, however, may be drawn and comprise it in like manner. Every such truth is the absolute *ens*, seen from one side; but it has innumerable sides. The central unity is still more conspicuous in actions. Words are finite organs of the infinite mind. They can not cover the dimensions of what there is in truth. They break, chop, and impoverish it. An action is the perfection and publication of thought. A right action seems to fill the eye and to be related to all Nature. 'The wise man in doing one thing' does all; or in the one thing he does rightly he sees the likeness of all which is done rightly."

One sentence in the foregoing extract should be borne in mind by any one who hopes to fairly enter into the philosophy of Emerson: "Every truth is the absolute *ens, seen from one side;* but it has innumerable sides." Without pausing to inquire whether a finite mind can ever attain to a view of all these innumerable sides at a glance, it is fairly to be doubted whether such a mind can ever express it in any form of human speech. We indeed remember the hope expressed by Emerson in his "Divinity Address": "I look for the new teacher that shall follow so far these shining laws that he shall see them come full circle; shall see their rounding, complete grace; shall see the world to be the mirror of the soul; shall see the identity of the law of gravitation with purity of thought; and show that the ought, that duty, is one thing with science, with beauty, and with joy." But while Emerson affirms perpetually that this is so—nay, if one pleases to hold, shows that it ought to be so—he has not to our feeling shown that it *is* really so. We own that we do not at all see that, for example, the law of gravitation is in any way identical with purity of heart.

A very notable chapter in this book of "Nature" is that upon "Idealism." At first thought one might suppose that there could be no reason for such a separate chapter, for Idealism runs through every other chapter like a golden thread. But he had, in fact, very good reasons for what he did. He plunges into the subject in the very opening sentence, which seems, at least hypothetically, to contravene everything which had gone before. Nature had been everywhere treated as though it were an absolute reality; but now he suggests the contrary idea, that it is only an appearance, or, as represented by the Hindoo sages, only a series of shows and deceptions, through which the Supreme Mind alternately reveals or conceals himself.

REALITY OR UNREALITY OF NATURE.

" A noble doubt perpetually suggests itself whether this end of discipline be not the final cause of the universe, and whether Nature outwardly exists. It is a sufficient account of that appearance which we call the world that God will teach a human mind, and so makes it the receiver of a certain number of congruent sensations, which we call sun and moon, man and woman, house and trade. In my utter impotence to test the authenticity of the report of my senses—to know whether the impressions they make upon me correspond with outlying objects—what difference does it make whether Orion is up there in heaven or some god paints the image in the firmament of the soul? The relations of parts and the end of the whole remaining the same, what is the difference whether land and sea interact and worlds revolve and intermingle without number or end—deep yawning under deep and galaxy balancing galaxy throughout absolute space—or whether, without relations of time and space, the same appearances are inscribed in the constant faith of man?"

In the last number but one of "The Dial," then edited by Mr. Emerson, is a paper on "The Preaching of Buddha," preceded by an extract from Eugene Bournouf's account of the purport of the doctrines of Buddha. These teachings carry the theory of ideality to the very utmost point conceivable by man. "This teaching," says Bournouf, "is that the visible world is in a perpetual change; that death proceeds to life, and life to death; that man, like all the living beings who surround him, revolves in the eternally round of transmigration; that he passes successively through all forms of life, from the most elementary up to the most perfect; that the place which he occupies in the vast scale of living beings depends on the merits of the actions which he performs in this world; that the rewards of heaven and the pains of hell, like all which this world contains, have only a limited duration; that time exhausts the merit of virtuous actions, and effaces the evil of bad actions; and that the fatal law of change brings back to earth both the god and the devil, to put both again on trial, and cause them to run a new course of transmigration. The hope which Buddha came to bring to men was the possibility of escaping from the law of transmigration by entering what he calls 'enfranchisement': that is to say, according to one of the oldest schools, the annihilation of the thinking principle as well as of the material principle. This annihilation is not entire until death; but he who was destined to attain to it possessed during his life an unlimited science, which gave him the pure view of the world as it is." And one of the earliest disciples of Buddha said, in phrase almost Emersonian : "Annihilation results from the comprehension of the equality of all laws ; there is only one, and not two or three. . . . Know that what is clearness is obscurity ; know also that what is obscurity is clearness. . . . What I have said is the supreme truth ; may my auditors arrive at complete annihilation !"

Emerson goes in a quite different direction. He assumes the actual unending existence of the *me*. Buddhism practically denies it, while nominally affirming it, for in no sense which we are capable of apprehending can that which was once a reptile, and may become so again, be identical with the *me* which is now a man. It lacks the essential quality of continuous self-consciousness ; and, moreover, absolute annihilation is the end to be striven for by all, and to be attained by those who are found worthy of it. Buddhism affirms the actual existence of the world without us; Emerson more than half doubts it. But, after all, he regards the question whether Nature be an absolute reality or merely an appearance to be of little consequence. Indeed, he seems rather to incline to the latter view, although either is satisfactory enough to him. He says :

SUBJECTIVE IDEALISM.

" Whether Nature enjoys a substantial existence without, or is only in the apocalypse of the mind, it is alike useful and alike venerable to me. Be it what it may, it is ideal to me so long as I can not try the accuracy of my senses. But, while we acquiesce entirely in the permanence of natural laws, the question of the absolute existence of Nature remains still open. It is the uniform effect of culture on the human mind not to shake our faith in the stability of particular phenomena, as of heat, water, azote, but to lead us to regard Nature as a phenomenon, not a substance; to attribute necessary existence to spirit; to esteem Nature as an accident and an effect."

He goes on to frame a defense of this ideal theory, as propounded by him:

DEFENSE OF IDEALISM.

"The frivolous make themselves merry with this ideal theory, as if its consequences were burlesque, as if it affected the stability of Nature. It surely does not. God never jests with us, and will not compromise the end of Nature by permitting any inconsequence in its procession. Any distrust of the permanence of laws would paralyze the faculties of man. Their permanence is sacredly respected, and his faith therein is perfect. The wheels and springs of man are all set to the hypothesis of the permanence of Nature. We are not built like a ship, to be tossed, but like a house, to stand. It is a natural consequence of this structure that, so long as the active powers predominate over the reflective, we resist with indignation any hint that Nature is more short-lived or mutable than spirit. The broker, the wheelwright, the carpenter, the tollman, are much displeased at the intimation. To the senses and the unrenewed

understanding belongs, indeed, a sort of instinctive belief in the absolute existence of Nature. In their view,
man and Nature are indissolubly joined. *Things* are
ultimate, and they never look beyond their sphere. The
presence of reason mars this faith. The first effort of
thought tends to relax this despotism of the senses,
which bends us to Nature as if we were a part of it, and
shows us Nature aloof and, as it were, afloat. Until this
higher agency intervenes, the animal eye sees with
wonderful accuracy sharp outlines and colored surfaces.
When the eye of reason opens, to outline and surface
are at once added grace and expression. These proceed
from imagination and reflection, and abate somewhat of
the angular distinctness of objects. If the reason be
stimulated to more earnest vision, outlines and surfaces
become transparent and are no longer seen; causes and
spirits are seen through them. The best moments of
life are those delicious awakenings of the higher powers,
and the reverential withdrawing of Nature before its
God."

From this ideal point of view Emerson goes
on to enumerate some special views as to the
effects of culture upon the human mind. Even
in the lower grades of culture, "Nature is made
to conspire with spirit to emancipate us. Certain
mechanical changes, a small alteration in our
local position, apprise us of a dualism. We are
strangely affected by seeing the shore from a moving ship, from a balloon, or through the tints of
an unusual sky. The least change in our point
of view gives the whole world a pictorial air. A

man who seldom rides needs only to get into a coach and traverse his own town, to turn the street into a puppet-show. What new thoughts are suggested by seeing a face of country quite familiar in the rapid movements of the railroad car!" And so on. "In these cases," says Emerson, "by mechanical means is suggested the difference between the observer and the spectacle, between man and Nature. Hence arises a pleasure mixed with awe. I may say that a low degree of the sublime is felt from the fact, probably, that the man is apprised that, while the world is a spectacle, something in himself is stable." But similar in kind, but far higher in effect, is the ideal ministry of poetry, philosophy, and religion.

THE IDEAL IN POETRY.

"In a higher manner the poet communicates the same pleasure. By a few strokes he delineates, as on air, the sun, the mountain, the camp, the city, the hero, the maiden—not different from what we know them, but only lifted from the ground and afloat before the eye. He unfixes the land and the sea, makes them revolve around the axis of his primary thought, and disposes them anew. Possessed himself by a heroic passion, he uses matter as symbols of it. The sensual man conforms thoughts to things; the poet conforms things to his thoughts. The one esteems Nature as rooted and fast; the other as fluid, and impresses his being thereon. To him the refractory world is ductile and flexible; he invests dust and stones with humanity, and makes them the words of the reason. The imagination may be defined to be the use which the reason makes of the material world. Shakespeare possesses the power of subordinating Nature for the purposes of expression beyond all poets. His imperial muse tosses the creation like a bauble from hand to hand, and uses it to embody any caprice of thought that is uppermost in his mind. The remotest spaces of Nature are visited, and the farthest-sundered things are brought together by a subtle spiritual connection. We are made aware that the magnitude of material things is relative, and all objects shrink and expand to serve the passion of the poet. The perception of real affinities between events (that is to say, of *ideal* affinities, for these only are real) enables the poet thus to make free with the most imposing forms and phenomena of the world, and to assert the predominance of the soul."

THE IDEAL IN PHILOSOPHY.

" Whilst the poet thus animates Nature with his own thoughts, he differs from the philosopher only herein: that the one proposes beauty as his main end; the other proposes truth. But the philosopher, not less than the poet, postpones the apparent order and relations of things to the empire of thought. 'The problem of philosophy,' according to Plato, 'is for all that exists conditionally to find a ground unconditioned and absolute.' It proceeds on the faith that a law determines all phenomena, which being known, the phenomenon can be predicted. That law, when in the mind, is an idea. Its beauty is infinite. The true philosopher and the true poet are one; and a beauty which is faith, and a truth which is beauty, is the aim of both. Is not the charm of one of Plato's or Aristotle's definitions strictly like the

'Antigone' of Sophocles? It is, in both cases, that a
spiritual life has been imparted to Nature; that the
solid-seeming block of matter has been pervaded and
dissolved by a thought; that this feeble human being
has penetrated the vast masses of Nature with an inform-
ing soul, and recognized itself in their harmony—that is,
seized their law. In physics, when this is attained, the
memory disburdens itself of its cumbrous catalogues of
particulars, and carries centuries of observation in a
single formula. Thus, even in physics, the material is
degraded before the spiritual. The astronomer, the geometer, rely on their irrefragable analysis, and disdain
the results of observation. The sublime remark of Eu-
ler on his law of arches: 'This will be found contrary
to all experience, yet it is true,' had already transferred
Nature into the mind, and left matter like an outcast
corpse."

THE IDEAL IN RELIGION AND ETHICS.

"Religion and ethics—which may be fitly called the
practice of ideas, or the introduction of ideas into life—
have an analogous effect with all lower culture in de-
grading Nature, and suggesting its dependence on spirit.
Ethics and religion differ herein: that the one is the
system of human duties commencing from man; the
other, from God. Religion includes the personality of
God; ethics does not. They are one to our present design. They both put Nature under foot. The first and
last lesson of religion is, 'The things which are seen are
temporal; the things which are unseen are eternal.' It
does that for the unschooled which philosophy does for
Berkeley and Viasa. The uniform language that may
be heard in the churches of the most ignorant sects is,
'Contemn the unsubstantial shows of the world; they

are vanities, dreams, shadows, unrealities; seek the realities of religion.' The devotee flouts Nature. Some
theosophists have arrived at a certain hostility toward
matter; as the Manichæans and Plotinus. In short,
they might say of all matter what Michel Angelo said of
external beauty: 'It is the frail and weary weed in
which God dresses the soul which he has called into
time.' "

ADVANTAGE OF THE IDEAL THEORY.

" The advantage of the ideal theory over the popular
faith is this: that it presents the world in precisely that
view which is most desirable to the mind. It is, in fact,
the view which reason, both speculative and practical—
that is, philosophy and virtue—take. For, seen in the
light of thought, the world is always phenomenal; and
virtue subordinates it to the mind. Idealism sees the
world in God. It beholds the whole circle of persons
and things, of actions and events, of country and religion,
not as painfully accumulated, atom after atom, act after
act, in an aged and creeping past, but as one vast picture, which God paints on the instant eternity for the
contemplation of the soul. Therefore, the soul holds
itself off from a too trivial and microscopic study of the
universal tablet. It respects the end too much to im-
merse itself in the means. It sees something more important in Christianity than the scandals of ecclesiastical
history or the niceties of criticism; and, very incurious
concerning persons or miracles, and not at all disturbed
by chasms of historical evidence, it accepts from God
the phenomenon as it finds it, as the pure and awful form
of religion in the world. It is not hot and passionate
at the appearance of what it calls its own good or bad
fortune, at the union or opposition of other persons.

No man is its enemy. It accepts whatsoever befalls as a part of its lesson. It is a watcher more than a doer, and it is a doer only that it may the better watch."

Thus closes the characteristic chapter on "Idealism," which certainly contains many things which seem to contravene much which has before been strenuously insisted upon. Most likely Emerson perceived this, and, if he ever condescended to explanations, he would have said that all these were but parts of the one universal truth, which could only be expressed in fragments. For, just before the last paragraph, urging the "advantages of the ideal theory over the popular faith," and repeating the affirmation that "motion, poetry, physical and intellectual science, and religion all tend to affect our convictions of the reality of the external world," he adds, as if half regretful that such was the case, "I own that there is something ungrateful too curiously to scan the particulars of the general proposition that all culture tends to imbue us with idealism. I have no hostility to Nature, but a child's love to it. I expand and live in the warm day like corn and melons. Let us speak her fair. I do not wish to fling stones at my beautiful mother, nor soil my gentle nest. I only wish to indicate the true position of Nature in regard to man, wherein to establish man all right education tends, as the ground which to attain is the object of human life—that is, of man's connection with Nature."

Yet still he holds by preference to the extreme
ideal theory. "Culture," he says, "inverts the
vulgar views of nature, and brings the mind to
call that *apparent* which it used to call *real*, and
that real which it use to call visionary. Children,
it is true, believe in the external world. The
belief that it *appears* only is an after-thought;
but with culture this faith will as surely arise on
the mind as did the first."

In the next brief chapter, entitled "Spirit,"
the much-vaunted *Idealism* is treated as quite in-
sufficient to solve all the problems put by Nature
to the mind:

INSUFFICIENCY OF IDEALISM.

"When we consider Spirit, we see that the views
already presented do not include the whole circumference of man. Three problems are put by Nature to the
mind: 'What is Matter? Whence is it? and Whereto?'
The first of these questions only the ideal theory answers. Idealism saith: 'Matter is a phenomenon, not a
substance.' Idealism acquaints us with the total dispar-
ity between the evidence of our own being and the evidence of the world's being. The one is perfect, the other
incapable of any assurance. The mind is a part of the
nature of things; the world is a divine dream, from
which we may presently awake to the glories and cer-
tainties of day. Idealism is a hypothesis to account for
Nature by other principles than those of carpentry and
chemistry. Yet, if it only deny the existence of matter,
it does not satisfy the demands of the spirit. It leaves

God out of me. It leaves me in the splendid labyrinth of my perceptions, to wander without end. Then the heart revisits it, because it balks the affections in denying substantive being to men and women. Nature is so pervaded with human life that there is something of humanity in all and in every particular. But this ideal theory makes Nature foreign to me, and does not account for that consanguinity which we acknowledge to it. Let it stand, then, in the present state of our knowledge, as a useful introductory hypothesis, serving to apprise us of the eternal distinction between the soul and the world."

But when Emerson again, in this chapter, comes to speak of Nature, he goes back to his original conception. It must not be overlooked that, as he forewarned his readers in the outset, he uses the term in a twofold sense—the common and the philosophic one. In the philosophic sense, every man is to every other man a part of Nature, as much so as the forms of matter, so that there are subjectively only three possible forms of existence : God, Myself, and Nature. In this broader sense, we are told that "The aspect of Nature is devout. Like the figure of Jesus, she stands with bended head and hands folded upon the breast. And all the uses of Nature admit of being summed in one. Through all her kingdoms, to the suburbs and outskirts of things, she is faithful to the cause whence she had her origin. She always speaks of spirit." But of spirit Emerson speaks in very vague terms. Thus :

WHAT SPIRIT IS.

"Of that ineffable essence which we call Spirit, he that thinks most will say least. We can foresee God in the coarse, as it were, distant phenomena of matter; but when we try to define and describe himself, both language and thought desert us, and we are as helpless as fools and savages. That essence refuses to be recorded in propositions; but, when man has worshiped him intellectually, the noblest ministry of Nature is to stand as the apparition of God. It is the organ through which the universal spirit speaks to the individual, and strives to lead back the individual to it. . . . But, when, following the invisible steps of thought, we come to inquire 'Whence is matter? and Whereto?' many truths arise to us out of the recesses of consciousness. We learn that the Highest is present in the soul of man; that the dread essence—which is not wisdom or love or beauty or power, but all in one, and each entirely, is that for which all things exist, and that by which they are; that Spirit creates; that behind Nature, throughout Nature, Spirit is present. One, and not compound, it does not act upon us from without—that is, in space and time—but spiritually, or through ourselves: therefore that Spirit—that is, the Supreme Being, does not build up Nature around us, but puts it forth through us, as the life of a tree puts forth new branches and leaves through the pores of the old. As a plant upon the earth, so a man rests upon the bosom of God. He is nourished by unfailing fountains, and draws, at his need, inexhaustible power. Who can set bounds to the possibilities of man? Once inhale the upper air, being admitted to behold the absolute natures of justice and truth, and we learn that man has access to the entire mind of the Creator; is himself the Creator in the finite."

This view seems to Emerson to be sufficient and adequate. He says, "It admonishes me where the sources of wisdom and power lie, and points to virtue as to

> "'The golden key
> Which opes the palace of Eternity';

carries upon its face the highest certificate of truth, because it animates me to create my own world through the purification of my soul." For the sake of setting forth at a glance the main utterances of Emerson upon this high theme, we group together several passages from other of his works bearing upon this point:

THE HUMAN SOUL AND THE DIVINE SPIRIT.

"The relations of the soul to the Divine Spirit are so pure that it is profane to seek to interpose helps. Whenever a mind is simple and receives a divine wisdom, all things pass away; means, teachers, texts, temples, fall; it lives now, and absorbs past and future into the present hour. . . . Let man learn the revelation of all Nature and all thought to his heart; this, namely, that the Highest dwells with him; that the sources of Nature are in his own mind, if the sentiment of duty is there. . . . Ineffable is the union of man and God in every act of the Soul; the simplest person who, in his integrity, worships God, becomes God; yet for ever and ever the influx of this better and universal self is new and unsearchable. . . . If we will not interfere with our thought, but will act entirely, or see how the thing stands with God, we know the particular thing, and everything, and every man. For the Maker of all things and of all persons stands behind us, and casts his dread omniscience through us over things. . . . The only mode of obtaining an answer to the questions of the senses is to forego all low curiosity, and, accepting the tide of being which floats us into the secret of Nature, work and live, work and live, and, all unawares, the advancing soul has built and forged for itself a new condition; and the question and answer are one. . . . We live in succession, in parts, in particles. Meantime within man is the soul of the whole; the wise silence; the universal beauty to which every part and particle is equally related—the eternal ONE. And this deep power in which we exist, and whose beatitude is all accessible to us, is not only self-sufficing and perfect in every hour, but the act of seeing and the thing seen, the seer and the spectacle, the subject and the object, are one."

Closely allied to the idea of the divine in the human soul is that of the immortality of the individual man. That Emerson fully believes this, in a sense, is clear; but it is not so clear in what specific sense. In his earlier utterances the subject is presented in terms not essentially differing from those in common use. But in later works the belief assumes a far less definite form. As thus, in the chapter on Worship, in his "Conduct of Life":

IMMORTALITY.

"Of Immortality, the soul, when well employed, is incurious. It *is* so well, that it is sure it *will be* well. It

asks no questions of the Supreme Power. The son of
Antiochus asked his father when he would join battle;
'Dost thou fear,' replied the king, 'that thou only in all
the army wilt not hear the trumpet?' It is a higher
thing to confide that, if it is best we should live, we shall
live. It is higher to have this conviction than to have
the lease of indefinite centuries and millenniums and æons.
Higher than the question of our duration is the question
of our deserving. Immortality will come to such as are
fit for it; and he who would be a great soul in the future
must be a great soul now. It is a doctrine too great to
rest on any legend—that is, on any man's experience but
our own. It must be proved, if at all, from our own activity and designs, which imply an interminable future
for their display."

In the chapter on Immortality in his latest
work, "Letters and Social Aims," he elaborates
the suggestion, and presents the natural argument
for the immortality of man as it is usually propounded. He says:

THE NATURAL ARGUMENT FOR IMMORTALITY.

"There is nothing in Nature capricious, or whimsical,
or accidental, or unsupported. Nature never moves by
jumps, but always in steady and supported advances.
The implanting of a desire indicates that the gratification
of that desire is in the constitution of the creature that
feels it. The wish for food, the wish for motion, the
wish for sleep, for society, for knowledge, are not random whims, but grounded in the structure of the creature,
and meant to be satisfied by food, by motion, by society,
by knowledge. If there is a desire to live, and in larger

sphere, with more knowledge and power, it is because life and knowledge and power are good for us, and we are the natural depositories of these gifts. The love of life is out of all proportion to the value set on a single day, and seems to indicate, like all our other experiences, a conviction of immense resources and possibilities proper to us, on which we have never drawn. . . . As a hint of endless being we may rank that novelty which perpetually attends life. The soul does not age with the body. On the borders of the grave the wise man looks forward with equal elasticity of mind or hope; and why not, after millions of years, on the verge of still newer existence? Most men are insolvent, or promise by their countenance and conversation, and by their early endeavor, much more than they ever perform, suggesting a design still to be carried out. The man must have new motives, new companions, new condition, and another term. Every really able man, in whatever direction he work—a man of large affairs, an inventor, a statesman, an orator, a poet, a painter—if you talk sincerely with him, considers his work, however much admired, as far short of what it should be. What is this better, this flying ideal, but the perpetual promise of the Creator?"

The argument is presented at length, and with unusual variety of illustration; but scattered through it are passages which indicate entire uncertainty as to the fundamental question of personal immortality. As this:

PERSONAL IMMORTALITY.

"I confess that everything connected with our personality fails. Nature never spares the individual. We are always balked of a complete success. No prosperity is promised to that. We have our indemnity only in the success of that to which we belong. *That* is immortal, and *we* only through that. The soul stipulates for no private good. That which is private I see not to be good. 'If truth live, I live; if justice live, I live,' said one of the old saints; 'and these by any man's suffering are enlarged and enthroned.' . . . Is immortality only an intellectual quality; or, shall I say only an energy, there being no passive? He has it, and he alone, who gives life to all names, persons, things, where he comes. No religion, not the wildest mythology, dies for him. He vivifies what he touches. Future state is an illusion for the ever-present state. It is not length of life, but depth of life. It is not duration, but a taking of the soul out of time, as all high action of the mind does."

Now, the idea of immortality, as thus set forth, while in no wise opposed to that of a conscious personal never-ending existence, does not at all imply it. Mr. Emerson even scouts at the belief that this was taught by Jesus. He says: "It is strange that Jesus is esteemed by mankind the bringer of the doctrine of immortality. He is never once weak or sentimental; he is very abstemious of explanation; he never preaches the personal immortality; whilst Plato and Cicero had both allowed themselves to overstep the stern limits of the spirit, and gratify the people with that picture." He cites, with apparent approval, two passages from Goethe. The one runs thus:

"To me the eternal existence of my soul is proved from my idea of activity. If I work incessantly till my death, Nature is bound to give me another form of existence when the present can no longer sustain my existence." But, in the other passage cited, something more is hinted than a doubt of any personal immortality : "It is to a thinking being quite impossible to think himself non-existent, ceasing to think and live. So far does every one carry in himself the proof of immortality, and quite spontaneously. But, so soon as the man will be objective and go out of himself, so soon as he will dogmatically grasp a personal duration to bolster up in cockney fashion that inward assurance, he is lost in contradiction."

The natural argument for the personal immortality of each individual man, as set forth by Emerson, may be briefly presented : "God has implanted in the nature of man a longing for immortality, and, by so implanting it, he has promised that this longing shall be realized ; he is always true to his promises ; and therefore man must be immortal." To us the argument is altogether inconclusive. If we rightly understand Emerson, it is inconclusive to him also, in so far at least as anything like personal immortality is concerned. He, moreover, more than intimates a doubt whether immortality is accorded to all men, or only to those who shall be found fit for it. We fail to see that the assumed longing for immortal-

ity is any sure proof that it will be satisfied. How
many of our most earnest longings are for ever un-
realized! All men long for and pray for comfort,
health, and length of days. Right and just objects of longing are all these; but to how many are
apportioned want, disease, and early death; their
longings unsatisfied, their prayers unanswered!

And again, this longing for immortality, in
any sense in which we can understand the word,
is far enough from being universal among mankind. To the five hundred millions of Buddhists,
Nirvana is the supreme object of longing and endeavor. As we understand it, the Buddhist idea
of *Nirvana* is by no means fitly represented by our
word "annihilation." We understand it to mean
a state of future being devoid of all which enters
into personality; individual thought, will, and
consciousness being absorbed in the infinite of the
Supreme Being, as a snow-flake, without annihilation, is absorbed and swallowed up in the ocean
into which it falls—"a moment white, then lost
for ever."

We believe most undoubtingly in the personal
immortality of every individual human being.
We believe in it intuitively and without proof
from any source without ourselves. We should
doubtless have believed it, had no direct revelation
been vouchsafed to us. What we accept as Divine
revelation only confirms and strengthens our belief
in immortality, just as it confirms and strengthens

our belief in the existence of the one God, eternal, immortal, and invisible, all-powerful, all-wise, and all-good. We call in question, not the truth of the belief in immortality, but the validity of Emerson's argument, and most especially the vague and unsatisfactory conclusion to which it leads him. If he is in any sense a "seer," his vision in this matter is dim.

Of the final short chapter, entitled "Prospects," which closes this book of Emerson, only brief mention is required; and that mainly for the sake of setting forth a particular phase of his mental processes. "Every surmise and vaticination of the mind," he affirms, "is entitled to a certain respect; and we learn to prefer imperfect theories and sentences, which contain glimpses of truth, to digested systems which have no one valuable suggestion. A wise writer will feel that the ends of study and composition are best answered by announcing undiscovered regions of thought, and so communicating, through hope, new activity to the torpid spirit. . . . At present man applies to Nature but half his force. He works with the understanding alone. He lives in it, and masters it by a penny-wisdom; and he that works most in it, he is but a half man. His relation to Nature, his power over it, is through the understanding; as by manure, the economic use of fire, wind, water, and the mariner's needle; steam, coal, chemical agriculture; the repairs of the human body by the dentist and the surgeon. This is such a resumption of power as if a banished king should buy his territories inch by inch, instead of vaulting at once into his throne." Still there are brighter prospects in store. He says:

PROSPECTS.

"Meantime, in the thick darkness there are not wanting gleams of a better light; occasional examples of the action of man upon Nature with his entire force—with reason as well as understanding. Such are the traditions of miracles in the earliest antiquity of all ages; the history of Jesus Christ; the achievement of a principle, as in religious and political revolutions, and in the abolition of the slave trade; the miracles of enthusiasm, as those reported of Swedenborg, Höhenlohe, and the Shakers; many obscure and yet contested facts now arranged under the name of animal magnetism; prayer, eloquence, self-healing, and the wisdom of children. These are examples of reason's momentary grasp of the sceptre; the exertion of a power which exists not in time or space, but in an instantaneous in-streaming power. The difference between the actual and the ideal force of man is happily figured by the schoolmen in saying, that the knowledge of man is 'an evening knowledge—*Vespertina cognitio*, but, that of God is a morning knowledge—*Matutina cognitio.*'"

The foregoing is certainly an odd enumeration of some of the gleams of a better light which foreshadow the coming day. Some of them seem to us, and most likely they have come to seem to

Emerson, to be beams of darkness flung forth from the depths of primal obscurity. But, as the sum and substance of all that had been before said, we have the following noble and hopeful passage; not the less noble because it retracts the derogatory expressions which had been now and then applied to Nature :

SOLUTION OF THE SPHINX PROBLEM.

"The problem of restoring to the world original and eternal beauty is solved by the redemption of the soul. The ruin or the blank which we see, when we look at Nature, is in our own eye. The axis of vision is not coincident with the axis of things; and so they appear not transparent, but opaque. The reason why the world lacks unity, and lies broken and in heaps, is because man is disunited with himself. He can not be a naturalist until he satisfies all the demands of the spirit. Love is as much its demand as perception; indeed, neither can be perfect without the other. In the uttermost meaning of the word, thought is devout, and devotion is thought. Deep calls unto deep; but in actual life the marriage is not celebrated. There are innocent men who worship God after the tradition of their fathers, but their sense of duty has not yet extended to the use of all their faculties. And they are patient naturalists; but they freeze their subject under the wintry light of the understanding. Is not prayer also a study of truth—a sally of the soul into the unfound infinite? No man ever prayed heartily without learning something.

"It will not need, when the mind is prepared for study, to search for objects. The invariable mark of

11

wisdom is to see the miraculous in the common. To
our blindness common things seem unaffecting. We
make fables to hide the baldness of the fact, and conform
it, as we say, to the higher law of the mind. But when
the fact is seen under the light of an idea, the gaudy fable
hides and shrivels. We behold the real higher law. To
the wise, therefore, a fact is pure poetry, and the most
beautiful of fables. These wonders are brought to our
own door. You are also a man. Man and woman, and
their social life, poverty, labor, fear, fortune, are known
to you. Learn that none of these things is superficial,
but that each phenomenon has its root in the faculties
and affections of the mind. While the abstract question
occupies your intellect, Nature brings it in the concrete
to be solved by your hands. It were a wise inquiry for
the closet to compare, point by point, especially in remarkable crises in life, our daily history with the rise
and progress of ideas in the mind."

The book closes with this jubilant strain; the
final end of the solution of the Sphinx problem;
for which we are willing to overlook the winding
paths by which it has been reached :

"So shall we come to look at the world with new
eyes. It shall answer the endless inquiry of the intellect, 'What is truth?' and of the affections, 'What is
good?' by yielding itself passive to the educated will.
Then shall come to pass what a poet said: 'Nature is
not fixed, but fluid. Spirit alters, molds, makes it. The
immobility or bruteness of Nature is the absence of
spirit; to pure spirit it is fluid, it is volatile, it is obe-
dient. Every spirit builds itself a house; and beyond
its house a world; and beyond its world a heaven.

Know, then, that the world exists for you; for it is the phenomenon perfect. What we are, that only can we see. All that Adam had, all that Cæsar could, you have and can do. Adam called his house heaven and earth; Cæsar called his house Rome; you perhaps call yours a cobbler's trade, a hundred acres of land, or a scholar's garret. Yet, line for line, and point for point, your dominion is as great as theirs, though without fine names."

Carlyle has expressed this idea still more tersely: "Louis was a ruler; but art thou not also one? His wide France, look at it from the fixed stars (themselves not yet Infinitude), is no wider than thy narrow brickfield, where thou didst faithfully or unfaithfully. Man, a 'symbol of eternity imprisoned into time!' it is not thy works, which are all mortal, infinitely little, and the greatest no greater than the least, but only the spirit thou workest in, that can have worth or continuance." Emerson thus concludes:

THE CONCLUSION.

"Build, therefore, your own world. As fast as you conform your life to the pure idea in your mind, that will unfold its vast proportions. A correspondent revolution in things will attend the influx of the spirit. So fast will disagreeable appearances: swine, spiders, snakes, pests, madhouses, prisons, enemies, vanish. They are temporary, and shall no more be seen. The sordes and the filths of Nature, the sun shall dry up, and the wind exhale. As when the summer comes from the south, the snow-banks melt, and the face of the earth becomes green before it, so shall the advancing spirit create ornaments along its path, and carry with it the beauty it visits, and the song which enchants it. It shall draw beautiful faces, warm hearts, wise discourses, and heroic acts around its way, until evil is no more seen. The kingdom of man over Nature, which cometh not with observation—a dominion such as now is beyond his dream of God—he shall enter without more wonder than the blind man feels who is gradually restored to perfect sight."

VIII.

THE ESSAYS.

THE two series, published in 1841 and 1847, contain twenty essays, upon a great variety of subjects. In most minds this is the work most distinctively associated with Emerson. It was this which slowly won the profound admiration of Hermann Grimm. The first thing which strikes the reader is the austere condensation of the style in contrast with the florid exuberance of that in "Nature." It bristles with sentences which are epigrams. If one wanted a text for a discourse upon almost any theme, he could scarcely fail to find it in one or another of these essays. We shall pass in rapid succession over some of the varied topics treated, dwelling mainly upon those which follow a different train of thought from that pursued in "Nature." The essay on "History" is to a great extent a more orderly setting forth the idea of the unity in variety existing throughout the entire realm of Nature. But there are passages which, leaving the domain of the ideal, come down to the generalization of isolated facts in human history. As this :

NOMADISM.

"In the early history of Asia and Europe, nomadism and agriculture are the two antagonist facts. The geography of Asia and Africa necessitated a nomadic life. But the nomads were the terror of all those whom the soil or the advantages of a market had induced to build towns. Agriculture was therefore a religious function because of the perils of the state from nomadism. And in these late and civil countries of England and America, the contest of these propensities still fights out the old battle in each individual. We are all rovers by turns—and pretty rapid turns. The nomads of Africa are constrained to wander by the attacks of the gadfly which drives the cattle mad, and so compels the tribe to emigrate in the rainy season, and drive off the cattle to the higher sandy regions. The nomads of Asia follow the pasturage from month to month. In America and Europe the nomadism is of trade and curiosity—a progress certainly from the gadfly of Astaboras to the Anglomania and Italo-mania of Boston Bay. The Persian court, in its magnificent era, never gave up the nomadism of its barbarous tribes, but traveled from Ecbatana, where the spring was spent, to Susa in summer, and to

Babylon for the winter. Sacred cities to which a periodical religious pilgrimage was enjoined, or stringent
laws and customs tending to invigorate the national
bond, were the check on the old rovers; and the cumu-
lative values of long residence are the restraints on the
itinerancy of the present day."

INTELLECTUAL NOMADISM.

"The antagonism of these two forms is not less active
in individuals, as the love of adventure or the love of
repose happens to predominate. A man of rude health
and flowing spirits has the faculty of rapid domestica-
tion, lives in his wagon, and roams through all latitudes
as easily as a Calmuc. At sea, or in the forest, or in the
snow, he sleeps as warm, dines with as good an appetite,
and associates as happily as beside his own chimneys.
Or perhaps his facility is deeper seated in the increased
range of his faculties of observation, which yield him
points of interest wherever fresh objects meet his eyes.
The pastoral nations were needy and hungry to despera-
tion; and this intellectual nomadism, in its success,
bankrupts the mind through the dissipation of power on
a miscellany of objects. The home-keeping wit, on the
other hand, is that continence or content which finds all
the elements of success on its own soil; and which has
its own perils of monotony and deterioration, if not
stimulated by foreign infusion."

There are some pregnant passages unfolding
the reason why men of our day feel such a deep
interest in the history of the Greeks. The following might have been written by Charles Emerson. It reads like the extract from his "Notes"

which have been quoted in an early part of this volume:

THE CHARM OF GREEK HISTORY.

"What is the foundation of that interest all men feel in Greek history in all its periods, from the Heroic or Homeric Age down to the domestic life of the Athenians or Spartans, four or five centuries later? What but this, that every man passes personally through a Grecian period? The Grecian state is the state of bodily nature—the perfection of the senses—of the spiritual nature unfolded in strict unity with the body. It existed in those human forms which supplied the sculptor with the models of Hercules, Phœbus, and Jove; not like the forms abounding in the streets of modern cities, wherein the face is a confused blur of features; but composed of incorrupt, sharply defined, and symmetrical features, whose eye-sockets are so formed that it would be impossible for such eyes to squint, and take furtive glances on this side and on that, but they must turn the whole head.

"The manners of that period are plain and fierce. The reverence exhibited is for personal qualities: courage, address, self-command, justice, strength, swiftness, a loud voice, a strong chest. Luxury and elegance are not known. A sparse population and want make every man his own valet, cook, butcher, and soldier; and the habit of supplying his own needs educates the body to wonderful performances. Such are the Agamemnon and Diomed of Homer; and not far different is the picture Xenophon gives of himself and his compatriots in the 'Retreat of the Ten Thousand': 'After the army had crossed the river Teleboas, in Armenia, there fell much snow, and the troops lay miserably on the ground cov-

ered with it. But Xenophon arose naked, and taking
an axe began to split wood; whereupon the others rose
and did the like.' Throughout his army exists a boundless liberty of speech. They quarrel for plunder; they
wrangle with the generals on each order; and Xenophon
is as sharp-tongued as any, and sharper-tongued than
most, and so gives as good as he gets. Who does not
see that this is a gang of great boys, with such a code of
honor and such lack of discipline as great boys have?"

To the same general principle of sympathy
is ascribed the charm of Greek literature and art:

THE CHARM OF GREEK LITERATURE AND ART.

"The costly charm of the ancient tragedy is that the
persons speak simply; speak as persons who have great
good sense without knowing it, before yet the reflective
habit has become the predominant habit of the mind,
Our admiration is not admiration of the old, but of the
natural. The Greeks are not reflective, but perfect in
their senses, with the finest physical organization in the
world. Adults acted with the simplicity and grace of
children. They made vases, tragedies, and statues, such
as healthy senses should—that is, in good taste. Such
things have continued to be made in all ages, and are
now, wherever a healthy physique exists; but as a class,
from their superior organization, the Greeks have surpassed all. They combine the energy of manhood with
the engaging unconsciousness of the child. The attraction of their manners is that they belong to man, and
are know to every man, in virtue of his being once a
child; besides that, there are always individuals who
retain these characteristics.

"A person of childlike genius and unborn energy is still a Greek, and revives our love of the Muse of Hellas. I admire the love of Nature in the 'Philoctetes.' In reading those fine apostrophes to sleep, to the stars, rocks, mountain, and waves, I feel time passing away as an ebbing sea. I feel the eternity of man, the identity of his thought. The Greek had, it seems, the same fellow-beings as I. The sun and moon, water and fire, met his heart precisely as they meet mine. Then the vaunted distinction between Greek and English, between classic and romantic schools, seems superficial and pedantic. When a thought of Plato becomes a thought to me, when a truth that fired the soul of Pindar fires mine, time is no more. When I feel that we two meet in a perception —that our two souls are tinged with the same hue, and do, as it were, run into one—why should I measure degrees of latitude? Why should I count Egyptian years?"

The same pregnant thought is presented with illustrations from all sides; and the essay thus concludes :

HOW HISTORY SHOULD BE READ AND WRITTEN.

"In the light of these two facts, that the mind is one, and that Nature is its correlative, history is to be read and written. The pupil shall pass through the whole cycle of experience. He shall collect into a focus the rays of Nature. History shall no longer be a dull book; it shall walk incarnate in every just and wise man. You shall not tell me by languages and titles a catalogue of the volumes you have read; you shall make me feel what periods you have lived. A man shall be the Temple of Fame. He shall walk, as the poets have described that goddess, in a robe painted all over with wonderful events and experiences; his own form and features, by that exalted intelligence, shall be that variegated vest. I shall find in him the fore-world; in his childhood the age of gold; the apples of knowledge; the Argonautic expedition; the calling of Abraham; the building of the Temple; the advent of Christ; the Dark Ages; the Revival of Letters; the Reformation; the discovery of new lands; the opening of new sciences and new regions in man. He shall be the priest of Pan, and bring with him into humble cottages the blessing of the morning stars, and all the recorded benefits of heaven and earth.

"Is there something overweening in this claim? Then I reject all I have written; for what is the use of pretending to know what we know not? But it is the fault of our rhetoric that we can not strongly state one fact, without seeming to belie some other. I hold our actual knowledge very cheap. What connection do the books show between the fifty or sixty chemical elements and the historical eras? Nay, what does history yet record of the metaphysical annals of man? What light does it shed on those mysteries which we hide under the names of death and immortality? Yet every history should be written in a wisdom which divined the range of our affinities, and looked at facts as symbols.

"I am ashamed to see what a shallow village tale our so-called history is. Broader and deeper must we write our annals—from an ethical reformation, from the influx of the ever-new, ever-sanative conscience—if we would truly express our central and wide-related nature, instead of this old chronology of selfishness and pride, to which we have too long lent our eyes. Already that exists for us, shines in on us unawares; but the path of science and of letters is not the way into Nature. The idiot, the Indian, the child, an unschooled farmer's boy, stand nearer to the light by which Nature is to be read than the dissector or the antiquary."

Here, again, we must guard ourselves against the constant persistency which permeates all of Emerson's mode of thought and way of expressing it. His conceptions vary with his moods and experiences; and here presents the one conception which he has at any particular time as the one which is not only true, but the truth. Thus, in a few pages before he has dwelt admiringly upon the Greek history; here history, as written, is almost less than worthless. This involves him in perpetual inconsistencies, and of this he is quite aware. But for consistency he has a most sovereign contempt, which he thus expresses in the essay upon "Self-Reliance."

CONSISTENCY.

"For non-conformity the world whips you with its displeasure; and therefore a man must know how to estimate a sour face. . . . The other terror that scares us from self-trust is our consistency; a reverence for past act or word, because the eyes of others have no other data for computing our orbit than our past acts, and we are loth to disappoint them. But why should you keep you head over your shoulder? Why drag about this corpse of your memory, lest you contradict somewhat you have stated in this or that public place?

Suppose you should contradict yourself; what then? It seems to be a rule of wisdom never to rely upon your memory even in acts of pure memory; but to bring the past for judgment into the thousand-eyed present, and live ever in a new day. In your metaphysics you have denied personality to the Deity; and yet when the devout motions of the soul come, yield to them with heart and life, though they should clothe God with shape and color. Leave your theory, as Joseph his coat in the hand of the harlot, and flee.

"A foolish consistency is the hobgoblin of little minds, adored by little statesmen and philosophers and divines. With consistency a great soul has little or nothing to do. He may as well concern himself with his shadow on the wall. Speak what you think now, in hard words; and to-morrow speak what to-morrow thinks, in hard words again, though it contradict everything you said to-day. 'Ah, so you shall be sure to be misunderstood!' Is it so bad, then, to be misunderstood? Pythagoras was misunderstood, and Socrates, and Jesus, and Luther, and Copernicus, Galileo, and Newton, and every wise spirit that ever took flesh. To be great is to be misunderstood."

This, again, is one of Emerson's half truths, or, rather, partial presentations of the truth. We certainly have the right to be more wise to-day than we were yesterday, and wiser to-morrow than we are to-day. But we hold that it is not wise to speak the thought of to-day until we are thoroughly assured that it is the true thought, or at least true so far as it goes. The wise man does not look upon other men as so many slop-bowls into which he may vomit the undigested ideas of the moment. When he has come to believe that these ideas are true ones, then, and then only, let him utter them. Should he in after-time come to consider them erroneous, then let him utter those which wider thought has convinced him to be true, although they should contravene anything or everything which he had before said. It may be the case that his first conception which he had expressed, and subsequently rejected, was, after all, the true one. Newton had elaborated his theory of gravitation; but when he came to apply it to certain essential facts of the case, as then known, he abandoned the theory for nearly twenty years. Then fresh physical investigation showed that the theory was correct, and that the fault lay in the erroneous observations of these important facts. Thus corrected, he returned to his original theory, and demonstrated it to be the true one, because it explained all the phenomena to which it related. Something like this has been the case with many, perhaps most, sincere thinkers.

We have thus far considered Emerson as a philosopher dwelling in ideal regions, propounding transcendental theories, which do not bear directly upon the affairs of the conduct of our daily life. But there is quite another side to his intellectual character. To requote the words of Mr. Whipple: "One side of his wisdom is worldly wisdom. The brilliant transcendentalist is evidently a man not easy to be deceived in matters pertaining to the ordinary course of human affairs. His observations on society, on manners, on character, on institutions, are stamped with sagacity, and indicate a familiar knowledge of the homely phases of life, which are seldom viewed in their poetical relations." And, moreover, his practical life has been directed by this homely philosophy. If speculatively he questions the actual reality of the phenomena which surround him, he practically acts as though they were real. The baker and the butcher, and their bread and meat, may all be mere appearances ; but none the less does he buy and consume their wares. He and his auditors and readers may be mere phantoms—an appearance speaking to or writing for appearances ; but none the less does he address them, and take his lecture fee or his copyright money. This phase of his philosophy appears prominent in the essays. Thus, in the one upon " Self-reliance," we read :

SELF-RELIANCE.

" Trust thyself; every heart vibrates to that iron string. Accept the place the Divine Providence has found for you—the society of your contemporaries, the connection of events. Great men have always done so, and confided themselves, childlike, to the genius of their age, betraying their perception that the absolutely trustworthy was seated at their heart, working through their hands, predominating in all their being. And we are now men, and must accept in the highest mind the same transcendent destiny; and not minors and invalids in a protected corner, not cowards fleeing before a revolution; but guides and redeemers and benefactors, obeying the almighty effort, and advancing on chaos and the dark. . . . These are the voices which we hear in solitude, but they grow faint and inaudible as we enter into the world. Society is a joint-stock company, in which the members agree, for the better securing of his bread to each shareholder, to surrender the liberty and comfort of the eater. The virtue in most request is conformity. Self-reliance is its aversion. It loves not realities and creators, but names and customs. Whoso would be a man must be a non-conformist. He who would gather immortal palms must not be hindered by the name of goodness, but must explore if it be goodness. Nothing is at last sacred but the integrity of your own mind. Absolve you to yourself, and you shall have the suffrage of the world."

And again, still following his theme along another path :

SELF-RELIANCE AND PRAYER.

"It is easy to see that a greater self-reliance must work a revolution in all the offices and relations of men: in their religion, their education; in their pursuits, their modes of living, their association; in their property, in their speculative views. In what prayers do men allow themselves! That which they call a holy office is not so much as brave and manly. Prayer looks abroad, and asks for some foreign addition to come through some foreign virtue, and loses itself in endless mazes of natural and supernatural and mediatorial and miraculous.

Prayer that craves a particular commodity—anything less than all good—is vicious. Prayer is the contemplation of facts of life from the highest point of view. It is the soliloquy of a beholding and jubilant soul; but prayer as a means to effect a private end is meanness and theft. It supposes dualism and not unity in nature and consciousness. As soon as a man is at unity with God, he will not beg. He will then see prayer in all action. The prayer of the farmer kneeling in his field to weed it, the prayer of the rower kneeling with the stroke of his oar, are true prayers, heard throughout nature, though for cheap ends."

FALSE PRAYERS.

"Another sort of false prayers are our regrets. Discontent is the want of self-reliance; it is infirmity of will. Regret calamities, if you can thereby help the sufferer; if not, attend your own work, and already the evil begins to be repaired. Our sympathy is just as base. We come to them who weep foolishly and sit down and cry for company, instead of imparting to them truth and health in rough electric shocks, putting them once more in communication with their own reason."

We suppose that Emerson would join heartily in the petitions of the Lord's Prayer; but we imagine that his devotions would quite as fully find expression in that comprehensive old Greek prayer which we find in the so-called "Homeric Fragments":

"O Sovran Jove! asked or unasked, supply all good;
  All evil—though implored—deny."

Another passage, bearing closely upon self-reliance, is this :

TRAVELING AND IMITATION.

"But the rage of traveling is a symptom of a deeper unsoundness affecting the whole intellectual action. The intellect is vagabond, and our system of education fosters restlessness. Our minds travel when our bodies are forced to stay at home. We imitate; and what is imitation but the traveling of the mind? Our houses are built with foreign taste; our shelves are garnished with foreign ornaments; our opinions, our tastes, our faculties, lean and follow the past and the distant. The soul created the arts wherever they have flourished. It was in his own mind that the artist sought his model. It was an application of his own thought to the thing that ought to be done and the conditions to be observed. And why need we copy the Doric or the Gothic model? Beauty, convenience, grandeur of thought, and quaint expression are as near to us as to any; and if the American artist will study with hope and love the precise thing to be done by him—considering the climate, the soil, the length of the day, the wants of the people, the habits, and the form of the government—he will create a house in which all of these will find themselves fitted, and taste and sentiment will be satisfied also."

Here, again, with all its keen shrewdness and wit, one may find traces of a one-sided view of the matter in hand. There is an advantage in traveling, even for amusement, provided always that the amusement does not take an ignoble

12

turn. The man who travels with no definite ulterior purpose of study or benevolence will yet not
fail to learn something of value. He sees man
and Nature under fresh aspects ; learns that the
narrow limits of his home do not include the
world ; that men are yet men, although they do
not eat and dress, speak and move just as he
does. The mere tourist, who goes from the east
to the west or from the west to the east, from
the north to the south or from the south to the
north, from America to Europe or from Europe
to America, can hardly fail to bring back something with him—something which has enlarged
his scope of vision, and made him more of a man.
It is something to have seen the strength or the
weakness of living empires, or to have stood by
the graves of dead empires ; to have seen St.
Peter's and the Cathedral of Cologne ; to have
looked at Luxor or Karnak, the ruins of the Parthenon or the Colosseum ; to have trod the Mount
of Olives or have seen the black stone at Mecca.
It gets a man, for a time at least, out of himself,
out of his old narrow ruts.

The other side of this view of traveling is elsewhere insisted upon by Emerson—as strongly insisted upon as we can do. His first visit to Europe
was made simply for recreation ; he went thither in order to bring back something which he did
not carry with him. He went to England just
that he might see, for a few minutes or hours,

half a dozen famous men whose writings he had read. This travel, undertaken with no definite intellectual purposes beyond seeing the people and the country, was no "fool's paradise." From it he brought back what he did not carry with him : restored health, recuperated spirits, a rejuvenated youth, which enabled him to perform the new duties which were to be imposed upon him in the new career to which he was to be called.

The essay on "Compensation" embodies some teaching which runs quite counter to very much which is commonly inculcated. He says :

ON COMPENSATION.

"Ever since I was a boy I have wished to write a discourse on 'Compensation'; for it seemed to me, when very young, that on this subject life was ahead of theology, and the people knew more than the preachers taught. It seemed to me also that in it might be shown to men a ray of divinity—the present action of the soul of the world, clean from all vestige of tradition ; and so the heart of man might be bathed by an inundation of eternal love, conversing with that which he knows *was* always, and always *must be*, because it really *is* now. It appears, moreover, that if this doctrine could be stated in terms with any resemblance to those bright intuitions in which this truth is sometimes revealed to us, it would be a star in many dark hours and crooked passages in our journey that would not suffer us to lose the way.

"I was lately confirmed in these desires by hearing a sermon at church. The preacher, a man esteemed for his orthodoxy, unfolded in the ordinary manner the doc-

trine of the last judgment. He assumed that judgment
is not executed in this world; that the wicked are successful; that the good are miserable; and then urged,
from reason and from Scripture, a compensation to be
made to both parties in the next life. No offense appeared to be taken by the congregation at this doctrine.
As far as I could observe, when the meeting broke up
they separated without remark on the sermon.

"Yet what was the import of this teaching? What
did the preacher mean by saying that the good are miserable in the present life? Was it that houses and lands,
offices, wine, horses, dress, luxury, are had by unprinci-
pled men, while the saints are poor and despised; and
that a compensation is to be made to these last hereafter, by giving them the like gratifications another day
—bank-stock and doubloons, venison and champagne?
This must be the compensation intended, for what else?
Is it that they have leave to love, and pray, and praise?
to love and serve men? Why, that they can do now.
The legitimate inference the disciple would draw was,
'We are to have *such* a good time as the sinners have
now'; or, to push it to its extreme point, 'You sin
now, we shall sin by and by; we would sin now, if we
could; not being successful, we expect our revenge to-
morrow.'

"The fallacy lay in the immense concession that the
bad are successful, that justice is not done now. The
blindness of the preacher consisted in deferring to the
base estimate of the market value of what constitutes a
manly success, instead of confronting and convicting the
world from the truth, announcing the presence of the
soul, the omnipotence of the will, and so establishing
the standard of good and ill, of success and falsehood."

At the outset Emerson states fairly the doctrine of compensation in the future life for any wrong or injury suffered in this, as laid down by the preacher and apparently accepted by the congregation. But when he puts forth his own version of it, and to "push it to its extreme import," the result is a caricature. Those who accept the doctrine do not believe that the compensation to be made to the good hereafter is to be of the same kind with the good which the wicked are assumed to enjoy here, and of which the good are deprived ; that, because the good are here without a penny, they shall have pocketfuls of doubloons in the hereafter ; that, because they have here eaten roots, and drank water, they shall in the hereafter revel in venison and champagne. But, on the contrary, they hold that the good which it is claimed they will enjoy will be infinitely higher, not in degree but in kind. For partial misery here, they shall have perfect bliss hereafter.

We agree as little as Emerson can do, even with this doctrine of compensation. To our minds there is no compensation in the case assumed, nor, indeed, could be. If a man defrauds me, so that for long years I undergo the hardest privations, and must perform the most irksome tasks, he makes me no compensation, if, at last, he not only restores what was mine, but thereto adds uncounted millions. If one so slanders me that I lose good name, and am esteemed an ingrate and a villain, he makes me no compensation for the wrong he had done me, if at some future day he shall give me a thousand certificates of my perfect integrity and virtue. If I have been wrongfully convicted of some great crime, and am confined for years as a felon, and, at length, my innocence being proved, not only are the prison doors opened to me, but the Government gives me a large pension, still there is no compensation in any true sense of the word. Those lost years of my life can never be restored to me.

Though I have suffered deep wrong, jury and judge may have done none, for they acted honestly and justly in view of the evidence before them. Not so in the case of the Divine Government. It knew all the facts in the case, and if, as is assumed, wrong has been done to the good, the Omniscient Ruler of all things has done it. The only escape from this conclusion is the denial of the assumption that any wrong has been done ; that, notwithstanding all appearances to the contrary, as judged by our finite minds, the Ruler and Judge of all rules as justly and judges as rightly in this world as he will in the future world.

But, when Emerson comes to the preparation of his long-meditated discourse on " Compensation," he shifts the meaning of the term from that sense in which it was employed by the preacher whom he had criticised. By compensation the preacher meant a making up in the future life for the wrongs inflicted in this. With Emerson, compensation is such a balance and adjustment of things, diverse, and sometimes apparently contrary, that in the constant result the right end is attained. The vari-colored rays of the solar spectrum, when combined in one, produce a perfect white ; the nice balance between the centripetal and the centrifugal forces keeps the planets in their predestined orbits and the stars in their courses, preserving the harmony of the most ancient heavens. This idea is elaborated in the essay on " Compensation," and in another upon " Spiritual Laws." The whole train of thought and the result of it are well summed up in three stanzas of verse which stand as mottoes for the two essays, and are also among the best and most characteristic of Emerson's poems.

COMPENSATION AND SPIRITUAL LAWS.

" The wings of Time are black and white,
Red with morning and with night.
Mountain tall and ocean deep,
Trembling balance duly keep.
In changing moon, in tidal wave,
Grows the feud of want and have.
Gauge more and less, through space
Electric star and pencil plays.

The lonely earth amid the balls
That hang through the eternal halls,
A makeweight, flying to the void,
Supplemental asteroid,
Or compensatory spark,
Shoots across the neutral dark.

" Man's the elm, and wealth the vine;
Stanch and strong the tendrils twine;
Though the frail tendrils thee deceive,
None from its stock that vine can reave.
Fear not, then, thou child infirm;
There's no god dare wrong a worm.
Laurel crown cleaves to deserts,
And power to him who power exerts;
Hast not thy share? On wingèd feet,
Lo! it rushes thee to meet;
And all that Nature made thy own,
Floating in air or pent in stone,
Will ride the hills and swim the sea,
And, like thy shadow, follow thee.

" The living heavens thy prayers respect;
House at once and architect;
Quarrying man's rejected hours,
Builds there with eternal towers;
   Sole and self-commanded works;
Fears not undermining days,
Grows by decays,
   And, by the famous might that lurks
In reaction and recoil,
Makes flame to freeze, and ice to boil;
Forging, through swart arms of offense,
The silver seal of innocence."

Thoughtful all this, and true as far as it goes ; but very far from what he had hoped—that this doctrine of compensation would be "a star in many dark hours and crooked passages in our journey, that would not suffer us to lose our way." Emerson seems to have been aware that he could only to a limited extent achieve what he had proposed ; for, almost at the opening of the essay, he says : " I shall attempt in this and the following chapter" (on Spiritual Laws) "to record some facts that indicate the path of the law of compensation ; happy beyond my expectation if I shall truly draw the smallest arc of this circle." And this expression of premonitory misgivings must stand also as the expression of his final judgment upon the completed result.

The essay on "Friendship" is a most delightful one. We may accept every word of it just as it stands without finding one representation apparently contradicted by another. We quote passages from a few paragraphs, omitting many others not less worthy of citation :

IS FRIENDSHIP IMMORTAL ?

" Will these, too, separate themselves from me again, or some of them? I know not, but I fear not, for my relation to them is so pure that we hold by simple affinity, and, the genius of my life being thus social, the same affinity will exert its energy on whomsoever is as noble as these men and women, wherever I may be. I confess to an extreme tenderness of nature on this point. It is

almost dangerous to me to 'crush the sweet poison of
the affections.' A new person is to me often a great
event, and hinders me from sleep. I have often had fine
fancies about persons, which have given me delicious
hours; but the joy ends with the day; it yields no fruit.
Thought is not born of it; my action is very little modi-
fied. I must feel pride in my friend's accomplishments
as if they were mine, and a property in his virtues. I
feel as warmly when he is praised as the lover when he
hears applause of his engaged maiden. We over-esti-
mate the conscience of our friend. His goodness seems
better than our goodness; his nature finer, his tempta-
tions less. Our own thought sounds new and larger from
his mouth. Yet the systole and the diastole of the heart
are not without their analogy in the ebb and flow of love.
Friendship, like the immortality of the soul, is too good
to be believed. The lover, beholding his maiden, half
knows that *she* is not verily that which he worships.
And, in the golden hour of friendship, we are surprised
with shades of suspicion and unbelief. We doubt that
we bestow on our hero the virtues in which he shines,
and afterward worship the form to which we have ascribed this divine inhabitation."

REAL FRIENDSHIPS.

"I do not wish to treat friendships daintily, but with
roughest courage. When they are real, they are not
glass threads or frost-work, but the solidest things we
know. The sweet sincerity of joy and peace which I
draw from this alliance with my brother's soul is the
nut itself whereof all Nature and all Thought is but the
husk and shell. Happy is the house which shelters a
friend! It might well be built, like a festal bower or

arch, to entertain him a single day. Happier if he
knows the solemnity of the occasion, and honors its law.
He who offers himself a candidate for that covenant
comes up like an Olympian, to the great games where
the first-born of the world are the competitors. He
proposes himself for contests where time, want, danger,
are in the lists; and he alone is victor who has truth
enough in his constitution to preserve the delicacy of his
beauty from the wear and tear of all these."

TRUTH IN FRIENDSHIP.

" There are two elements that go to the composition
of friendship, each so sovereign that I can detect no
superiority in either, no reason why either should be
first named. One is *truth*. A friend is a person with
whom I may be sincere. Before him I may think aloud.
I am arrived at last in the presence of a man so real and
equal that I may drop even those undermost garments of
dissimulation, courtesy, and second thought, which men
never put off, and may deal with him with the simplicity
and wholeness with which one chemical atom meets
another."

TENDERNESS IN FRIENDSHIP.

" The other element of friendship is *tenderness*. We
are holden to men by every sort of tie; by blood, by
pride, by fear, by hope, by lucre, by lust, by hate, by
admiration; by every circumstance, and badge, and
trifle; but we can scarce believe that so much character
can subsist in another as to draw us by *love*. Can
another be so blessed, and we so pure, that we can offer
him tenderness? I find very little written directly to
this matter in books; and yet I have one test which I

can not choose but remember. My author says: 'I offer
myself faintly and bluntly to those whose effectually I
am; and tender myself least to him to whom I am the
most devoted.'   The end of friendship is a commerce the
most strict and homely that can be joined; more strict
that any of which we have experience. It is for aid and
comfort through all the relations and passages of life and
death.   It is fit for serene days and graceful gifts, and
country rambles; but also for rough roads and hard fare,
shipwreck, poverty, and persecution.   It keeps company
with the sallies of the wit and the trances of religion.
We are to dignify to each other the daily needs and offices
of man's life, and embellish it by courage, wisdom, and
unity.   It should never fall into something usual and
settled, but should be alert and inventive, and add rhyme
and reason to what was drudgery."

CONVERSATION IN FRIENDSHIP.

"Friendship may be said to require natures so rare and
costly, each so well-tempered and so happily adapted, and
withal so circumstanced, that its satisfaction can very seldom be assured. It can not subsist in its perfection—say
some of those who are learned in the warm lore of the
heart—betwixt more than two.   I am not quite so strict
in my terms perhaps, because I have never known so high
a fellowship as others.   I please my imagination more
with a circle of godlike men and women variously related
to each other, and between whom exists a lofty intelligence.   But I find this law of *one to one* peremptory to
conversation, which is the practice and consummation of
friendship.   Do not mix waters too much.   The best mix
as ill as good and bad.   You shall have very useful and
cheering discourse at several times with two several men;

but let the three of you come together, and you shall not have one new and hearty word. Two may talk, and one may hear; but three can not take part in a conversation of the most sincere and hearty sort. In good company there is never such discourse between two across the table as takes place when you leave them alone. In good company the individuals merge their egotism into a social soul exactly coextensive with the several consciousnesses there present. No partialities of friend to friend, no fondness of brother to sister, of wife to husband, are there pertinent, but quite otherwise. Only he may then speak who can sail on the common thought of the party, and is not poorly limited to his own. Now, this convention, which good sense demands, destroys the high freedom of great conversation, which requires an absolute running of two souls into one."

SOME AFTER-THOUGHTS ON FRIENDSHIP.

"It has seemed to me lately more possible than I knew, to carry a friendship greatly on one side, without due correspondence on the other. Why should I cumber myself with regrets that the receiver is not capacious? It never troubles the sun that some of his rays fall wide and vain into ungrateful space, and only a small part on the reflecting planet. Let your greatness educate the cold and crude companion. If he is unequal, he will presently pass away. It is thought a disgrace to love unrequited. But the great will see that true love can not be unrequited. True love transcends the unworthy object, and dwells and broods on the eternal; and, when the poor interposed mask crumbles, it is not sad, but feels rid of so much earth, and feels its independency the surer. Yet these things may hardly be said without a

sort of treachery to the relation. The essence of friendship is entireness, a total magnanimity and trust. It
must not surmise or provide for infirmity. It treats its
object as a god that it may deify both."

The essay on "Prudence" is practical enough
to suit the most strenuous materialist. At the
outset Emerson makes a sort of half apology for
writing upon such a theme. "What right have
I," he says, "to write on prudence, whereof I
have little, and that of the negative sort? My
prudence consists in avoiding and going without,
not in adroit steering, not in gentle repairing. I
have no skill to make money spend well, no genius
in my economy; and whoever sees my garden discovers that I must have some other garden. Yet
I love facts, and hate lubricity, and people without perception. Then I have the same right to
write on prudence that I have to write on poetry
or holiness. We write from aspiration and antagonism, as well as from experience. We paint those
qualities which we do not possess. Moreover, it
would be hardly honest in me not to balance these
fine lyric words of love and friendship with words
of coarser sound, and whilst my debt to my senses
is real and constant, not to own it in passing."
The nature and objects of prudence are characteristically set forth:

PRUDENCE—WHAT AND WHY IT IS.

"Prudence is the virtue of the senses. It is the
science of appearances. It is the outmost action of the

inward life. It is God taking thought of oxen. It moves matter after the laws of matter. It is content to seek health of body by complying with physical conditions, and health of mind by the laws of the intellect. The world of the senses is a world of shows; it does not exist for itself, but has a symbolical character; and a true prudence, or law of shows, recognizes the co-presence of other laws, and knows that its own office is subaltern; knows that it is surface and not center where it works. Prudence is false when detached. It is legitimate when it is the natural history of the soul incarnate; when it unfolds the beauty of laws within the narrow scope of the senses. Prudence does not go behind Nature, and ask whence it is. It takes the laws of the world, whereby man's being is conditioned, as they are, and keeps these laws, that it may enjoy their proper good. It respects space and time, climate, want, sleep, the law of polarity, growth, and death.

"We are instructed by the petty experiences which usurp the hours and years. The hard soil and four months of snow make the inhabitant of the northern temperate zone wiser and abler than his fellow who enjoys the fixed smile of the tropics. The southern islander may ramble all day at his will. At night he may sleep on a mat under the moon; and, wherever a wild date-tree grows, Nature has, without a prayer even, spread a table for his morning meal. The northerner is perforce a householder. He must brew, bake, salt, and preserve his food, and pile wood and coal. But as it happens that not one stroke can labor lay to without some new acquaintance with Nature, and as Nature is inexhaustibly significant, the inhabitants of these climates have always excelled the southerner in force.

"Such is the value of these matters, that a man who knows other matters can never know too much of these. Let him, if he have hands, handle; if eyes, measure and discriminate. Let him accept and hive every fact of chemistry, natural history, and economics. The more he has, the less is he disposed to spare any one; time is always bringing occasions that disclose their value. Some wisdom comes out of every natural and innocent action. The domestic man who loves no music as well as his kitchen clock, and the airs which the logs sing to him as they burn on the hearth, has solaces which others never dream of. The application of means to ends insures victory, and the songs of victory, not less in a farm or a shop than in the tactics of party or of war. Let a man keep the law—any law—and his way will be strewn with satisfactions. On the other hand, Nature punishes any neglect of prudence. If you think the senses final, obey their law. If you believe in the soul, do not clutch at sensual sweetness before it is ripe on the slow tree of cause and effect. The beautiful laws of Nature, once dislocated by our inaptitude, are holes and dens. If the hive be disturbed by rash and stupid hands, instead of honey, it will yield us bees. Our words and actions to be fair must be timely. A gay and pleasant sound is the whetting of the scythe in the mornings of June; and yet what is more lonesome and sad than the sound of a whetstone or mower's rifle when it is too late in the season to make hay?

But, besides genuine prudence, there are base and spurious prudences, which are touched upon in sharp phrases:

BASE AND SPURIOUS PRUDENCE.

"The world is filled with the proverbs and acts and winkings of a base prudence, which is a devotion to matter, as if we possessed no other faculties than the palate, the nose, the touch, the eye, the ear; a prudence which adores the rule of three; which never subscribes, which never gives, which rarely tends; and asks but one question: 'Will it bake bread?' This is a disease like the thickening of the skin until the vital organs are destroyed. The spurious prudence, making the senses final, is the god of sots and cowards. It is Nature's joke, and therefore literature's. The true prudence limits this sensual by admitting the knowledge of an internal and real world. This recognition once made—the order of the world and the distribution of affairs and times being studied with the co-perception of their subordinate place, will reward any degree of attention. For our existence, thus apparently attached in Nature to the sun and the returning moon, and the periods which they mark—so susceptible to climate and to country; so alive to social good and evil; so fond of splendor, and so tender to hunger and cold and debt—reads all its primary lessons out of these books."

PRUDENCE AND COURAGE.

"So in regard to disagreeable and formidable things, prudence does not consist in evasion or in flight, but in courage. He who wishes to walk in the most peaceful paths of life with any serenity must screw himself up to resolution. Let him front the object of his worst apprehension, and his stoutness will commonly make his fear groundless. The Latin proverb says that 'in battles the

eye is first overcome.' Entire self-possession may make
a battle very little more dangerous to life than a match
with foils or at football. The terrors of the storm are
chiefly confined to the parlor and the cabin. The drover,
the sailor, buffets it all day, and his health renews itself
at as vigorous a pulse under the sleet as under the sun
of June.

"In the occurrence of unpleasant things among neighbors, fear comes readily to the heart, and magnifies the
consequence of the other party; but it is a bad counselor.
Every man is actually weak and apparently strong. To
himself he appears weak; to others formidable. You
are afraid of Grim; but Grim is also afraid of you. You
are solicitous of the good-will of the meanest person, un-
easy at his ill-will. But the sturdiest offender of your
peace and of the neighborhood, if you rip up *his* claims,
is as thin and timid as any; and the peace of society is
often kept because, as children say, 'one is afraid and
the other dares not.' Far off, men swell, bully, and
threaten; bring them hand to hand, and they are a feeble
folk."

PRUDENCE AND LOVE.

"It is a proverb that 'Courtesy costs nothing'; but
calculation might come to value love for its profit. Love
is not a hood but an eye-water. If you meet a sectary,
or a hostile partisan, never recognize the dividing lines;
but meet on what common ground remains. If they set
out to contend, Saint Paul will lie and Saint John will
hate. What low, poor, paltry, hypocritical people an argument on religion will make of the pure and chosen
souls! They will shuffle and crow, crook and hide; feign
to confess here only that they may brag and conquer

there; and not a thought has enriched either party, and not an emotion of bravery, modesty, or hope."

PRUDENT COMPLIANCES.

" So neither should you put yourselves in a false position with your contemporaries by indulging in a vein of hostility and bitterness. Though your views are in straight antagonism with theirs, assume an identity of sentiment, assume that you are saying precisely what all think, and in the flow of wit and love roll out your paradoxes in solid column, with not the infirmity of a doubt. So, at least, you get an adequate deliverance. Assume a consent, and it shall presently be granted, since really and underneath their external diversities all men are the same."

We have quoted this last paragraph only that we may express our utter dissent from it, except under the very widest limitations. Every day we are confronted with sentiments and opinions which we can not honestly assume to be identical with our own. Could Elijah honestly tell the priests of Baal that his God and theirs was the same? Could Luther blandly assure Eck and Tetzel that he agreed exactly, or in any degree even, with them in the matter of indulgences? Could Milton say to Salmasius that both of them were of one mind in regard to the great act of judgment executed by the people of England upon Charles the First? Could Emerson and Brigham Young —assuming that both were honest and sincere in their opinions—honestly and sincerely assure each

other that there was no difference between them ?
Should I, who abhor assassination, assure a Nihil-
ist that my views respecting the slaying of the
Czar of Russia differed in nowise from his own ?
It may be, and often is, a matter of the highest
and best wisdom to refrain from expressing one's
sentiments, for there is a time to be silent and a
time to speak.   One is not bound of necessity to
assail the dogma of the Real Presence when standing under the dome of St. Peter's, or to denounce
Mohammed as a false prophet before the portals
of the temple at Mecca.   But, if a man will or
must speak at all, only the basest and most unworthy prudence will sanction his speaking other
than the truth.   There are times and emergen-
cies when the best and highest prudence must
give way to something higher and better ; times
when this half virtue would be a whole crime. It
was imprudent for John the Baptist to denounce
Herod for having taken to himself his brother's
wife ; for Leonidas with his three hundred to hold
the pass of Thermopylæ ; for Luther to nail up
his eighty-five theses on the doors of the Wittem-
berg Cathedral and to go to Worms ; for John
Wesley to persist in open-air preaching ; for Gar-
rison to denounce slavery in Boston.   Yet all
these things had to be done, and were done, because the way of duty lay in the paths of impru-
dence.   But in the closing paragraph of this essay
Emerson sums up in brief the true doctrine of

all prudence worthy to be so called, in ordinary cases :

THE ULTIMATE OF PRUDENCE.

" Wisdom will never let us stand with any man or men on unfriendly terms. We refuse sympathy and intimacy with people, as if we waited for some better sympathy and intimacy to come. But whence and when? To-morrow will be as to-day. Life wastes itself while we are preparing to live. Let us suck the sweetness of those affections and consuetudes that grow near us. These old shoes are easy to the feet. Undoubtedly we can easily pick faults in our company ; can easily whisper names prouder, and that tickle the fancy more. Every man's imagination hath its friends, and life would be dearer with such companions. But, if you can not have them on good, mutual terms, you can not have them. If not the Deity, but our ambition, hews and shapes the new relations, then virtue escapes, as strawberries lose their flavor in garden-beds.

" Thus, truth, courage, love, humility, and all the virtues range themselves on the side of prudence, or the art of securing a present well being. I do not know if all matter will be found to be made of one element—as oxygen and hydrogen—at last, but the world of manners is wrought of one stuff; and, begin where we will, we are pretty sure, in a short space, to be mumbling our Ten Commandments."

The essay on " Experience " is many-sided, treating upon many topics and from many points of view. It is full of sharp epigrammatic sayings, not unfrequently flung together with little apparent law of logical cohesion. We cite a single sarcastic passage :

THE WORLD TO THE SCHOLAR.

"The mid-world is best. Nature, as we know her, is no saint. The Lights of the Church, the Ascetics, Gentoos, and Corn-eaters, she does not distinguish by any favor. She comes eating and drinking and sinning. Her darlings—the great, the strong, the beautiful—are not the children of our law; do not come out of the Sunday-schools, nor weigh their food, nor punctually keep the Commandments. If we will be strong with her strength, we must not harbor such disconsolate consciences, borrowed, too, from the consciences of other nations. We must set up the strong present tense against all the rumors of wrath, past or to come. So many things are unsettled which it is of the first importance to settle; and, pending their settlement, we will do as we do. While the debate goes forward on the equity of commerce, and will not be closed for a century or two, New and Old England may keep shop. Law of copyright and international copyright is to be discussed; and, in the interim, we will sell our books for the most we can. Expediency of literature, lawfulness of writing down a thought is questioned; much is to say on both sides, and, while the fight waxes hot, thou, dearest scholar! stick to thy foolish task; add a line every hour, and between whiles add a line. Right to hold land, right of property is disputed, and the conventions convene; and, before the vote is taken, dig away in your garden, and spend your earnings as a waif or a godsend to all serene and beautiful purposes. Life itself is a bubble and a skepticism, and a sleep within a sleep. Grant it, and as much more as thou wilt; but thou, God's darling! heed thy private dream; thou wilt not be missed in the scorning and the skepticism; there are enough of them; stay there in thy closet, and toil until the rest are agreed what to do about it. Thy sickness, they say, and thy puny habit require that thou do this or avoid that; but know that thy life is a flitting state, a tent for the night; and do thou, sick or well, finish that stint. Thou art sick, but shalt not be worse, and the universe, which holds thee dear, shall be the better."

This, of course sarcastically stated, is what experience teaches some men. Quite different is what experience had taught Emerson at three-and-forty, when this essay was written. Experience had taught him much, but only a mere fragment of what he wished to learn. He had read only the preface to the mighty book of the universe. He thus, half mournfully, half hopingly, sums up what he thought he had learned:

NET RESULT OF PRESENT EXPERIENCE.

"Illusion, temperament, succession, surface, surprise, reality, subjectiveness—these are the thread on the loom of time, these are the lords of life. I dare not assume to give them order, but I name them as I find them in my way. I know better than to claim any completeness for my picture. I am a fragment, and this is a fragment of me. I can very confidently announce one or another law, which throws itself into relief and form; but I am too young yet, by some ages, to compile a code. I gossip for my hour concerning the eternal politics. I

have seen many fair pictures not in vain. A wonderful
time I have lived in. I am not the novice I was fourteen
years, nor yet seven years ago. Let who will ask where
is the fruit? I find a private fruit sufficient. This is a
fruit—that I should not ask for a rash effect for my
meditations, counsels, and the hivings of truths. I
should feel it pitiful to demand a result on this town and
county, an overt effect on the instant, month, and year.
The effect is deep and secular as the cause. It works on
periods in which mortal lifetime is lost. I *am* and I
have; but I do not *get*, and, when I fancied I had gotten
something, I found that I did not. That hankering after
an overt or practical effect seems to me an apostasy. In
good earnest, I am willing to spare myself this most un-
necessary deal of doing. Life wears to me a visionary
face. Hardest, roughest action is visionary also. It is
but a choice between soft and visionary dreams. People
disparage knowing and the intellectual life, and urge
doing. I am very content with *knowing*, if only I could
know. That is an august entertainment, and would
suffice me a great while. To know a little would be
worth the expense of this world.

"I know that the world I converse with in the city
and on the farms is not the world I *think.* I observe
that difference, and shall observe it. One day I shall
know the value and law of this discrepance. But I have
not found that much was gained by manipular attempts
to realize the world of thought. Many eager persons
make an experiment this way, and make themselves
ridiculous. Worse, I observe that in the history of mankind there is not a solitary example of success—taking
their own tests of success. I say this polemically, or in
reply to the inquiry, 'Why not realize your world?'"

This reads very differently from much that we have cited, and much more that we have not cited, from Emerson, insisting upon doing as well as, and even more than, thinking. But let that pass. Both views are the genuine expressions of a susceptible mind in different moods, and looking at different sides of the same thing. The essay concludes in a strain which, in a measure, harmonizes the thoughts of both moods :

FINAL VICTORY.

"But far from me the despair which prejudges the law by a paltry empiricism, since there never was a right endeavor but it succeeded. Patience and patience, and we shall win at last. We must be very suspicious of the deceptions of the element of time. It takes a good deal of time to eat, or to sleep, or to earn a hundred dollars, and a very little time to entertain a hope which becomes the light of our life. We dress our garden, eat our dinners, discuss the household with our wives, and these things make no impression—are forgotten next week; but, in the solitude to which every man is always returning, he has a sanity and revelation which, in his passage into new worlds, he will carry with him. Never mind the ridicule; never mind the defeat; up again, old heart! It seems to say, 'There is a victory yet for all justice; and the true romance which the world exists to realize will be the transformation of genius into practical power.'"

The motto which is prefixed to the essay upon Experience is both text and peroration for the discourse. It is also, perhaps, the most Emersonian of all of Emerson's poems, for its pregnant thought, rugged rhythm, and swift changes :

THE LORDS OF LIFE.

" The Lords of Life, the Lords of Life:
    I saw them pass
      In their own guise,
    Like and unlike,
    Portly and grim,
      Use and surprise,
    Surface and dream.
Succession swift, and spectral wrong,
Temperament without a tongue,
And the inventor of the game,
Omnipresent without name.
Some to see, some to be guessed,
They marched from east to west.
Little man, least of all,
Among the legs of his guardians tall,
Walked about with puzzled look ;
Him by the hand kind Nature took:
Dearest Nature, strong and mild,
Whispered, ' Darling, never mind!
To-morrow they will wear another face:
The founder thou ! these are thy race.' "

The essay on " Nature " is well worthy of comparison with Emerson's book of the same title, written some eight or ten years before. They are alike and unlike. But the exuberance of the style of the book is toned down in the essay to the extremest of condensation; and the very essence of the condensation is again distilled down into the ten lines of verse which form the motto :

THE MYSTERY OF NATURE.

" The rounded world is fair to see,
    Nine times ᴌolded in mystery :
    Though baffled seers cannot impart,
    The secret of its laboring heart,
    Throb thine with Nature's throbbing breast,
    And all is clear from east to west.
    Spirit that lurks each form within
    Beckons to the spirit of its king,
    Self-kindled every atom glows,
    And hints the future which it owes."

After the conclusion of the essays, a new phase in the intellectual character of Emerson is apparent ; or, at least, his thoughts were turned into new channels. We read little upon the lofty topics of abstract speculation with which he had been occupied ; little of questionings whether Nature was a reality or only an appearance. Using the word in a noble sense, and not an ignoble one, he seems to have come to the conclusion that this " mid-world," in which our human life is passed —the only one respecting which man has any clear knowledge from within or from without— this world, with its institutions, its laws, its customs, its forms, its habits, its aims, failures, and successes, its great men, and even those who were

not very great—was quite worth the attention of
the thinker, and affords topics worthy to be dis-
coursed of by him.   In default of any other special profession, he had entered successfully upon
the pursuit of the lecturer.   The New England
"lyceum" system was introduced into Great
Britain, and in 1847 Emerson made his second
visit to England—this time as a public lecturer.
From this visit resulted the writing of " English
Traits," which, although not published as a book
until 1856, was really the production of several
years before.   In the interval (in 1850) he had
published a volume entitled, " Representative
Men."   The " English Traits " was really the
earlier work ; it will be first considered.

IX.

ENGLISH TRAITS.

EMERSON describes the very practical motives
which induced him to make this visit.   In Lan-
cashire and Yorkshire the " Mechanics' Institutes" had formed a " Union," which embraced
twenty or thirty towns, and presently extended
into the Middle Counties, and northward into
Scotland.   " I was invited," he said, " on liberal
terms, to read a series of lectures before them all.

The remuneration was equivalent to the fees at that time paid in this country for the like services. At all events, it was sufficient to cover my traveling expenses ; and the proposal offered an excellent opportunity of seeing the interior of England and Scotland, by means of a home and a committee of intelligent friends awaiting me in every town." The invitation was not at once accepted ; but, continues Emerson, " the invitation was repeated and pressed at a moment of more leisure, and when I was a little spent by some unusual studies. I wanted a change and tonic, and England was proposed to me. Besides, there were at least the dread attraction and salutary influences of the sea. I did not go very willingly. I am not a good traveler, nor have I found that long journeys yield a fair share of reasonable hours." However, the resolve was made, and in the autumn of 1847 he sailed from Boston in a packet-ship, thus entering upon what he had not long before stigmatized as the " fool's paradise " of traveling, which was certainly no such thing to him, but was, on the contrary, productive of great and lasting benefits.

With the exception of the chapter in which the visit of Emerson to Stonehenge in company with Carlyle has already been quoted, there is in the " English Traits " hardly a bit of any special information as to individuals or places. It is in no sense a book of travel or incident, but

an attempt to seize and emphasize the characteristics of the English people and mind. The land
and the people who inhabit it are not treated from
any ideal point of view. It is nowhere intimated
that either of them may be a mere appearance ;
but they are throughout represented as actual
existences, quite worthy of being studied even
though the study took a hundred years. Only a
few pages can be devoted to some of the topics
treated of.

PHYSICAL ENGLAND.

"As soon as you enter England, which, with Wales,
is no larger than the State of Georgia, this little land
stretches by an illusion to the dimensions of an empire.
The innumerable details, the crowded succession of
towns, cities, cathedrals, castles, and great and decorated
estates, the number and power of the guilds, the military
strength and splendor, the multitude of rich and remarkable people, the servants and the equipages—all these
catching the eye, and never allowing it to pause, hide all
boundaries by the impression of magnitude and endless
wealth. It is stuffed full, in all corners, with towns,
towers, churches, villas, palaces, hospitals, and charity
houses. In the history of art it is a long way from a
cromlech to York Minster, yet all the intermediate steps
may still be traced in this all-preserving island.

"The territory has a singular perfection.· The climate is warmer by many degrees than it is entitled to
by latitude. Neither hot nor cold, there is no hour in
the whole year when one cannot work. Here is no winter, but such days as we have in Massachusetts in No-

vember — a temperature which makes no exhausting demands on human strength, but allows the attainment of the largest stature. Charles the Second said: ' It invites men abroad more days in the year and more hours in the day than another country.' Then England has all the materials of a working country except wood. The constant rain—a rain with every tide in some parts of the island—keeps its multitude of rivers full, and brings agricultural production up to the highest point. It has plenty of water, of stone, of potter's clay, of coal, of salt, and of iron. The land naturally abounds with game, and the shores are enlivened by water-birds. The rivers and the surrounding sea spawn with fish. In the northern lochs the herring are in innumerable shoals. At one season the country people say, ' The lakes contain one part water and two parts fish.'

"Factitious climate, factitious position. England resembles a ship in its shape; and, if it were one, its best admiral could not have worked it or anchored it in a more judicious or effective position. England is anchored at the side of Europe, and right in the heart of the modern world. The sea, which, according to Virgil's famous line, divided the poor Britons utterly from the world, proved to be the ring of marriage with all nations. On a fortunate day, a wave of the German Ocean burst the old isthmus which joined Kent and Cornwall to France, and gave to this fragment of Europe its impregnable sea-wall, cutting off an island eight hundred miles in length, with an irregular breadth reaching to three hundred miles ; a territory large enough for independence, so near that it can see the harvests of the continent, and so far that who would cross the strait must be a mariner, ready for tempests."

COMMERCIAL ADVANTAGES.

"As America, Europe, and Asia lie, these Britons have precisely the best commercial position on the whole planet, and are sure of a market for all the goods they can manufacture. And to make these advantages avail, the river Thames must dig its spacious outlet to the sea from the heart of the kingdom, giving road and landing to innumerable ships, and all conveniency to trade. When James the First declared his purpose of punishing London by removing his court, the Lord Mayor replied that, 'in removing his royal presence from his lieges, they hoped he would leave them the Thames.'"

This and much more of like import was written a generation ago. Since then, by availing themselves of natural advantages, supplementing these by artificial means, the relative superiority of England to the rest of the world has been largely diminished, not to say overcome. We judge that, within a time not very far remote, New York, and the other cities which line the banks of its harbor and bay, will come to be the center and *entrepôt* of the world's busy life. But, in any case, it is not so much the physical structure and position of England which have made that country what it is, as the race of men who have held and now hold it. On this general matter of race, Emerson has much to say. We extract a few sentences, omitting the connecting passages which bind the whole together :

THE ENGLISH RACE.

"Men gladly hear of the power of 'blood' or 'race.' Everybody likes to know that his advantages can not be attributed to air, soil, sea; or to local wealth, as mines and quarries; nor to laws and traditions; nor to fortune —but to superior brain, as it makes the praise more personal to him. We anticipate in the doctrine of Race something like that law of physiology that, wherever bone, muscle, or essential organ is found in one healthy individual, the same part or organ may be found, in or near the same place, in its congener; and we may look to find in the son every mental and moral property that existed in the ancestor. Then first we care to examine the pedigree and copy heedfully the training—what food they ate, what nursing, school, and exercise they had—which resulted in this mother-wit, delicacy of thought, and robust wisdom. How came such men as King Alfred and Roger Bacon, William of Wykeham, Walter Raleigh, Philip Sidney, Isaac Newton, William Shakespeare, George Chapman, Francis Bacon, George Herbert, Henry Vane, to exist here? What made these delicate natures? Was it the air? Was it the sea? Was it the parentage? For it is certain that these men are samples of their contemporaries."

Race—that is, in its simplest form of expression, the descent of physical and moral qualities from father to son—is an important factor in the problems of human life and action. "Race," says Emerson, "avails much, if that be true which is alleged, that all Celts are Catholics and all Saxons are Protestants, that Celts love unity

14

of power and Saxons the representative principle. Race is a controlling influence with the Jew, who for two millenniums, under every climate, has preserved the same character and employments. It is race, is it not? that puts the hundred millions of India under the dominion of a remote island in the north of Europe." But, in the strict ethnological sense of the word, there is no such thing as an English race. In its very broadest acceptation, it is a compound people, made up in quite modern times from an intermixture of races proper. Emerson says:

MIXTURES IN THE ENGLISH RACE.

"The sources from which tradition derives their stock are three. First, they are of the oldest blood in the world—the Celts or Sidonians, of whose beginning there is no memory, and their end is likely to be still more remote in the future, for they have endurance and productiveness. They planted Britain, and gave to the seas and mountains names which are poems and imitate the pure voices of Nature. They had no violent feudal tenure, but the husbandman owned the land. They had an alphabet, astronomy, priestly culture, and a sublime creed. They made the best popular literature of the Middle Ages, in the songs of Merlin, and the tender and delicious mythology of Arthur. But the English come mainly from the Germans, whom the Romans found it hard to conquer—say, impossible to conquer, when one remembers the long sequel; a people about whom, in the old empire, the rumor ran, 'there was never any that meddled with them that repented it not.'"

Of the Norsemen, who, under the name of Danes and the like, have played a considerable part in the building up of the English race, Emerson has a good word or two to say, though with much by way of abatement :

THE NORSEMEN.

" The Norsemen are excellent persons in the main, with good sense, steadiness, wise speech, and prompt action ; but they have a singular turn for homicide ; their chief end of man is to murder or to be murdered. Oars, scythes, harpoons, crowbars, peat-knives, and hay forks are valued by them all the more for their charming aptitude for assassination. Never was poor gentleman so surfeited with life, so furious to get rid of it, as the Northman. It was a proverb of ill condition to die the death of old age.

"It took many generations to trim, comb, and perfume the first boat-load of Norse pirates into Royal Highnesses and most noble Knights of the Garter, but every sparkle of ornament dates back to the Norse boat. There will be time enough to mellow this strength into civility and religion. The children of the blind see, the children of felons have a healthy conscience ; many a mean, dastardly boy is at the age of puberty transformed into a serious and generous youth."

But for the Normans, that is, the Northmen who had settled themselves in France, Emerson has a supreme aversion. He says :

THE NORMANS.

"The Normans came out of France into England worse men than they went into it one hundred and sixty years before. They had lost their own language, and learned the Romance or barbarous Latin of the Gauls, and had acquired, with the language, all the vices it had names for. The Conquest has obtained in the chronicles the name of the 'memory of sorrow.' Twenty thousand thieves landed at Hastings. These founders of the House of Lords were greedy and ferocious dragoons, sons of greedy and ferocious pirates. They were all alike. They took everything they could carry; they burned, harried, violated, tortured, and killed, until everything English was brought to the verge of ruin. Such, however, is the illusion of antiquity and wealth, that decent and dignified men now existing boast their descent from these filthy thieves, who showed a far juster conviction of their own merits by assuming for types the swine, goat, jackal, leopard, wolf, and snake, which they severally resembled."

Mr. Emerson generalizes at first pretty largely concerni g the elements which enter into the composition of the English people, but he soon limits the subject to a small circle. He says: "What we think of when we talk of ' English Traits' really narrows itself to a small district. It excludes Ireland and Scotland and Wales, and reduces itself at last to London, that is, to those who come and go thither. The portraits that hang on the walls of the Academy Exhibition at London, the figures in ' Punch's ' drawings of the public men or of the club-houses, the prints in the shop-windows, are distinctive English, and not American, nor Scotch, nor Irish ; but it is a very restricted nationality. As you go north into the manufacturing and agricultural districts, and to the population that never travels, as you go into Yorkshire, as you enter Scotland, the world's Englishman is no longer found. In Scotland there is a rapid loss of all grandeur of mien and manners ; a provincial eagerness and acuteness appear ; the poverty of the country makes itself remarked, and a coarseness of manners. In Ireland are the same soil and climate as in England, but less food, no right relation to the land, political dependence, small tenantry, and an inferior or misplaced race." One might thus almost say that the title of the book should have been " London Traits," instead of " English Traits." Bearing this in mind, we shall present a few of these traits as they presented themselves to the eye and fancy of Emerson :

BODILY TRAITS OF THE ENGLISH.

" The English at the present day have great vigor of body and endurance. Other countrymen look slight and undersized beside them, and invalids. They are bigger men than the Americans. I suppose a hundred English, taken at random out of the street, would weigh a fourth more than so many Americans. Yet I am told the skeleton is not larger. They are round, ruddy, and handsome; at least the whole bust is well formed, and there is a tendency to stout and powerful frames. It is the fault of their forms that they grow stocky, and the women have that disadvantage—few tall, slender figures of flowing shape, but stunted and thickset persons. The French say that the Englishwomen have two left hands. But in all ages they are a handsome race. They have a vigorous health, and last well into middle and old age. The old men are as red as roses, and still handsome. A clear skin, a peach-bloom complexion, and good teeth are found all over the island."

ENGLISH LOVE OF UTILITY.

"They have a supreme eye to facts; their mind is not dazzled by its own means, but locked and bolted to results. Their practical vision is spacious, and they can hold many threads without entangling them. Their self-respect, their faith in causation, and their realistic logic, or coupling of means to ends, have given them the leadership of the modern world. The bias of the nation is a passion for utility. They love the lever, the screw and pulley, the Flanders draught-horse, the waterfall, windmills, tide-mills; the sea and the wind to bear their freight ships. More than the diamond they prize that dull pebble, which is wiser than a man, and whose axis is parallel to the axis of the world."

ARTIFICIALITY OF ENGLISH INSTITUTIONS.

"The nearer we look, the more artificial is their social system. Their law is a network of fictions. Their property a scrip or certificate of right to interest on money which no man ever saw. Their social classes are made by statute. Their ratios of power are historical and legal. The last Reform Bill took away political

power from a mound, a ruin, and a stone wall, while
Birmingham and Manchester, whose mills paid for the
wars of Europe, had no representative. Purity in the
elective Parliament is secured by the purchase of seats.
Sir Samuel Romilly, purest of English patriots, decided
that the only independent mode of entering Parliament
was to buy a seat, and he bought Horsham. Foreign
power is kept by armed colonies; power at home by a
standing army of police. The pauper lives better than
the free laborer; the thief better than the pauper; and
the transported felon better than one under imprison-
ment. The crimes are factitious: as smuggling, poach-
ing, non-conformity, heresy, and treason. Better, they
say in England, 'kill a man than a hare.' The sovereignty of the seas is maintained by the impressment of
seamen. Solvency is maintained by a national debt, on
the principle, 'If you will not lend me money, how
can I pay you?' Their system of education is factitious.
The universities galvanize dead languages into a sem-
blance of life. Their Church is artificial. The manners
and customs of society are artificial—made-up men with
made-up manners. And thus the whole is Birming-
hamized, and we have a nation whose existence is a work
of art; a cold, barren, almost arctic isle being made the
most fruitful, luxurious, and imperial land in the whole
earth."

It will be seen that Mr. Emerson is by no
means fastidious about making his statements
literally harmonize with each other. Of this
"cold, barren, and almost arctic isle" he had
said, only a few pages before : "Neither hot nor
cold, there is no hour in the whole year in which

man can not work ; no winter but such days as
we have in November ; while the constant rain
brings agricultural production up to the highest
point." In English manners Emerson finds
pluck the most characteristic feature. He says :

ENGLISH PLUCK.

"I find the Englishman to be him of all men who
stands firmest in his shoes. They have in themselves
what they value in their horses—mettle and bottom.
And what I heard first, I heard last ; and the one thing
which the English value is *pluck.* The word is not
beautiful, but on the quality they signify by it the nation
is unanimous. The cabmen have it ; the merchants have
it ; the bishops have it ; the women have it. The 'Times'
newspaper, they say, 'is the pluckiest thing in England.'
They require you to be of your own opinion ; and they
hate the practical cowards who can not in affairs answer
directly, Yes or No. They dare to displease ; nay, will
let you break all the commandments, if you do it
natively and with spirit. You must be somebody ; then
you may do this or that as you will."

English manners are set forth under a variety
of phases, not always perfectly congruous. The
people, we are told in one place, "are positive,
methodical, cleanly, and formal ; loving routine
and conventional ways ; loving truth and religion, to be sure, but inexorable on all points of
form." On the very next page we are assured
that "each man walks, eats, drinks, and shaves ;
dresses, gesticulates, and in every manner acts

and suffers without reference to the bystanders.
Every man in this polished country consults only
his own convenience, as much as a solitary pioneer
in Wisconsin. I know not where any personal
eccentricity is so freely allowed, and no man
gives himself any concern about it. An Englishman walks in the pouring rain, swinging his
closed umbrella like a walking-stick; wears a
wig, or a shawl, or a saddle, or stands on his
head, and no remark is made." Mr. Emerson's
typical Englishman, putting everything together,
is, to our apprehension, a rude, polished, rough-
and-ready, conventional person; doing just what
he pleases, and letting everybody also do what
he pleases, but inexorable upon points of form;
afraid of nobody, but in mortal terror of Mrs.
Grundy. Just as the climate of this almost arctic
island is neither cold nor hot, has no winter, and
its barren soil is highly fertile, and while there
is no day in the year in which the Englishman
may not live out of doors; yet "the harsh and
wet climate in which he is born keeps him indoors whenever he is at rest." Quite the most
charming thing which Mr. Emerson sees in English life is its domesticity. He says:

ENGLISH DOMESTICITY.

"Born in a harsh and wet climate, which keeps him
indoors whenever he is at rest, and being of an affectionate and loyal temper, he dearly loves his house. If he is

rich, he buys a demesne and builds a hall; if he is in middle condition, he spares no expense on his house. An English family consists of a very few persons, who from youth to age are found revolving within a few feet of each other, as if tied by some tie tense as that cartilage which we have seen attaching the two Siamese. England produces, under favorable conditions of ease and culture, the finest women in the world. And as the men are affectionate and true-hearted, the women inspire and refine them. Nothing can be more delicate without being fantastical, nothing more firm and based in nature and sentiment, than the courtship and mutual carriage of the sexes."

All this is very charming. We have no doubt that Mr. Emerson was brought much into the intimacy of such homes as he has described ; and that he saw them in their very best aspects ; for, as he tells us, he found a committee of intelligent friends awaiting him in every town which he visited during his lecturing tour. But, if we can put faith in what we read in history, this delightful domesticity is quite as rare in England as elsewhere. Predominant among the traits of the English people, Emerson finds that of truthfulness :

ENGLISH TRUTHFULNESS.

"Their practical power rests on their national sincerity. Veracity derives from instinct, and marks superiority in organization. Nature has endowed some men with cunning as a compensation for strength withheld; but it has provoked the malice of all others, as if avengers of public wrong. In the nobler kinds, where strength could be afforded, her races are loyal to truth. Beasts, that make no truce with man, do not break faith with each other. English veracity seems to rest on a sounder animal structure, as if they could afford it. They are blunt in saying what they think, sparing of promises; and they require plain-dealing of others. They confide in each other. English believes in English. The French feel the superiority of this probity. Madame de Staël says that the English irritated Napoleon mainly because they had found out how to unite success with honesty. At St. George's festival in Montreal, where I happened to be a guest, I observed that the chairman complimented his compatriots by saying that 'they confided that, wherever they met an Englishman, they found a man who would speak the truth.' The English, of all classes, value themselves on this trait, as distinguishing them from the French, who, in the popular estimation, are more polite than true. An Englishman understates, avoids the superlative, checks himself in compliments, alleging that in the French language one can not speak without lying."

Now, as Emerson knows next to nothing of the French people, and has seen only the better sort of the English, and that too in their best aspects, his broad generalizations must be accepted with very much of allowance. It is not a little singular that in his "Representative Men," he selects the French Montaigne as the exemplar of straightforward truthfulness. "Montaigne," he says, "is the frankest and honestest of all writers." Mr. Frothingham says : "Montaigne has been a favorite author with Emerson on account of his sincerity." A few more miscellaneous excerpts must be made from these "English Traits."

ENGLISH GRAVITY.

"The English race are reputed morose. I do not know that they have sadder brows than their neighbors of northern climates. They are sad by comparison with the singing and dancing nations; not sadder, but slow and staid, as finding their joys at home. They too believe that where there is no enjoyment of life, there can be no vigor and art in speech or thought; that your merry heart goes all the way, your sad one tires in a mile. This trait of gloom has been fixed on them by French travelers, who, from Froissart, Voltaire, Le Sage, Mirabeau, down to the lively journalists of the *feuilletons*, have spent their wit on the solemnity of their neighbors. The French say, 'Gay conversation is unknown in their island; the Englishman finds no relief from reflection except in reflection; when he wishes for amusement, he goes to work; his hilarity is like an attack of fever.'

"I suppose their gravity of demeanor and their few words have obtained this reputation. As compared with the Americans, I think them cheerful and contented. Young people in America are much more prone to melancholy. The English have a mild aspect and a ringing, cheerful voice. They are large-natured, and not so easily amused as the southerners, and are among them as grown people among children, requiring war, or trade, or engineering, or science, instead of frivolous games. They are proud and private, and, even if disposed to recreation, will avoid the open garden. 'They sported sadly—*ils s'amusaient tristement, selon la cou-*

tume de leur pays,' says Froissart; and I suppose never
nation built their party-walls so thick, or their garden
fences so high. Meat and wine produce no effect upon
them; they are just as cold, quiet, and composed at the
end as at the beginning of dinner."

For all these and many other apparently contradictory statements of the traits of the Englishmen, Emerson himself gives an explanation,
satisfactory enough as far as it goes : "They are con-
tradictorily described as sour, splenetic, and stubborn, and as mild, sweet, and sensible. The truth
is, they have great range and variety of character.
Commerce sends abroad multitudes of different
classes. The choleric Welshman, the fervid Scot,
the bilious resident in the East or the West In-
dies, are wide of the perfect behavior of the educated and dignified man of family. So is the
burly farmer; so is the country squire, with his
narrow and violent life. In every inn is the commercial room, in which 'travelers' or bagmen,
who carry patterns and solicit orders for the man-
ufacturers, are wont to be entertained. It easily
happens that this class should characterize England to the foreigner, who meets them on the
road and at every public-house, whilst the gentry
avoid the taverns, or seclude themselves whilst in
them. But," he continues, "these classes are
the right English stock, and may fairly show the
national qualities before yet art and education
have dealt with them."

ENGLISH WHIMSICALITY.

"The English are a nation of humorists. Individual right is pushed to the outermost bound compatible with public order. Property is so perfect that it seems the craft of that race, and not to exist elsewhere. The king can not step on an acre which the peasant refuses to sell. A testator endows a dog or a rookery, and Europe can not interfere with his absurdity. Every individual has his particular way of living, which he pushes to folly; and the decided sympathy of his compatriots is engaged to back up Mr. Crump's whim by statutes, and chancellors, and horse-guards. There is no freak so ridiculous but some Englishman has attempted to immortalize it by money and law. Mr. Cockayne is very sensible of this. That pursy man means by freedom the right to do as he pleases, and does wrong in order to feel his freedom, and makes a conscience of persisting in it."

Perhaps Mr. Emerson would say that, when Mr. Cockayne and others of his ilk insulted and almost mobbed Lady Burdette - Coutts in the streets of London because she had contracted a marriage which did not suit their fancy, they were only exercising their own inalienable right of letting her know what they thought of the matter. Mr. Emerson has something to say about English self-conceit and braggadocio, quoting as quite apposite what was written nearly three centuries ago by a Venetian traveler: "The English are great lovers of themselves, and of everything belonging to them. They think there are no other men than themselves, and no other world but

England." Speaking in his own person, Emerson proceeds :

ENGLISH SELF-CONCEIT.

"I have found that Englishmen have such a good opinion of England that the ordinary phrases, in all good society, of postponing or disparaging one's own things in talking with a stranger, are seriously mistaken by them for an insuppressible homage to the merits of their own nation; and the New Yorker or Pennsylvanian who modestly laments the disadvantage of a new country— log-huts and savages—is surprised by the instant and unfeigned commiseration of the whole company, who plainly account all the world out of England a heap of rubbish. The same insular limitation pinches his foreign politics. He sticks to his traditions and usages; and, so help him God! he will force his island by-laws down the throat of great countries, like India, China, Canada, Australia; and not only so, but impose Wapping on the Congress of Vienna, and trample down all nationalities with his taxed boots. In short, I am afraid that English nature is so rank and aggressive as to be a little incompatible with every other."

This trait crops out everywhere. "There are," says Emerson, "really no limits to this conceit, though brighter men among them make painful efforts to be candid. At all events, they feel themselves at liberty to assume the most extraordinary tone on the subject of English merits." This they do, not only at home, but when abroad. "An English lady on the Rhine, hearing a German speaking of her party as 'foreigners,' exclaimed, 'No, we are not foreigners, we are English; it is you who are foreigners!' He adds: "France is, by its natural contrast, a kind of blackboard, on which the English character draws its own traits in chalk. This arrogance habitually exhibits itself in allusions to the French. I suppose that all men of English blood in America, Europe or Asia have a secret joy that they are not French natives." Closely allied to this omnipresent self-conceit—and, indeed, only a very disagreeable mode of expressing it—is another trait:

ENGLISH BRAGGADOCIO.

"But, beyond this nationality, it must be admitted that the island offers a daily worship to the old Norse god Brage, celebrated among our Scandinavian forefathers for his eloquence and majestic air. They tell you daily, in London, the story of the Frenchman and the Englishman who quarreled. Both were unwilling to fight, but their companions put them up to it. At last it was agreed that they should fight alone, in the dark, and with pistols. The candles were put out, and the Englishman, to make sure not to hit anybody, fired up the chimney, and brought down the Frenchman. They have no curiosity about foreigners, and answer any information you may volunteer with, 'Oh, oh!' until the informant makes up his mind that they shall die in their ignorance for any help he will offer."

Mr. Emerson finds thus much to say even in favor of this particular English trait: "There is this benefit in brag, that the speaker is unconsciously expressing his own ideal. Humor him by all means, draw it all out, and hold him to it. Nature makes nothing in vain, and this little superfluity of self-regard in the English brain is one of the secrets of their power and history. For it sets every man on being and doing what he really is and can. It takes away a dodging, skulking, secondary air, and encourages a frank and manly bearing; so that each man makes the most of himself, and loses no opportunity for want of pushing." The English have certainly lost nothing for want of pushing, though, perhaps, they are beginning to feel that they are like to lose by over-pushing, and by trying to hold on to what they have apparently won. Speaking of English rule abroad, and some kindred matters, Emerson says :

ENGLISH NARROWNESS.

" But this childish patriotism costs something, like all narrowness. The English sway of their colonies has no root of kindness. They govern by their arts and their ability; they are more just than kind, and whenever an abatement of their power is felt they have not conciliated the affection on which to rely. The English dislike the American structure of society, whilst yet trade, mills, public education, and Chartism are doing what they can to create in England the same social condition. America is the paradise of economists, is the favorable exception invariably quoted to the rules of ruin.

15

But, when he speaks directly of the Americans, the islander forgets his philosophy, and remembers his disparaging anecdotes."

One need not go far to find instances of the unkindness of England toward every people with whom she has had to do with power to execute her will, but it is not so easy to find examples of her justice. Mr. Emerson sums up pithily what he has to say in regard to the general relations of England to the rest of the world : " In short, I am afraid that the English nature is so rank and aggressive as to be a little incompatible with every other. The world is not wide enough for two " ; that is, we suppose, for the English and anybody else.

Of the immense wealth accumulated in England Mr. Emerson speaks in terms of wonder, and he noticed particularly the universal homage paid to it.

ENGLISH HOMAGE TO WEALTH.

" There is no country in which so absolute a homage is paid to wealth. In America there is a touch of shame when a man exhibits the evidences of a large property ; as if, after all, it needed apology. But the Englishman has pure pride in his wealth, and esteems it a final certificate. A coarse logic rules throughout all English souls : ' If you have merit, can you not show it by your good clothes, and coach and horses? How can a man be a gentleman without a pipe of wine?' Haydon says, ' There is a fierce resolution to make every man live according to the means he possesses.' There is a mixture of religion in it. They are under the Jewish law; and read with sonorous emphasis that their days shall be long in the land; they shall have sons and daughters, flocks and herds, wine and oil.'

"In exact proportion is the reproach of poverty. They do not wish to be represented except by opulent men. An Englishman who has lost his fortune is said to have 'died of a broken heart.' The last term of insult is, ' a beggar.' Nelson said, ' The want of fortune is a crime I can not get over.' Sydney Smith said, ' Poverty is infamous in England.' And one of their recent writers speaks, in reference to a private and scholastic life, of ' the grave moral deterioration which follows an empty exchequer.' You shall find this sentiment, if not so frankly put, yet deeply implied in the novels and romances of the present century; and not only in these, but in biography, and in the notes of public men, in the tone of preaching, and in the table-talk."

Mr. Emerson is no despiser of wealth, but of the inordinate estimate put upon the personal possession of it, he says :

VALUES OF WEALTH.

"The creation of wealth in England during the last ninety years is a main fact in modern history. The wealth of London determines prices all over the globe. All things precious or useful or amusing or intoxicating, are sucked into this commerce, or floated into London. A hundred thousand palaces adorn the island. All that can feed the senses and passions; all that can succor the talent or arm the hands of the intelligent middle class, who never

share in what they buy for their own consumption ; all
that can aid science, gratify taste, or soothe comfort, is
in open market.   Whatever is excellent and beautiful in
civil, rural, or ecclesiastical architecture ; in fountain, garden, or grounds, the English noble crosses sea and land
to see and copy at home.   The taste and science of
thirty peaceful generations are in the vast auction ; and
the hereditary principle heaps on the owner of to-day
the benefit of ages of owners.   The present generation
of owners are to the full as absolute as their fathers in
choosing and producing what they like."

THE BEST RESULTS OF ENGLISH WEALTH.

" But the proudest result of this creation has been
the great and refined forces it has put at the disposal of
the private citizen.   In the social world an Englishman
to-day has the best lot.   He goes with the most powerful protection, keeps the best company, is armed by the
best education, is seconded by wealth ; and his English
name and accidents are like a flourish of trumpets announcing him.   I much prefer the condition of an English gentleman of the better class to that of any potentate in Europe—whether for travel, or for opportunity
of society, or for access to means of science or study, or
for mere comfort and easy, healthy relation to people at
home."

Yet under this mighty and seemingly so firm
structure of British wealth are hidden manifold
perils and evils.   Most perilous of all is the fact
that for every man who enjoys these undisputed
advantages, there are a hundred, perhaps a thou-

sand, who have no share in them. Emerson, in looking back at the mighty progress of the ninety years which preceded the writing of this book, has to look on the other side of the picture. And this is among the things which could not be over-looked. It was among the sad things which inspired Carlyle in the writing of his "Chartism" only a few years before.

WEALTH AND THE ENGLISH PEOPLE.

"In the culmination of national prosperity, in the annexation of countries; building of ships, depots, towns; in the influx of tons of gold and silver; amid the chuckle of chancellors and financiers, it was found that bread rose to famine prices; that the yeoman was forced to sell his cow and pig, his tools and his acre of land; and the dread barometer of the poor-rates was touching the point of ruin. The poor-rate was sucking in the solvent classes, and forcing an exodus of farmers and mechanics. What befalls from the violence of financial crises, befalls daily in the violence of artificial legislation."

This, and the citation which follows, was evidently written after Emerson's return from Europe, say some thirty years ago. Since then it has received an added emphasis of stern truth : a truth also which it concerns us to ponder well in our own behoof ; for the United States in this year 1881 have come rapidly to approximate to the England of 1851.

RESPONSIBILITIES OF WEALTH.

"Such a wealth has England earned — ever new, bounteous, and augmenting. But the question recurs, Does she take the step beyond; namely, to the wise use, in view of the supreme wealth of nations? We estimate the wisdom of nations by seeing what they did with their surplus capital. And in view of these injuries, some compensation has been attempted in England. A part of the money earned returns to the brain, to buy schools, libraries, bishops, astronomers, chemists, and artists with ; and a part to repair the wrongs of this intemperate weaving, by hospitals, saving-banks, mechanics' institutes, public grounds, and other charities and amenities. But the antidotes are frightfully inadequate, and the evil requires a deeper cure, which time and a simpler social organization must supply. At present she does not rule her wealth. She is simply a good England, but no divinity, or wise and instructed soul. She, too, is in the stream of fate—one victim more in a common catastrophe.

"But being in the fault, she has the misfortune of greatness to be held as the chief offender. England must be held responsible for the despotism of expense. Her prosperity, the splendor which so much manhood and talent and perseverance has thrown upon vulgar aims, is the very argument of materialism. Her success strengthens the hands of base wealth. Who can propose to youth, poverty and wisdom, when mean gain has arrived at the conquest of letters and arts? when English success has grown out of the very renunciation of trifles, and the dedication to outsides? Hardly the bravest among them have the manliness to resist it successfully. Hence it has come that not the aims of a manly life, but the means of meeting a ponderous expense, is that to be considered by a youth in England emerging from his minority. A large family is reckoned a misfortune; and it is a consolation in the death of the young that a source of expense is closed."

Of the aristocracy of England—using the term in its limited sense, to indicate that class who owe their position rather to birth than to personal qualities—Emerson speaks half in admiration and half in kindly deprecation. "The feudal character of the English State, now that it is getting obsolete, glares a little in contrast with the democratic tendencies. The inequality of power and property shocks republican nerves. Palaces, halls, villas, walled parks, all over England, rival the splendor of royal seats. Many of the halls, like Herdon or Redleston, are beautiful desolations. The proprietor never saw them, or never lived in them. Primogeniture built those sumptuous piles, and, I suppose, it is the sentiment of every traveler, as it is mine, ' 'Twas well to come ere these were gone.' "

ENGLISH PRIMOGENITURE.

" Primogeniture is a cardinal rule of English property and institutions. Laws, customs, manners, the very persons and faces affirm it. The frame of society is aristocratic, the taste of the people is loyal. The estates, names, and manners of the people flatter the fancy of the people, and conciliate the necessary support. In spite of broken faith, stolen charters, and the devastation of so-

ciety by the profligacy of the court, we take sides, as we
read, for the loyal England, and King Charles's 'return
to his right' with his cavaliers—knowing what a heart-
less trifler he is, and what a crew of God-forsaken robbers they are. The people of England knew as much,
but the fair idea of a settled government, connecting
itself with heraldic names, with the written and oral history of Europe, and at last with the Hebrew religion
and the oldest traditions of the world, was too pleasing a
tradition to be shattered by a few offensive realities, and
the politics of shoemakers and costermongers."

BOND BETWEEN COMMONERS AND NOBLES.

" The hopes of the commoners take the same direction
with the interest of the patricians. Every man who becomes rich buys land, and does what he can to fortify
the nobility, into which he hopes to rise. The Anglican
clergy are identified with the aristocracy. Time and law
have made the joining and molding perfect in every
part. The cathedrals, the universities, the national music, the popular romances, conspire to uphold the her-
aldry which the current politics of the day are, sapping.
The taste of the people is conservative. They are proud
of the castles and of the language and symbols of chiv-
alry. Even the word 'lord' is the luckiest style that is
used in any language to designate a patrician. The superior education and manners of the nobles recommend
them to the country."

CHANGES IN THE NOBILITY.

" The Norwegian pirate got what he could, and held it
for his son. The Norman noble, who was the Norwegian

pirate baptized, did likewise. There was this advantage of Western over Oriental nobility, that this was recruited from below. English history is aristocracy with the doors open. Who has courage and capacity, let him come in. Of course, the terms of admission to this club are hard and high. The selfishness of the nobles comes in aid of the interest of the nation to require signal merit. Piracy and war gave place to trade, politics, and letters of the war-lord to the law-lord, the law-lord to the merchant and mill-owner ; but the privilege was kept, while the means of obtaining it were changed."

The successive changes in the manner of getting place among the nobles are briefly touched upon. We abbreviate them still more :

THE OLD WAR-LORDS.

"The foundations of these families lie deep in Norwegian exploits by sea, and Saxon sturdiness on land. All nobility, in its beginnings, was somebody's natural superiority. The things these English have done were not done without peril of life, nor without wisdom and conduct ; and the first hands, it may be presumed, were often challenged to show their right to their honors, or yield them to better men. And I make no doubt that the feudal tenure was no sinecure, but baron, knight, and tenant often had their memories refreshed in regard to the service by which they held their lands. The war-lord earned his honors, and no donation of land was large, as long as it brought the duty of protecting it hour by hour against a terrible enemy. In France and England the nobles were, down to a late day, bred to war, and the duel, which in peace still held them to the risks of war, diminished the envy that, in trading and studious nations, would have else pried into their title. They were looked upon as men who played high for a great stake."

Partly succeeding to, partially accompanying, and to a great extent superseding, these old war-lords are the comparatively modern peace-lords, of whom Emerson says :

THE MODERN PEACE-LORDS.

"The new age brings new qualities into request. The virtues of pirates give way to those of planters, merchants, senators, and scholars. Comity, social talent, and fine manners, no doubt, have had their part also. I have met somewhere with a historiette, which, whether more or less true in its particulars, carries a general truth. 'How came the Duke of Bedford by his great landed estates? His ancestor, having traveled on the continent—a lively, pleasant man—became the companion of a foreign prince, wrecked on the Devonshire coast, where a Mr. Russell lived. The prince recommended him to Henry the Eighth, who, liking his company, gave him a large share of the plundered church lands.' The pretense is that the noble is of unbroken descent from the Norman, and has never worked for eight hundred years. But the fact is otherwise. Where is Bohun? Where is De Vere? The lawyer, the farmer, the silk-mercer, lies *perdu* under the coronet, and winks to the antiquary to say nothing; especially skillful lawyers, nobody's sons, who did some piece of work, at a nice time, for Government, and were rewarded with ermine."

This illustrative "historiette" is substantially true; and is told at some length in Burke's "British Peerage." The "foreign prince wrecked on the Devonshire coast," was the Archduke Philip of Austria, only son of the Emperor Maximilian I, and husband of the mad Juana, daughter of Ferdinand and Isabella of Spain, and the father of the Emperor Charles V. This John Russell, recommended by the Archduke Philip, entered the service of Henry VIII, and in 1538 was raised to the peerage as Baron Russell. In 1540, when the great monasteries were dissolved, his lordship obtained a grant to himself, his wife, and their heirs, of the site of the Abbey of Tavistock, and of extensive possessions belonging thereunto. In 1550 he was made Earl of Bedford, and in 1694 his descendant, the fifth earl, was created Duke of Bedford. There are few English houses who have within the last two centuries played so great a part in history as this of Bedford, founded by an untitled gentleman. Among the most notable of this family were the patriot William, Lord Russell, son and heir of the first Duke of Bedford, who was judicially murdered in 1683; and the statesman long famous as Lord John Russell, third son of the sixth Duke of Bedford, and who died as Earl Russell.

Emerson is ready to grant that the English peerage, as such, has had and still has its uses. He says: "If one asks, in the critical spirit of

the day, what service this class have rendered?
uses appear, or they would have perished long
ago. Some of these are easily enumerated, others
more subtle make a part of unconscious history.
Their institution is one step in the progress of
society. For a race yields a nobility in some
form, however we name the lords, as surely as it
yields women." The most noticeable present use
of the peerage he thinks is that it forms a recognized school of manners; and "whatever tends
to form manners, or to finish men, has a great
value."

MANNERS OF THE PEERAGE.

"The English nobles are high-spirited, active, educated men, born to wealth and power, who have run
through every country, and kept in every country the
best of company. You can not wield great agencies
without lending yourself to them, and when it happens
that the spirit of the earl meets his rank and duties, we
have the best examples of behavior. Power of any kind
readily appears in the manners; and beneficent power
—*le talent de bien faire*—gives a majesty which can not
be concealed or resisted. 'The upper classes,' say the people here, 'have only birth, and not thoughts.' Yes, but
they have manners, and it is wonderful how much talent
runs into manners; nowhere and never so much as in
England. They have the sense of a superiority, the absence of the ambitious effort which disgusts in the aspir-
ing classes, a pure tone of thought and feeling, and the
power to command, among their other luxuries, the
presence of the most distinguished men at their festive
meetings. The economist who asks, 'Of what use are

lords?' may learn to ask, with **Franklin**, 'Of what use is a baby?' They have been a social church, proper to inspire sentiments mutually honoring the lover and the loved. Politeness is the ritual of society as prayers are of the Church, a school of manners, and a gentle blessing to the age in which it grew. It is a romance adorning English life with a fairer horizon; a midway heaven fulfilling to their sense their fairy tales and poetry. This, just as far as the breeding of the nobleman, really made him brave, handsome, accomplished, and great-hearted."

Yet there is presented also quite another aspect of the manners of the English aristocracy. And this other aspect must be noted. At court, and in the very highest circles, as far as we can judge, the code of manners, except in so far as those belonging to those narrow circles are concerned, is the height of ill-breeding. Emerson touches upon this side briefly but emphatically.

THE NOBLES AND THE COMMONERS.

" Most of the nobles are only chargeable with idleness, which, because it squanders such vast power of benefits, has the mischief of crime. My friend [whom we suppose to be Carlyle] said: 'They might be little providences upon earth, and they are for the most part jockeys and fops.' Campbell says: 'Acquaintance with the nobility I could never keep up; it requires a life of idleness, dressing, and attendance on their parties.' A man of wit, who is also one of the celebrities of wealth and fashion, confessed to his friend that he could not enter their houses without being made to feel that they were great lords, and he a low plebeian. With the tribe of *artistes*, including the musical tribe, the patrician *morgue* keeps no terms, but excludes them. When Julia Grisi and Mario sang at the houses of the Duke of Wellington and other grandees, a ribbon was stretched between the singer and the company."

THE UNTITLED NOBILITY.

" I suppose, too, that a feeling of self-respect is driving men out of this society, as if the noble were slow to receive the lesson of the times, and had not learned to disguise his pride of place. A multitude of English, educated at the universities, bred into their society, with manners, ability, and the gifts of fortune, are every day confronting the peers, and outstripping them, as often, in the race of honor and influence. That cultivated class is large and ever enlarging. It is computed that, with titles and without, there are seventy thousand of these people coming and going in London, who make up what is called 'high society.' They can not shut their eyes to the fact that an untitled nobility possesses all the power, without the inconveniences, that belong to rank; and the rich Englishman goes over the world at the present day, drawing more than all the advantages which the strongest of his kings could command.

" The revolution in society has reached this class. The great powers of industrial art have no exclusion of name or blood. The tools of our time, namely, steam, ships, printing, money, and popular education, belong to those who can handle them; and their effect has been that the advantages once confined to men of family are now open to the whole middle class. The road that grandeur levels for his coach, toil can travel in his cart."

The political status of the House of Peers is worthy of consideration. At the time of Emerson's visit, the list numbered five hundred and seventy. But he says, " On ordinary days there were only twenty or thirty in attendance. ' Where are the others ?' I asked. " At home on their estates, devoured with *ennui,* or in the Alps, or up the Rhine, in the Harz Mountains, or in Egypt, or in India, on the Ghauts.' ' But with such interests at stake, how can these men afford to neglect them ?' ' Oh,' replied my friend, ' why should they work for themselves, when every man in England works for them, and will suffer before they come to harm." Still these six hundred peers, not one in ten of whom has reached that place except by reason that his father before him was a peer, have, in theory at least, fully as much weight in the Government as all the rest of Great Britain. Upon this point Emerson says :

THE STATUS OF THE PEERS.

" The existence of the House of Peers as a branch of the Government entitles them to fill half the Cabinet; and their weight of property and station give them a virtual nomination of the other half; whilst they have their share in the subordinate offices as a school of training. This monopoly of political power has given them their intellectual and social eminence in Europe. A few law-lords and a few political lords take the brunt of public business. In the army the nobility fill a large part of the high commissions, and give to these a tone of expense and splendor, and also of exclusiveness. They have borne their full share of danger and duty in the service. For the rest, the nobility have the lead in matters of state and expense; in questions of taste, in social usages, in convivial and domestic hospitalities. In general, all that is required of them is to sit securely, to preside at public meetings, to countenance public charities, and to give the example of that decorum so dear to the British heart."

Of the religion of England, as crystallized in the rites of the Established Church, Emerson has many things to say, and some not altogether laudatory. To his view it is not the embodiment of a system of faith. "English life," he says, "does not grow out of the Athanasian Creed, or the Articles, or the Eucharist. . . . In the barbarous days of a nation some *cultus* is formed or imported : altars are built, tithes are paid, priests ordained. The education and expenditure of the country takes that direction ; and when wealth, refinement, great men, and ties to the world supervene, its prudent men say, 'Why fight against fate, or lift those absurdities which are now mountains ? Better find some niche or crevice in this mountain of stone which religious ages have quarried and carved wherein to bestow yourself, than attempt anything ridiculously and dangerously above your strength, like removing it.'" Still the Church of England has in it a mighty power, as he acknowledges :

DEVELOPMENT OF THE ANGLICAN CHURCH.

"The Catholic Church, thrown on this serious, toiling people, has made in fourteen centuries a massive system, close-fitted to the manners and genius of the country, at once domestical and stately. In the long time it has blended with everything in heaven above and the earth beneath. It moves through a zodiac of feasts and fasts; names every day of the year, every town and market and headland and monument; and has coupled itself with the almanac, that no court can be held, no field plowed, no horse shod, without some leave from the Church. All maxims of prudence or shop or farm are fixed and dated from the Church. Hence its strength in the agriculturial dstricts. The distribution of lands into parishes enforces a church sanction to every civil privilege; and the gradation of the clergy—prelates for the rich, and curates for the poor—with the fact that a classical education has been secured to the clergymen, makes them, as Wordsworth says, 'the link that unites the sequestered peasantry with the intellectual advancement of the age.'"

THE OLD CHURCH AND THE PEOPLE.

"The English Church has many certificates to show of humble, effective service in humanizing the people, in cheering and refining men, feeding, healing, and educating. It has the seal of martyrs and confessors; the noblest book; a sublime architecture; a ritual marked by the same secular merits—nothing cheap or purchasable. From the slow-grown Church important reactions proceed; much for culture, much for giving a direction to the nation's affection and will to-day. The carved and pictured chapel—its entire surface animated with image

16

and emblem—made the parish church a sort of book and
Bible to the people's eye.

"Then, when the Saxon instinct had secured a service in the vernacular tongue, it was the tutor and uni-
versity of the people. The reverence for the Scriptures
is an element of civilization; for thus has the history of
the world been preserved, and is preserved. Here in
England every day a chapter of Genesis, and a leader in
the 'Times.' This is binding the old and new to some
purpose."

THE CHURCH AND LOYALTY.

"From his infancy every Englishman is accustomed
to hear daily prayers for the Queen, for the royal family, and the Parliament, by name; and the life-long con-
secration of these personages can not be without influence on his opinions. The universities, also, are parcel
of the ecclesiastical system, and their first design is to
form the clergy. Thus the clergy for a thousand years
have been the scholars of the nation.

"The national temperament deeply enjoys the unbroken order and tradition of its Church; the liturgy, ceremony, architecture; the sober grace, the good company,
the connection with the throne, and with history, which
adorn it. And while it thus endears itself to men with
more taste than activity, the stability of the English nation is passionately enlisted to its support, from its inex-
tricable connection with the cause of public order, with
politics, and with the funds."

ENGLISH AGES OF FAITH.

"Good churches are not built by bad men; at least,
there must be probity and enthusiasm somewhere in society. These minsters were neither built nor filled by

atheists. No church has had more learned, industrious, or devoted men; plenty of 'clerks and bishops,' as Fuller says, 'who, out of their gowns, would turn their backs on no man.' Their architecture still glows with faith in immortality. Heats and genial periods arrive in history; or, shall we say? plenitudes of divine presence, by which high tides are caused in the human spirit, and great virtues and talents appear, as in the eleventh, twelfth, thirteenth, and again in the sixteenth and seventeenth centuries, when the nation was full of genius and piety."

In Emerson's judgment those pious ages are no more; and the Anglican Church of the present is not what it was:

THE PRESENT ANGLICAN CHURCH.

"But the age of the Wycliffes, Oobhams, Arundels, Beckets; of the Latimers, Mores, Cranmers; of the Taylors, Leightons, Herberts; of the Sherlocks and Butlers, is gone. Silent revolutions in opinion have made it impossible that men like these should return or find a place in their once sacred stalls. The spirit which once dwelt in this Church has glided away to animate other activities; and they who come to the old shrines find apes and players rustling the old garments."

A CHURCH OF MANNERS.

"The religion of England is part of good-breeding. When you see on the Continent the well-dressed Englishman come into his ambassador's chapel, and put his face, for silent prayer, into his smooth-brushed hat, one can not help feeling how much of national pride prays

with him, and the religion of a gentleman. So far is he
from attaching any meaning to the words, that he believes he has done almost the generous thing, and that it
is very condescending in him to pray to God. A great
duke said, on the occasion of a victory, that he thought
the Almighty God had not been well used by them, and
that it would become their magnanimity, after so great
successes, to take order that a proper acknowledgement
be made."

THE CHURCH OF THE RICH.

" It is a church of the gentry, and not a church of
the poor. The operatives do not own it; and gentlemen
lately testified in the House of Commons, that in their
lives they never saw a poor man in a ragged coat inside
a church. The torpidity on the side of religion of the
vigorous English understanding shows how much wit
and folly can agree in one brain."

Here, once more, we find a marked example
of the lofty way in which Emerson is wont to
deal with facts. He forms the widest generalizations from a few instances, in no wise typical. If
an English gentleman, when he enters the chapel
of the British embassy abroad, puts his face into
his hat for silent prayer, what right has Mr. Emerson to suppose that he is " far from attaching
any meaning to the words," even though that hat
be a well-brushed one ? Quite likely also, the
gentlemen testified truly in Parliament that they
" never saw a poor man in a ragged coat inside a
church " ; but to our mind this merely shows that

even the poor men who attend public worship have a coat that is not ragged. In a certain sense the Anglican Church is the church of the rich ; and it is well that it is so. But it is a stretch of statement to say that "it is not the church of the poor" also. Else how does it happen that this Church has such "strength in the agricultural districts," where the majority of the people certainly can not be rich ?

In writing of the Church of Old England, Mr. Emerson reiterates, in substance, what he had said almost twenty years before, in his "Divinity Address," of the Churches of New England. The burden of all is the decay of worship. This decay, if it exist at all, has existed a long time—as far back as the seventeenth century, in Mr. Emerson's judgment. If this were so, in the middle of the nineteenth century the consequences of this "wasting unbelief" of which he spoke would by this time have come to be apparent : "When all things go to decay genius leaves the temple to haunt the senate or the market. Literature becomes frivolous. Science is cold. The eye of youth is not lighted by the hope of other worlds, and age is without honor. Society lives to trifles, and when men die we do not mention them." Does England present this aspect, upon Mr. Emerson's own showing ?

Emerson is apparently sensible that these "traits" do not cover the broad field of English national character, for in the closing chapter, entitled "Results," he says :

"England is the best of actual nations. It is no ideal framework; it is an old pile, built in different ages, with repairs, additions, and makeshifts; but you see the poor best you have got. The power of performance has not been exceeded—the creation of value. The English have given importance to individuals, a principal end and fruit of every society. 'Magna Charta,' said Rushmore, 'is such a fellow that he will have no sovereign.' By this sacredness of individuals, they have in seven hundred years evolved the principles of freedom. It is the land of patriots, martyrs, sages, and bards; and if the ocean out of which it emerged should wash it away, it will be remembered as an island famous for immortal laws, for the announcements of original right, which make the stone tables of liberty."

Shortly after Emerson's arrival in England, late in 1847, he was a guest at the annual dinner given by the Manchester Athenæum, and was invited, among others, to address the assemblage. The times wore a gloomy outlook. There was great commercial disaster and unwonted distress. He recognized all this, and yet, as was to be expected on such an occasion, his remarks took a hopeful turn. But as he has appended this address to the "English Traits," we may assume that it represents the real views held by him after an interval of nearly ten years. He says :

HAIL AND FAREWELL TO ENGLAND.

" Holiday though it be, I have not the smallest interest in any holiday, except as it celebrates real and not pretended joys; and I think it just, in this time of gloom and disaster, of affliction and beggary in these districts, that, on these very accounts I speak of, you should not fail to keep your literary anniversary. I seem to hear you say that ' for all is come and gone, we will not reduce by one chaplet, or by one oak leaf, the braveries of our annual feast.'

" For I must tell you, I was given to understand in my childhood, that the British Island from which my forefathers came was no lotus garden, no paradise of serene sky, and roses and music and merriment all the year round: no, but a cold, foggy, mournful country, where nothing grew well in the open air but robust men and virtuous women, and these of a wonderful fiber and endurance; that their best parts were slowly revealed; they did not strike twelve the first time; good lovers and good haters, and you could know little about them till you had seen them long, and little good of them until you had seen them in action; that in prosperity they were moody and dumpish, but in adversity they were grand.

" Is it not true, sir, that the wise ancients did not praise the ship parting with flying colors from the port, but only that brave sailer which came back with torn sheets and battered sides, stripped of her banners, but having ridden out the storm. And so, gentlemen, I feel in regard to this aged England, with the possessions, honors, and trophies, and also with the infirmities, of a thousand years gathering around her; irretrievably committed, as she now is, to many old customs which can

not be suddenly changed; pressed upon by the transitions
of trade, and new and all incalculable modes, fabrics,
machines, and competing populations. I see her, not
dispirited, not weak, but well remembering that she has
seen dark days before; indeed, with a kind of instinct
that she sees a little better in a cloudy day; and that in
storm and calamity she has a secret vigor, and a pulse
like a cannon. I see her in her old age, not decrepit, but
young, and still daring to believe in her power of endurance and expansion.

"Seeing all this, I say all hail! mother of nations,
mother of heroes, with strength and skill equal to the
time; still wise to entertain and swift to execute the
policy which the mind and heart of mankind requires in
the present hour; and thus only hospitable to the foreigner, and truly a home to the thoughtful and generous
who are born on her soil. So be it! So let it be! If it
be not so; if the courage of England goes with the
chances of a commercial crisis, I will go back to the
capes of Massachusetts, and to my own Indian stream,
and say to my countrymen, 'The old race are all gone,
and the elasticity and hopes of mankind must henceforth
remain on the Alleghany ranges or nowhere.'"

X.

REPRESENTATIVE MEN.

IN 1850 Emerson published a volume entitled
"Representative Men," which, Mr. Whipple says,

"is a series of masterly mental portraits, with some of the features overcharged." These representative men are : " Plato, the Philosopher "; "Swedenborg, the Mystic"; "Montaigne, the Skeptic "; Shakespeare, the Poet "; " Napoleon, the Man of the World "; and " Goethe, the Writer." The volume opens with an introductory chapter on the "Uses of Great Men," from which we extract a few passages, taken somewhat out of their connection, but grouped together so as to present some idea of the general scope of the whole :

USES OF GREAT MEN.

"It is natural to believe in great men. If the companions of our childhood should turn out to be heroes, and their condition regal, it would not surprise us. All mythology opens with demigods, and the circumstance is high and poetic; that is, their genius is paramount. Nature seems to exist for the excellent. The world is upheld by the veracity of good men; they make the earth wholesome. They who lived with them found life glad and nutritious. Life is sweet and tolerable only in our belief in such society; and, actually or ideally, we manage to live with superiors.

" The search after great men is the dream of youth, and the occupation of manhood. We travel into foreign parts to find their works—if possible, to get a glimpse of them; but we are put off with fortune instead. I do not travel to find comfortable, rich, and hospitable people, or clear sky, or ingots that cost too much. But if there were any magnet that would point to the countries and houses where are intrinsically rich and powerful, I would sell all and buy it, and put myself on the road to-day. The race goes with us on their credit. The knowledge that in the city is a man who invented the railroad, raises the credit of all the citizens. Our religion is the love and cherishing of these patrons. The gods of fable are the shining monuments of great men. Our colossal theologies of Judaism, Christism, Buddhism, Mohammedanism, are the necessary and structural action of the human mind. Our theism is the purification of the human mind."

WHO IS THE GREAT MAN.

"I count him a great man who inhabits a higher sphere of thought, into which other men rise with labor and difficulty. He has but to open his eyes to see things in a true light, and in large relations; while they must make painful corrections, and keep a vigilant eye on many sources of error. But the great man must be related to us. I can not tell what I would know; but I have observed that there are persons who, in their character and actions, answer questions which I have not skill to put. One man answers some questions which none of his contemporaries put, and is isolated."

CLASSES OF GREAT MEN.

"I admire great men of all classes: those who stand for facts and for thoughts. I like rough and smooth: 'Scourges of God' and 'Darlings of the human race.' I like the first Cæsars and Charles the Fifth of Spain, and Charles the Twelfth of Sweden, Richard Plantagenet, and Bonaparte in France. I applaud a sufficient man, an officer equal to his office; captains, ministers, senators. Sword and staff, or talents sword-like or staff-

like, carry on the work of the world. But I find him
greater when he can abolish himself and all his heroes,
by letting in the element of reason, irrespective of persons—this subtilizer and irresistible upward force, into
our thought—destroying individualism; the power so
great that the potentate is nothing. Then he is a mon-
arch who gives a constitution to his people; a pontiff
who preaches the equality of souls, and releases his people from their barbarous homages; an emperor who can
share his empire."

ULTIMATE USE OF GREAT MEN.

"For a time our teachers serve us personally, as
metres or milestones of progress. Once they were angels
of knowledge, and their figures touched the sky. Then
we drew near; saw their means, culture, and limits;
and they yielded their place to other geniuses. Happy,
if a few names remain so high that we have not been
able to read them nearer; and age and comparison have
not robbed them of a ray. But, at last, we shall cease
to look in men for completeness, and shall content ourselves with their social and delegated quality. All that
respects the individual is temporary and prospective,
like the individual himself, who is ascending out of his
limits into a catholic existence.

"We have never come at the true and best benefits of
any genius, so long as we believe him an original force.
In the moment when he ceases to help us as a cause
he begins to help us more as an effect; then he appears
as an exponent of a vaster mind and will. Yet, within
the limits of human education and agency, we may say
that great men exist that there may be greater men.
The destiny of organized nature is amelioration; and

who can tell its limits? It is for man to tame the chaos;
on every side, while he lives, to scatter the seeds of
cience and of song, that climate, corn, animals, men,
may be milder, and the germs of love and benefit may be
multiplied."

Of Plato, who heads Emerson's list of representative men, he writes at first with undiscrimi-
nating eulogy.

SUPREMACY OF PLATO.

"Among books, Plato only is entitled to Omar's fa-
natical compliment to the Koran, when he said, 'Burn
the libraries; for their value is in this book.' These
sentences contain the culture of nations; these are the
corner-stone of schools; these are the fountain-head of
literatures. A discipline is it in logic, arithmetic, taste,
symmetry, poetry, languages, rhetoric, ontology, morals,
or practical wisdom. There never was such range of
speculation. Out of Plato come all things that are still
written and debated among men of thought. Great
havoc makes he among our originalities. We have
reached the mountain from which all these drift-bowl-
ders were detached. For it is fair to credit the broadest
generalizer with all the particulars deducible from his
genius.

"Plato is philosophy, and philosophy Plato—at once
the glory and the shame of mankind, since neither Saxon
nor Roman have availed to add any idea to his categories. No wife, no children has he; and the thinkers of
all civilized nations are his posterity, and are tinged with
his mind. How many great men Nature is incessantly
sending up out of night to be *his men*—Platonists! The

Alexandrians, a constellation of genius; the Elizabeth-
ans, not less; Sir Thomas More, Henry More, John
Hales, John Smith, Francis Bacon, Jeremy Taylor, Ralph
Cudworth, Sydenham, Thomas Taylor, Marcilius Ficinus,
and Picus Mirandola. Calvinism is in his 'Phædo';
Christianity is in it. Mohammedanism draws all its
philosophy, in its hand-book of morals—the *Akhlak-y-
Jalaly*—from him. Mysticism finds in Plato all its texts.
The citizen of a town in Greece is no villager nor patriot.
An Englishman reads, and says, 'How English!' a
German, 'How Teutonic!' an Italian, 'How Roman
and how Greek!' As they say that Helen of Argos had
that universal beauty that everybody felt related to her,
so Plato seems, to a reader in New England, an American genius. His broad humanity transcends all sectional
lines."

This broad statement is illustrated under a
variety of forms. Thus:

ORIGINALITY OF PLATO.

" Plato, like every great man, consumed his own times.
What is a great man but one of great affinities, who takes
up into himself all arts, all sciences, all knowables, as his
food. He can spare nothing; he can dispose of everything. What is not good for virtue is good for knowledge. Hence his contemporaries tax him with plagia-
rism. But the inventor only knows how to borrow; and
society is glad to forget the innumerable laborers who
ministered to this architect, and reserves all its gratitude
for him. When we are praising Plato we are praising
quotations from Solon and Sophron and Philolaus. Be
it so. Every book is a quotation; and every house is a

quotation from all forests and mines and stone-quarries; and every man is a quotation from all his ancestors. And this grasping inventor puts all nations under contribution."

UNIVERSALITY OF PLATO.

"Plato absorbed the learning of his times—Philolaus, Timæus, Heraclites, Parmenides, and what else; then his master, Socrates; and finding himself still capable of a larger synthesis—beyond all example then or since —he traveled into Italy to gain what Pythagoras had for him; then into Egypt, and perhaps still farther east to import the other element, which Europe wanted, into the European mind. This breadth entitles him to stand as the representative of philosophy. Every man who would do anything well must come to it from a higher ground. A philosopher must be more than a philosopher. Plato is clothed with the powers of a poet, stands upon the highest place of a poet, and (though I doubt he wanted the decisive gift of lyric expression) mainly is not a poet because he chose to use the poetic gift to an ulterior purpose."

PLATO'S ECLECTICISM.

"Plato, in Egypt and in Eastern pilgrimages, imbibed the idea of One Deity, in which all are absorbed. The unity of Asia and the detail of Europe; the infinitude of the Asiatic soul, and the defining, result-loving, machine-making, surface-seeking, opera-going Europe. Plato came to join, and, by contrast, to enhance the energy of both. The excellence of Europe and Asia is in his brain. Metaphysics and natural philosophy expressed the genius of Europe; he substructs the religion of Asia as its base.

" If he loved abstract truth, he saved himself by propounding the most popular of all principles—the absolute
good, which rules rulers, and judges the judge.   If he
made transcendental distinctions, he fortified himself by
drawing his illustrations from sources disdained by ora-
tors and polite conversers—from mares and puppies,
from pitchers and soup-ladles, from cooks and criers;
the shops of potters, horse-doctors, butchers, and fish-
mongers.

"Thought seeks to know unity in unity; poetry, to
show it in variety; that is, always by an object or a
symbol.   Plato keeps the two vases, one of æther and
one of pigment, at his side, and invariably uses both.
Things added to things—as statistics, civil history—are
inventories.   Things used as language are inexhaustibly
attractive.   Plato turns incessantly the obverse and the
reverse of the medal of Jove."

PLATO'S CENTRAL DOCTRINE.

"To take an example: The physical philosophers
had sketched each his theory of the world; the theory
of atoms, of fire, of flux, of spirit—theories mechanical
and chemical in their genius.   Plato, a master of mathematics, and studious of all natural laws and causes, feels
these, as second causes, to be no theories of the world,
but bare inventories and lists.   To the study of Nature
he therefore prefixes the dogma: 'Let us declare the
cause which led the Supreme Ordainer to produce and
compose the universe.   He was good, and he who is
good feels no kind of envy.   Exempt from envy, he
wished that all things should be as much as possible
like himself.   Whosoever, taught by wise men, shall
admit this as the prime cause of the origin and founda-

tion of the world, will be in the truth. . . . All things
are for the sake of the good, and it is the cause of everything beautiful.' This dogma animates and impersonates
his philosophy."

But, after all, Emerson admits that there
were grave defects in Plato as a teacher; and
these are just the ones which the warmest Emersonian must find in Emerson :

ONE DEFECT IN PLATO.

"It remains to say, that the defect of Plato in power
is only that which results inevitably from his quality.
He is intellectual in his aim, and therefore, in his expression, literary. Mounting into heaven, diving into
the pit, expounding the laws of the state, the passion of
love, the remorse of crime, the hope of the parting soul
—he is literary, and never otherwise. It is almost the
sole deduction from the merit of Plato that his writings
have not—which is, no doubt, incident to this pregnancy
of intellect in his work—the vital authority which the
screams of prophets and the sermons of unlettered Arabs
and Jews possess. There is an interval; and to cohesion
contact is necessary. I know not what can be said in
reply to this criticism, but that we have come to a fact
in the nature of things: An oak is not an orange; the
qualities of sugar remain with sugar, and those of salt
with salt."

A SECOND DEFECT.

"In the second place, he has not a system. The
dearest defenders and disciples are at fault. He attempted a theory of the universe, and his theory is not
complete or self-evident. One man thinks he meant
this; and another, that. He has said one thing in one

place, and the reverse of it in another place. He is charged with having failed to make the transition from ideas to matter. Here is the world, sound as a nut, perfect, not the smallest piece of chaos left; never a stitch nor an end; not a mark of haste or botching, or second-thought; but the *theory* of the world is a thing of threads and patches."

A THIRD DEFECT.

"The longest wave is quickly lost in the sea. Plato would willingly have a Platonism—a known and accurate expression for the world—and it should be accurate. It shall be the world passed through the mind of Plato—nothing less. Every atom shall have the Platonic tinge; every atom, every relation or quality you knew before, you shall know again, and find here new ordered; not Nature, but Art. And you shall feel that Alexander indeed overran with men and horses some countries of the planet; but the countries and things of which countries are made—elements, planets themselves, laws of planet and of men—have passed through this man as bread into his body; so all this mammoth morsel has become Plato. He has clapped copyright on the world. But the mouth-ful proves too large. *Boa Constrictor* has good will to eat, but he is foiled. He falls abroad in the attempt, and, biting, gets strangled. The bitten world holds the biter fast by his own teeth. There he perishes; unconquered Nature lives on and forgets him. So it fares with all; so must it fare with Plato. In view of external nature, Plato turns out to be philosophical exercitations. He argues on this side and on that. The acutest German, the lovingest disciple, could never tell what Platonism was. Indeed, admirable texts can be quoted on both sides of every great question from him."

17

PLATO SUMMED UP.

"These things we are forced to say, if we must consider the effort of Plato, or of any philosopher, to dispose of Nature—which will not be disposed of. No power of genius has yet had the smallest success in explaining existence. The perfect enigma remains. But there is an injustice in assuming this ambition for Plato. Let us not seem to treat with flippancy his venerable name. Men, in proportion to their intellect, have admitted his transcendent claims. The way to know him is to compare him not with Nature, but with others. How many ages have gone by, and he remains unapproached!"

In a brief supplementary chapter, entitled "Plato, New Readings," Emerson reiterates and enlarges upon some of the points before treated, but closes with this depreciatory remark : "In his eighth book of the 'Republic' he throws a little mathematical dust in our eyes. I am sorry to see him, after such noble superiorities, permitting the lie to governors. Plato plays Providence a little with the baser sort, as people allow themselves with their dogs and cats."

SWEDENBORG, THE MYSTIC.

Second in Emerson's Category of Representative Men stands the name of Emanuel Swedenborg, "the mystic." He prefaces his special consideration of this man by speaking of certain broad types of thinking men who are not "what the world calls producers. They have nothing in

their hands; they have not cultivated corn nor
made bread; they have not led out a colony nor
invented a loom." But still higher "in the estimation and love of this city-building, market-
going race of mankind are the poets, who from
the intellectual kingdom feed the thought and
the imagination with ideas and pictures which
raise men out of the world of coin and money,
and console them for the shortcomings of the day,
and meanness of labor and traffic." Then also is
the philosopher, " who flatters the intellect of this
laborer by engaging him with subtleties which
instruct him in new faculties; others may build
cities, he is to understand them and keep them in
awe." But, he adds, "There is a class who lead
us into another region—the world of morals or of
will. What is singular about this region of
thought is its claim. Wherever the sentiment
of right comes in, it takes precedence of everything else. For other things, I make poetry of
them; but the moral sentiment makes poetry of
me." This last class of men are the mystics. In
a certain sense, Emerson seems to include Moses
and Menu, Jesus and Mohammed, among the
mystics. Of mysticism in general he thus
speaks:

ON MYSTICISM.

"The path is difficult, secret, and beset with terror.
The ancients called it *ecstasy* or ' absence '— a getting out
of their bodies to think. All religious history contains

traces of the trance of saints—a beatitude, but without
any sign of joy; earnest, solitary, even sad. 'The flight,'
Plotinus called it, of the Alone to the Alone; μύεσις, the
'closing of the eyes,' whence our word 'mystic.' The
trances of Socrates, Plotinus, Porphyry, Behmen, Bun-
yan, Fox, Pascal, Guyon, Swedenborg, will readily come
to the mind. But what as readily comes to the mind is
the accompaniment of disease. This beatitude comes in
terror and with shock to the mind of the receiver. ' It
o'erinforms the tenement of clay,' and drives the man
mad; or gives a certain violent bias, which taints his
judgment. In the chief examples of religious illumination somewhat morbid has mingled, in spite of the un-
questionable increase of mental power. Must the highest good drag after it a quality which neutralizes and
discredits it? Shall we say that the economical mother
disburses so much earth and so much fire by weight and
metre to make a man, and will not add a pennyweight,
though a nation is perishing for a leader? Therefore,
the men of God purchased their science by folly or pain.
If you will have pure carbon, carbuncle, or diamond, to
make the brain transparent, the trunk and organs shall
be so much the grosser: instead of porcelain, they are
potter's earth, clay, or mud."

EMANUEL SWEDENBORG.

"In modern times no such remarkable example of
this introverted mind has occurred as in Emanuel Swedenborg, born in Stockholm, in 1688. This man, who
appeared to his contemporaries a visionary, and elixir of
moonbeams, no doubt led the most real life of any man
then in the world. And now, when the royal and ducal
Fredericks, Christierns, and Brunswicks of that day have

slid into oblivion, he begins to spread himself into the minds of thousands. As happens in great men, he seemed, by the variety and extent of his powers, to be a composition of several persons, like the giant fruits which are matured in our gardens by a composition of several blossoms. His frame is on a large scale, and possesses the advantage of size. As it is easier to see the reflection of the great sphere in large globes, though defaced by some crack or blemish, than in drops of water, so men of large caliber, though with some eccentricity or madness, like Pascal or Newton, help us more than ordinary, balanced minds."

Emerson states briefly the main outward facts in the life of Swedenborg; tells how the devotion of his youth and manhood, down to far beyond middle life, was paid to physical science; how he "goes grubbing into mines and mountains, prying into chemistry, optics, physiology, mathematics, astronomy, and theology"; how he anticipated much of the science of the nineteenth century, as in astronomy, magnetism, chemistry, and anatomy. "But in 1743, when he was fifty-four years old, what is called his 'Illumination' began. All his metallurgy and transportation of vessels overland was absorbed into this ecstasy. He ceased to publish any more scientific books, and devoted himself to the writing and publication of his voluminous theological works." He was held in high esteem by men of all classes and orders—men of science and learning perhaps ex-

cepted—and died of apoplexy in London, in his
eighty-fifth year.

THE GENIUS OF SWEDENBORG.

"The genius which was to penetrate the science of
the age with a far more subtle science; to pass the
bounds of space and time; venture into the dim Spirit-
realm, and attempt to establish a new religion in the
world, began its lessons in quarries and forges, in the
smelting-pot and crucible, in ship-yards and dissecting-
rooms. No one man is perhaps able to judge of the merits of his work on so many subjects. One is glad to
learn that his books on mines and metals are held in the
highest esteem by those who understand such matters."

HIS UNIVERSALITY AND UNITY.

"A colossal soul, he lies vast abroad on his times,
uncomprehended by them, and requires a long focal distance to be seen; suggests, as Aristotle, Bacon, Selden,
Humboldt, that a certain vastness of learning, or *quasi*-
omnipotence of the human soul in Nature is possible.
His superb speculation, as from a tower over Nature and
Arts, without ever losing sight of the texture and se-
quence of things, almost realizes his own picture in his
'Principia,' of the original integrity of man. One of the
missouriums and mastodons of literature, he is not to be
measured by whole colleges of ordinary scholars. Our
books are false by being fragmentary; their sentences
are *bon mots*, and not parts of natural discourse; childish
expressions of surprise or pleasure in Nature; or, worse,
owing a brief notoriety to their petulance, or aversion
from the order of Nature, and purposely framed to excite surprise, as jugglers do by concealing their means.

But Swedenborg is systematic, and respective of the world in every sentence. All the means are orderly given; his faculties work with astronomic punctuality; and this admirable writing is pure from all pertness and egotism."

SOME OF SWEDENBORG'S TEACHINGS.

"Swedenborg was born into an atmosphere of great ideas. The thoughts in which he lived were the universality of each law of Nature; the Platonic doctrine of the scale or degrees; the version or conversion of each into the other, and so the correspondence of all the parts; the fine secret that little explains large, and large, little; the centrality of man in Nature, and the connection that exists in all things. He saw that the human body was strictly universal, or an instrument through which the soul feeds, and is fed by the whole of matter; so that he held, in exact antagonism to the Skeptics, that 'the wiser a man is, the more will he be a worshiper of the Deity.' In short, he was a believer in the identity-philosophy, which he held not idly, as the dreamers of Berlin and Boston, but which he experimented with, and established through years of labor, with the heart and strength of the rudest Viking that his rough Sweden ever sent to battle. This theory dates from the oldest philosophers and derives, perhaps, its best illustration from the newest. It is this: That Nature iterates her means perpetually on successive planes. In the old aphorism, *Nature is always self-similar.*"

Emerson illustrates this theory from several operations of Nature. Thus: "In the plant, the 'eye,' or germinating point, opens to a leaf, then to another leaf, with the power of transforming the leaf into radicle, stamen, pistil, petal, bract, sepal, or seed. The whole art of the plant is still to repeat leaf on leaf without end ; the more or less of heat, light, moisture, and food determining the form it shall assume." So, too, in the animal creation. "In the animal, Nature makes a vertebræ, or a spine of vertebræ, and helps herself still more by a new spine, with a limited power of modifying its form—spine on spine to the end of the world."

Emerson insists that the same general law holds in the complex physical and intellectual constitution of man : " Nature recites her lessons once more in a higher mood. The mind is a finer body, and resumes its functions of feeding, digesting, absorbing, excluding, and generating, in a new and ethical element. Here, in the brain, is all the process of alimentation repeated, in the acquiring, composing, digesting, and assimilating of experience. Here, again, is the mystery of generation repeated. In the brain are the male and female faculties; here is marriage, here is fruit. And there is no limit to this ascending scale, but series on series. Everything, at the end of one use, is taken up into the next, each series punctually repeating every organ and process of the last. We are adapted to infinity, and love nothing which ends ; and in Nature is no end ; but everything at the end of one use is lifted into a superior ; and the ascent of these things climbs into demoniac and celestial natures. Creative force, like a musical composer, goes on unweariedly repeating a simple air or theme, now high, now low, in solo, in chorus, ten thousand times reverberated, till it fills earth and heaven with the chant." In this comment upon the philosophy of Swedenborg we think that Emerson has made the largest of what Mr. Whipple styles his "fragmentary contributions to the Philosophy of the Infinite."

Still Emerson makes many grave objections to the philosophy of Swedenborg, as he had done to that of Plato. We cite some of these objections, retaining his own words, but with many omissions :

DEFECTS IN SWEDENBORG'S PHILOSOPHY.

"In the 'Conjugal Love,' he has unfolded the science of marriage. Of this book one would say that, with the highest elements, it has failed of success. It came near to be the hymn of love which Plato attempted in 'The Banquet'; the love which, Dante says, Casella sang among the angels in paradise. The book had been grand if the Hebraism had been omitted, and the laws stated without Gothicism, as ethics, and with that scope for ascension of state which the nature of things requires. Yet Swedenborg, after his mode, pinned his theory to a temporary form. He exaggerates the circumstances of marriage ; and, though he finds false marriages on earth, fancies a wiser choice in heaven."

HEAVEN AND HELL.

"In his 'Animal Kingdom' he surprised us by declaring that he loved analysis and not synthesis; and now, after his fiftieth year, he falls into jealousy of his intellect; makes war on his mind; takes the part of conscience against it; and on all occasions traduces and blasphemes it. He was wise, but wise in his own despite. There is an air of infinite grief, and infinite wailing, all over and through this lurid universe. A bird does not more readily weave its nest, or a mole bore into the ground, than this sea of souls substructs a new hell and pit, each more abominable than the last, round every new crew of offenders. He was let down through a column that seemed of brass—but it was formed of angelic spirits —that he might descend safely among the unhappy, and witness the devastation of souls. He saw the hell of jugglers; the hell of assassins; the hell of robbers, who kill and boil men; the infernal tun of the deceitful; the excrementitious hells; the hell of the revengeful, whose faces resembled a round, broad cake, and their arms rotate like a wheel. Except Rabelais and Swift, nobody ever had such a science of filth and corruption.

"These books should be used with caution. It is dangerous to sculpture these effervescent images of thought. True in transition, they become false if fixed. It requires, for his just apprehension, almost a genius equal to his own. But when his visions become the stereotyped language of multitudes of persons of all degrees of age and capacity, they are perverted. An ardent and contemplative young man of eighteen or twenty years might read once these books of Swedenborg—these mysteries of love and conscience—and then throw them aside forever."

And much more to the same general purport, if not quite so strongly expressed. Of Swedenborg's so-called "Revelations," Emerson speaks with not a little contempt:

SWEDENBORG'S REVELATIONS.

"For the anomalous pretension of revelations of the other world, only his probity and genius can entitle it to any serious regard. His revelations destroy their credit by running into detail. If a man say that the Holy Ghost has informed him that the last judgment (or the last of the judgments) took place in 1757, or that the Dutch in the other world live in a heaven by themselves—I reply that the spirit, which is holy, is reserved, taciturn, and deals in laws. The rumors of ghosts and hobgoblins gossip and tell fortunes; the teachings of the high spirit are abstemious, and, in regard to particulars, negative. Socrates's genius did not advise him to act or to find; but, if he purposed to do somewhat not advantageous, it dissuaded him. 'What God is,' he said, 'I know not; what he *is not*, I know.' The Hindoos have denominated the Supreme Being the 'Internal Check.' The illuminated Quakers explained their light, not as somewhat which leads to any action, but it appears as an obstruction to anything unfit. The secret of heaven is kept from age to age. No imprudent, no sociable angel, ever dropped an early syllable to answer the longings of saints, the fears of mortals. Behmen is healthily and beautifully wise, notwithstanding the mystical narrowness and incommunicableness. Swedenborg is disagreeably wise, and, with all his accumulated gifts, paralyzes and repels."

Yet, notwithstanding all these manifold objections, which to our mind—assuming them to be well-founded—seem conclusive, Emerson, in conclusion, awards to Swedenborg a high place not merely among the representative men, but among the representatives of good and wise men —at least, after a fashion :

FINAL ESTIMATE OF SWEDENBORG.

"His books have no melody, no emotion, no humor, no relief to the dead, prosaic level. The entire want of poetry in so transcendent a mind betokens the disease; and, like a hoarse voice in a beautiful person, is a kind of warning. I think sometimes he will not be read longer. His great name will turn a sentence. His books have become a monument. His laurel is so largely mixed with cypress, a charnel-breath so mingles with the temple incense, that boys and maidens will shun the spot.

"Yet in this immolation of genius and fame at the shrine of conscience is a merit sublime beyond praise. He lived to purpose; he gave a verdict. He elected goodness as the clew to which the soul must cling in all this labyrinth of Nature. I think of him as of some transmigrating votary of Indian legend, who says, 'Though I be dog, or jackal, or pismire in the last rudiments of nature, under what integument or ferocity, I cleave to right as a sure ladder that leads up to man and to God.'

"Swedenborg has rendered a double service to mankind, which is now only beginning to be known. By the science of experiment and use he made his first steps. He observed and published the laws of nature, and, ascending by just degrees from events to their summits and causes, he was fired with piety at the harmonies he felt, and abandoned himself to their joys and worship. This was his first service. If the glory was too bright for his eyes to bear, if he staggered under the trance of delight, the more excellent is the spectacle he saw—the realities of Being which beam and blaze through him, and which no infirmities of the prophet are suffered to obscure; and he renders a second passive service to men not less than the first—perhaps, in the great circle of being, and in the retribution of spiritual Nature, not less glorious or less beautiful to himself."

MONTAIGNE, THE SKEPTIC.

We need not dwell upon what Emerson has to say of Shakespeare, or Napoleon, or Goethe. But a little space must be given to Montaigne, "the skeptic." Skepticism, in Emerson's vocabulary, is "not at all unbelief; not at all universal doubting—doubting even that one doubts; least of all, scoffing and profligate jeering at all that is stable and good." The skeptic is the considerer, the prudent—taking in sail, counting stock, husbanding his means, and combining in himself many admirable qualities. He says that all these qualities meet in Montaigne. He avows a great personal regard for the admirable gossip of the skeptic, and tells how it began and grew:

"A single odd volume of Cotton's translations of the essays remained to me from my father's library when a

boy. It lay long neglected until, after many years, when
I was newly escaped from college, I read the book, and
procured the remaining volumes. I remember the delight and wonder in which I lived with it. It seemed to
me that I had myself written the book in some former
life, so sincerely it spoke to my thought and experience."

Certainly many men of very diverse natures
have been great admirers of Montaigne. In the
cemetery of Père la Chaise, Emerson came upon
the monument of Auguste Collignon, upon which
was inscribed that "he lived to do right, and had
formed himself to virtue on the essays of Montaigne." John Sterling, from love to Montaigne,
made a pilgrimage to his château, and copied
from the walls of the library the inscriptions
which Montaigne had written there two hundred
and fifty years before. One of the autographs of
Shakespeare is in a copy of Florio's translation of
Montaigne, which is the only existing book posi-
tively known to have been in the possession of
Shakespeare. Another copy of this same translation contains on the fly-leaf the autograph of
Ben Jonson. The only great writer of modern
times that Byron read with avowed satisfaction
was Montaigne. And Gibbon says that, in the
bigoted times in which Montaigne lived, he and
Henry IV were the only liberal men in France.
Emerson thus characterizes these essays of Montaigne :

MONTAIGNE'S ESSAYS.

" Montaigne is the freest and honestest of all writers. His French freedom runs into grossness, but he has anticipated all censure by the bounty of his confessions. In his times books were written to one sex only, and almost all were written in Latin; so that, in a humorist, a certain nakedness of statement was permitted, which our manners, of a literature addressed equally to both sexes, do not allow. But though a biblical plainness, coupled with a most uncanonical levity, may shut his pages to many sensitive readers, yet the offense is superficial. He parades it; he makes the most of it; nobody can think or say worse of him than he does. He pretends to most of the vices; and, if there be any virtue in him, he says it got in by stealth. There is no man, in his opinion, who has not deserved hanging five or six times; and he pretends to no exception in his own behalf. 'Five or six as ridiculous stories,' he says, 'can be told of me as of any man living. . . . When I the most religiously confess myself, I find that the best virtue I have has in it some tincture of vice; and I am afraid that Plato, in his purest virtue, if he had listened and laid his ear close to himself, would have heard some jarring sound of human mixture, but faint and remote, and only to be perceived by himself.' "

MONTAIGNE'S DOWNRIGHTNESS.

" Here is an impatience and fastidiousness at color or pretense of any kind. He has been in courts so long as to have conceived a furious disgust at appearances; he will indulge himself with a little cursing and swearing; he will talk with sailors and gypsies, use flash and

street ballads. Whatever you get here will smack of the
earth and real life—sweet, or smart, or stinging. He
makes no hesitation to entertain you with the records
of his disease; his journey to Italy is quite full of that
matter. He took and kept this position of equilibrium.
Over his name he drew an emblematic pair of scales, and
wrote ' *Que sçais je ?* ' under it.

"The essays are an entertaining soliloquy on every
random topic that comes into his head ; treating everything without ceremony, yet with masculine sense. There
have been men with deeper insight, but, one would say,
never a man with such an abundance of thoughts. He
is never dull, never insincere, and has the genius to make
the reader care for all that he cares for. The sincerity
and marrow of the man reaches to his sentences. I know
not anywhere the book that seems less written. It is the
language of conversation transferred to a book. One has
the same pleasure in it that we have in listening to the
necessary speech of men about their work, when any unusual circumstance gives momentary importance to their
dialogue. At thirty-three he married, not because he
wished to, he says, 'but because the common custom and
the use of life will have it so. Most of my actions are
guided by example, not choice.' In the hour of death he
gave the same weight to custom, causing the Mass to be
celebrated in his chamber."

We can well understand how Montaigne should
have come to be a favorite author during the two
unfastidious centuries after his death ; and how,
as Emerson says, "the world has endorsed his
book by translating it into all tongues, and printing seventy-five editions of it in Europe ; and

that, too, a circulation somewhat chosen, namely, among courtiers, soldiers, princes, and men of the world, and men of generosity." It is a kind of seventeenth century "Spectator," full of keen observation and cutting wit; not indeed free from impurity, like the English "Spectator," but not defaced by the pruriency of Boccaccio or the shameless obscenity of Rabelais. But still a question will come up which is thus put by Emerson : "Shall we say that Montaigne has spoken wisely, and given the right and permanent expression of the human mind on the Conduct of Life ?" This question he appears to answer in the affirmative, and essentially on the ground of what, we suppose, he would style the Rational Skepticism of Montaigne. As heretofore, we isolate several passages, which taken together seem to fairly express the purport of the whole :

BELIEF AND SKEPTICISM.

" We are natural believers. Truth, or the connection of cause and effect, alone interests us. We are persuaded that a thread runs through all things; all worlds are strung upon it, as beads; and men, and events, and life, come to us only because of that thread; they pass and repass, only that we may know the direction and continuity of that line. A book or statement which goes to show that there is no line, but random and chaos—a calamity out of nothing, a prosperity and no account of it, a hero born from a fool, a fool from a hero—dispirits us. Seen or unseen, we believe that the tie exists.

18

Talent makes counterfeit ties; genius makes the real ones.

But, though we are natural conservers and causationists, and reject a sour, dumpish unbelief, the skeptical class, which Montaigne represents, have reason, and every man at some time belongs to it. Every superior mind will pass through this domain of equilibrium; I should rather say, will know how to avail himself of the checks and balances in Nature, as a natural weapon against the exaggeration and formalism of bigots and blockheads.

"Skepticism is the attitude assumed by the student in relation to the particulars which society adores, but which he sees to be reverend only in their tendency and spirit. The ground occupied by the skeptic is the vestibule of the temple. Society does not like to have any breath of question blown on the existing order. But the interrogation of custom at all points is an inevitable stage in the growth of every superior mind, and is the evidence of its perception of the flowing Power which remains itself in all changes."

Emerson goes on to speak of several kinds of irrational skepticism. He says :

"I mean to celebrate this calendar-day of our Saint Michael de Montaigne by counting and describing these doubts and negations. I wish to ferret them out of their holes and sun them a little. We must do with them as the police do with old rogues, who are shown up to the public at the marshal's office. They will never be so formidable when once they have been entered and registered. But I mean honestly by them; that justice shall be done to their terrors. I shall not take sundry objections, made up on purpose to be put down. I shall take the worst I can find, whether I can dispose of them or they of me. I do not press the skepticism of the Materialist. I know the quadruped opinion will not prevail. It is of no importance what bats and oxen think."

But there are dangerous forms of irrational skepticism.

LEVITY OF INTELLECT.

"The first dangerous symptom I report is levity of intellect, as if it were fatal to earnestness to know too much. Knowledge is the knowing that we cannot know. The dull pray, the geniuses are light mockers. How respectable is earnestness on every platform! but intellect kills it. This is hobgoblin the first, and though it has been the subject of much eulogy in our nineteenth century, I confess it is not very affecting to my imagination, for it seems to concern the shattering of baby-houses and toy-shops. What flutters the Church of Rome, or of England, or of Geneva, or of Boston may have, may yet be very far from touching, any principle of faith. I think the wiser a man is, the more stupendous he finds the natural and moral economy, and lifts himself to a more absolute reliance."

THE POWER OF MOODS.

"There is the power of moods, each setting at naught all but its own tissue of facts and beliefs. The beliefs and unbeliefs appear to be structural. Our life is March weather, savage and serene each hour. We go forth austere, serene, dedicated; believing in the iron links of destiny, and will not turn on our heel to save our life.

But a book or a bust, or only the sound of a name, shoots a spark through the nerves, and we suddenly believe in will; 'Fate is for imbeciles; all is possible to the resolved mind.' Presently a new experience gives a new turn to our thoughts; common-sense resumes its tyranny; we say, 'Well, the army, after all, is the gate to fame, manners, and poetry; and look you, on the whole, selfishness plants best, prunes best, makes the best commerce, and the best citizen.' Are the opinions of men on right and wrong, on fate and causation, at the mercy of a broken sleep or an indigestion? Is his belief in God and duty no deeper than a stomach evidence? And what guaranty for the permanence of his opinions? I like not the French celerity—a Church and a State once a week. This is the second negation; and I shall let it pass for what it will."

FATE OR DESTINY.

"The word fate, or destiny, expresses the sense of mankind in all ages—that the laws of the world do not always befriend, but often hurt and crush us. Fate, in the shape of *Kinde* or Nature, grows over us like grass. We paint Time with a scythe; Love and Fortune, blind; Destiny, deaf. We have too little power of resistance against this ferocity which champs us up. What front can we make against these unavoidable, victorious, maleficent forces? What can I do against the influence of race in my history? What can I do against hereditary and constitutional habits; against scrofula, lymph, impotence; against climate, against barbarism in my country? I can reason down or deny everything except this perpetual Belly; feed he must and will, and I cannot make him respectable."

ILLUSIONISM.

"But the main resistance which the affirmative impulse finds—and one including all others—is in the doctrine of the illusionists. There is a painful rumor in circulation that we have been practised upon in all the principal performances of life, and free-agency is the emptiest name. The mathematics, it is complained, leave the mind where they find it: so do all sciences; and so do all events and actions. I find a man who has passed through all the sciences the churl he was, and through all the offices, learned, civil, and social, can detect the child. We are not the less necessitated to dedicate life to them. In fact, we may come to accept it as the fixed rule and theory of our state of education that God is a substance, and his method is illusion. The eastern sages owned the goddess Yoganidra, the great illusory energy of Vishnu, by whom, as utter ignorance, the whole world is beguiled; or shall I state it thus: The astonishment of life is the absence of any appearance of reconciliation between the theory and the practice of life."

Twenty years before, Emerson had thought—or at least thought that he thought—that all these obstinate questionings of things outward and inward could be easily resolved. In his "Nature" he had said : "Undoubtedly we have no questions to ask which are unanswerable; whatever curiosity the order of things has awakened, the order of things can satisfy. The true theory will explain all phenomena." Now everything is unexplained, and apparently as inexplicable as ever. And so every sound man must perforce be a skeptic. "Shall we," he asks, "because a good nature in-

clines to virtue's side, say 'There are no doubts,'
and lie for the right? Can you not believe that
a man of earnest and burly habit may find small
good in tea, essays, and catechism, and wants a
rougher instruction to make things plain to him?
And has he not a right to be convinced in his
own way? When he is convinced he will be
worth the pains."

Montaigne, as we read him, was never much
vexed with any of these doubts and questionings;
or, if he was vexed by them, never came to be
convinced. He lived his threescore years, took
things as he found them, and did not try to
mend them. He married because he saw that
other men of his years and station were wont to
marry; and partook of the sacrament when on
his deathbed, because that was the custom in
France. For things which lay close around him
he had a keen perception, and had a sharp way of
expressing his perception. But for all higher
matters, if to his chosen motto, " *Que sçais je?* "
(What do I know?) we add, "And what do I
care?" we shall have the measure of the man.
We are not sure what direct answer Emerson
would have given to his own question: " Has
Montaigne spoken wisely, and given the right
and permanent expression of the human mind on
the conduct of life?" But our answer, and the
answer of the whole scope of Emerson's teachings
is, "He has not so done."

XI.

THE CONDUCT OF LIFE.

EMERSON'S " Conduct of Life," published in 1860, consists of nine essays upon various topics, such as "Fate," "Power," "Wealth," "Culture," "Beauty," "Worship," and "Illusions." They may properly be regarded as a third series of his "Essays." The old topics are treated under somewhat new aspects, with less of apparent inconsistency in form. Years had enlarged the scope of his vision and changed his standpoint, so that he could take in at a glance more than one facet of the prism. The mottoes prefixed to several of these essays are indicative of their scope and tendency.

FATE.

" Delicate omens, traced in air,
　To the lone bard true witness bare;
　Birds, with auguries on their wings,
　Chanted undeceiving things,
　Him to beckon, him to warn;
　Well might then the poet scorn
　To learn of scribe or courier
　Hints writ in vaster character;
　And on his mind, at dawn of day,
　Soft shadows of the evening lay;
　For the prevision is allied
　Unto the thing so signified;
　Or say, the foresight that awaits
　Is the same genius that creates."

A single quatrain stands as the motto to the essay on " Power :"

POWER.

" His tongue was framed to music,
  And his hand was armed with skill ;
  His face was the mould of beauty,
  And his heart the throne of will."

The motto to the essay on " Wealth " is much longer.   We quote only the conclusion :

WEALTH.

" All is waste and worthless, till
  Arrives the wise, selecting Will,
  And out of time and chaos, wit
  Draws the threads of fair and fit.
  Then temples rose, and towns and marts,
  The shop of toil, the hall of arts ;
  Then flew the sail across the seas,
  To feed the North from tropic trees—
  The storm-wind wove, the torrent span,
  Where they were bid the rivers ran ;
  New slaves fulfilled the poet's dream—
  Galvanic wire, strong-shouldered steam.
  Then docks were built, and crops were stored,
  And ingots added to the hoard.
  But, though light-headed man forget,
  Remembering matter pays her debt ;
  Still, through her motes and masses draw
  Electric thrills and ties of law,
  Which bend the strength of Nature wild
  To the conscience of a child."

The motto to the essay on "Behavior" is especially Emersonian in its irregularity of rhythm and rhyme :

BEHAVIOR.

"Grace, Beauty, and Caprice
  Built this wonderful portal;
Graceful women, chosen men,
  Dazzle every mortal:
Their sweet and lofty countenance
  His enchanting food;
He need not go to them, their forms
  Beset his solitude.
He seldom looketh in their face,
  His eyes explore the ground,
The green grass is a looking-glass
  Whereon their traits are found.
Little he says to them—
  So dances his heart in his breast;
Their tranquil mien bereaveth him
  Of wit, of words, of rest.
Too weak to win, too fond to shun
  The tyrants of his doom,
The much-deceived Endymion
  Slips behind a tomb."

Of the noble essay on "Worship" something has already been said in connection with the spiritual philosophy of Emerson.   Its motto is :

WORSHIP.

" This is he who, felled by foes,
  Sprung harmless up, refreshed by blows:

He to captivity was sold,
But him no prison-bars would hold :
Though they sealed him on a rock,
Mountain chains he can unlock :
Thrown to lions for their meat,
The crouching lion kissed his feet :
Bound to the stake, no fears appalled,
But arched o'er him an honoring vault.
This is he men miscall **Fate**,
Threading dark ways, arriving late;
But ever coming in time to crown
The truth, and hurl wrong-doers down.
He is the oldest and best known,
More near than aught thou call'st thy own.
Yet, greeted in another's eyes,
Disconcerts with glad surprise.
This is Jove, who, deaf to prayers,
Floods with blessings unawares.
   Draw, if thou canst, the mystic line
   Severing rightly his from thine.
   Which is human, which Divine?"

The essay on "Illusions" is mystical enough in subject and treatment : quite as mystical as is its motto ; and the unrhymed lines have a weird, almost impalpable, rhythm :

ILLUSIONS.

"Flow, flow the waves hated;
   Accursed, adored,
The waves of mutation :
   No anchorage is.
Sleep is not, Death is not;
   Who seem to die, live.

"House you were born in,
    Friends of your spring-time,
Old man and young maid,
    Day's toil and its guerdon,
Fleeing to fables, cannot be moored.

"See the stars through them,
    Through treacherous marbles.
        Know, the stars everlasting
        Are fugitive also,
    And emulate vaulting
    The lambent heat-lightning
    And fire-fly's flight.

"When thou dost return
    On the wave's circulation,
    Beholding the shimmer,
        The wild dissipation,
    And out of endeavor
    To change and to flow,
        The gas becomes solid,
        And Phantoms and Nothings
        Return to be Things,
        And endless imbroglio
    Is Law and the World.
        Then first shalt thou know
    That in the wild turmoil,
        Horsed upon Proteus,
    Thou ridest to power
        And to endurance."

But even in illusions Emerson finds uses. He
says: "The intellect is stimulated by the statement of truth in trope, and the will by clothing

the laws of life in illusions. But the unities of truth and right are not broken by the disguise. There need never be any confusion in *these*. In a crowded life of many parts and performances, on a stage of nations or in the obscurest hamlet of Maine and California, the same elements offer the same choices to each new-comer ; and, according to his election, he fixes his fortune in absolute Nature." Then follows a maxim which might have been framed by Montaigne in one of his best moods : "It would be hard to put more mental and moral philosophy than the Persians have thrown into a sentence—

 'Fooled thou must be, though the wisest of the wise:
  Then be the fool of virtue, not of vice.' "

The essay and the book close with this—often said in substance elsewhere :

ILLUSIONS THEMSELVES ILLUSIONARY.

"There is no chance and no anarchy in the universe. Every god is there sitting in his sphere. The young mortal enters the hall of the firmament; there he is alone with them alone ; they pouring on him benedictions and gifts, and beckoning him up to their thrones. On the instant, and incessantly, fall snow-storms of illusions. He fancies himself in a vast crowd, which sways this way and that, and whose movement and doings he must obey ; he fancies himself poor, orphaned, insignificant. The mad crowd drives him hither and thither; now furiously commanding this thing to be done, now that. What is he that he should resist their will and think or act for himself? Every moment new changes and new showers of deceptions to baffle and distract him. And when, by and by, for an instant, the air clears and the cloud lifts a little, there are the gods still sitting around him on their thrones—they alone with him alone."

———

XII.

SOCIETY AND SOLITUDE.

"Society and Solitude" was published in 1870. It consists of twelve chapters, and may be regarded as a fourth series of the "Essays." The topics relate mainly to matters of every-day life and common experience, such as "Civilization," "Art," "Domestic Life," "Farming," "Clubs," "Success," and "Old Age." The tone is calm and serene, rising not unfrequently into grave eloquence, less brilliant and striking than was displayed in his earlier writings. It is a book to be taken up in those halcyon hours which sometimes come to severest thinker when he longs for a temporary repose. The closing chapter on "Old Age" breathes the very spirit of the closing stanza of Wordsworth's ode on the "Intimation of Immortality":

" The clouds which gather round the setting sun
    Do take a silver coloring from an eye
    Which hath kept watch o'er man's mortality.
Another race is run, and other palms are won.
    Thanks to the human heart by which we live—
Thanks to its tenderness, its joys, and fears—
    To me the meanest flower that blows can give
Thoughts that do often lie too deep for tears."

Somewhat after the manner of Cicero, in the "De Senectute," Emerson enumerates some of the consolations and blessings of a serene old age. We cite only one of these :

ACCOMPLISHED PURPOSES.

"Another felicity of age is that it has found expression. The youth suffers not only from ungratified desires, but from powers untried, and from a picture in his mind of a career which has as yet no outward reality. He is tormented with the want of correspondence between things and thoughts. Michel Angelo's head is full of masculine and gigantic figures as of gods walking, which make him savage until his furious chisel can render them into marble; and of architectural dreams, until a hundred stone-masons can lay them in courses of travertine.

"There is the like tempest in every good head in which some great benefit for the world is planted. The throes continue until the child is born. Every faculty new to each man thus goads and drives him out into doleful deserts until it finds proper vent. All the functions of human duty irritate and lash him forward, bemoaning and chiding, until they are performed. He

wants friends, employment, knowledge, power, house
and land, wife and children, honor and fame; he has
religious wants, æsthetic wants, domestic, civil, humane
wants. One by one, day after day, he learns to coin
his wishes into facts. He has his calling, homestead,
social connection, and personal power; and thus, at the
end of fifty years, his soul is appeased by seeing some
sort of correspondence between his wish and his possession. This makes the value of age, the satisfaction it
slowly offers to every craving. He is serene who does
not feel himself pinched and wronged, but whose condition, in particular and in general, allows the utterance
of his mind. In old persons, when thus fully expressed,
we often observe a fair, plump, perennial, waxen complexion, which indicates that all the ferment of earlier
days has subsided into serenity of thought and behavior."

All this, of course, relates only to persons who
have attained in some good measure to the ideal
of a serene old age. Not a few fail wholly of this,
some by reason of faults patent to all, some by
reason of circumstances seemingly quite beyond
their control. Among great men who have fairly
attained to this blessing we may cite the names of
Wordsworth, Gibbon, Milton, Franklin, Bryant,
Longfellow, John Adams, and Emerson. A very
pleasant sketch is given of John Adams, at the
age of almost ninety. It is all the more interesting because it is a transcript of what had been
written by Emerson forty-five years before—he
then being only twenty-two. He says: "I have

lately found in an old note-book a record of a visit to ex-President John Adams in 1825, soon after the election of his son to the Presidency. It is but a sketch, and nothing important passed in the conversation ; but it reports a moment in the life of an heroic person who in extreme old age appeared still erect, and worthy of his fame."

JOHN ADAMS AT NINETY.

"To-day, at Quincy, with my brother, by invitation of Mr. Adams's family. The old President sat in a stuffed arm-chair, dressed in a blue coat, black small-clothes, white stockings; a cotton cap covered his bald head. We made our compliment, told him he must let us join our gratulations and congratulations to those of the nation on the happiness of his house.

"He thanked us, and said: 'I am rejoiced because the nation is happy. The time of gratulation and congratulation is nearly over with me. I am astonished that I have lived to see and know of this event. I have lived now nearly a century—a long, harassed, and eventful life.' I said: 'The world thinks a good deal of joy has been mixed with it.' 'The world does not know,' he replied, 'how much toil, anxiety, and sorrow I have suffered.' I asked if Mr. Adams's letter of acceptance had been read to him. 'Yes,' he said; and added, 'My son has more political prudence than any man I know who has existed in my time. He was never put off his guard, and I hope he will continue such; but what effect age may work in diminishing the power of his mind, I do not know. He has been very much on the stretch ever since he was born. He has always been very laborious, child and man, from infancy.' When Mr. J. Q. Adams's age was mentioned, he said: 'He is now fifty-eight, or will be in July'; and remarked, 'all the Presidents were of the same age. General Washington was about fifty-eight, I was about fifty-eight, and Mr. Jefferson, and Mr. Madison, and Mr. Monroe.' We inquired when he expected to see Mr. Adams. He said: 'Never; Mr. Adams will not come to Quincy, except to my funeral. It would be a great satisfaction to me to see him; but I don't wish him to come on my account.'"

The interview lasted about an hour, the conversation touching upon a great variety of topics.

"He spoke of Mr. Lechmere, whom he 'well remembered to have seen come down daily, at a great age, to walk in the old town-house'; adding, 'he was collector for the customs for many years under the Royal Government.' Edward said, 'I suppose, sir, you would not have taken his place, even to have walked as well as he.' 'No,' he answered, 'that was not what I wanted.'

"He talked of Whitefield, and remembered, when he was a freshman at college, to have come into town to the Old South Church to hear him, but could not get into the house. 'I, however, saw him,' he said, 'and distinctly heard all. He had a voice such as I never heard before or since. He cast it out so that you could hear it at the meeting-house'—pointing toward the Quincy Meeting-house, 'and he had the grace of a dancing-master, of an actor of plays.'—'And were you pleased with him, sir?' —'Pleased! I was delighted beyond measure.' We asked if at Whitefield's return the same popularity continued. 'Not the same fury,' he said, 'not the same wild enthusiasm as before; but a greater esteem, as he became

19

more known. He did not terrify, but was admired.'
He spoke of the new novels of Cooper, and 'Peep at the
Pilgrims,' and 'Saratoga,' with praise, and named with
accuracy the characters in them.

"He speaks very distinctly for so old a man; enters
bravely into long sentences, which are interrupted by
want of breath; but carries them invariably to a conclusion, without correcting a word. He likes to have a
person always reading to him, or company talking in
his room; and is better next day after having visitors in
his chamber from morning to night."

This chapter closes with the following general
summation of the attainable blessings of old age :

OLD AGE AFTER A WELL-SPENT LIFE.

"When life has been well-spent, age is a loss which
it can well spare—muscular strength, organic instincts,
gross bulk, and works that belong to these. But the
central wisdom, which was old in infancy, is young in
fourscore years; and, dropping off obstructions, leaves,
in happy subjects, the mind purified and wise. I have
heard that whoever loves is in no condition old. I have
heard that whenever the name of man is mentioned, the
doctrine of immortality is announced; it cleaves to the
constitution. The mode of it baffles our wit, and no
whisper comes to us from the other side. But the inference from the intellect, living knowledge, living
skill—at the end of life just ready to be born—affirms
the inspirations of affection and of the moral sentiment."

XIII.

LETTERS AND SOCIAL AIMS.

In 1875 Emerson published a volume entitled "Letters and Social Aims." It consists of eleven chapters, and is really the fifth series of his "Essays." Probably the date of publication indicates only approximately that when they were composed. Some of the chapters bear evident impresses of an earlier period. Some of them read like stray waifs which had lain hidden in his portfolios and note-books. Some seem to have been carefully elaborated, and only awaited the time of publication. Among the latter class is the thoughtful essay on "Immortality" which closes the volume. Of this we have spoken at some length in a preceding chapter. But the position given to it seems to indicate that, with all its doubts and questionings, it embodies Emerson's maturest thoughts and convictions upon this subject. In the essay on "Poetry and Imagination," Emerson gives his idea of what essentially constitutes poetry:

POETRY.

"Poetry is the perpetual endeavor to express the spirit of the thing; to pass the brute body, and search the life and reason which cause it to exist; to see that

the object is always flowing away, whilst the spirit or
necessity which causes it subsists. Its essential mark is
that it betrays in every word instant activity of mind,
shown in new uses of every fact and image; in preter-
natural quickness or perception of relations. All its
words are poems. It is the presence of mind that gives
a miraculous command of all means of uttering the
thought and feeling of the moment. The poet squanders
on the hour an amount of life that would more than
furnish the seventy years of the man that stands next
him.

"The thoughts are few, the forms many; the large
vocabulary or many-colored coat of the indigent Unity.
In the presence and conversation of a true poet, teeming
with images to express his enlarging thought, his person, his form, grows larger to our fascinated eyes. And
thus begins that deification which all nations have made
of their heroes of many kind—saints, poets, law-givers,
and warriors. Our best definition of poetry is one of
the oldest sentences, and claims to have come down
from the Chaldæan Zoroaster, who wrote it thus:
'Poets are standing transporters, whose employment
consists in speaking to the Father and to matter; in
producing apparent imitations of apparent natures, and
inscribing things unapparent in the apparent fabrication
of the world.' "

This is the ideal of what poetry should be; an
ideal seldom realized fully in the greatest of poets,
and then only in the very greatest of parts of
their best poems. But there are certain adjuncts
to poetry which are so general that they may be
regarded as indispensable. Among these are:

MELODY AND FORM.

"Music and rhyme are among the earliest pleasures of the child, and, in the history of literature, poetry precedes prose. Every one may see, as he rides on the highway through an uninteresting landscape, how a little water instantly relieves the monotony, no matter what objects are near it—a gray rock, a grass-patch, an alder-bush, a stake—they become beautiful by being reflected. It is rhyme to the eye, and explains the charm of rhyme to the ear. Shadows please us as still finer rhymes. Architecture gives the like pleasure by the repetition of equal parts in a colonnade, in a row of windows, or in wings; gardens, by the symmetric contrasts of the beds and walks. In society you have this figure in a bridal company, where a choir of white-robed maidens gives the charm of living statues; in a funeral procession, where all wear black; in a regiment of soldiers in uniform."

RHYME AND RHYTHM.

"The universality of this taste is proved by our habit of casting our facts into rhyme to remember them better, as so many proverbs may show. Who would hold the order of the almanac so fast, but for the ding-dong 'Thirty days hath September,' etc.; or of the zodiac, but for 'The ram, the bull, the heavenly twins,' etc.? We are lovers of rhyme and return, period and musical reflection. The babe is lulled to sleep by the nurse's song. Sailors can work better for their 'Yo-heave-o!' Soldiers can march better for the drum and the trumpet."

METRE.

"Metre begins with pulse-beat, and the length of lines in songs and poems is determined by the inhalation and exhalation of the lungs. If you hum or whistle the rhythm of the common English metres—of the decasyllabic quatrain or the octosyllabic with alternate sexisyllabic, or other rhythms, you can easily believe these measures to be organic, derived from the human pulse, and to be therefore not proper to one nation, but to mankind. I think you will also find a charm—heroic, plaintive, pathetic—in these cadences, and be at once set on searching for the words that can rightly fill the vacant beats."

It is further shown that the so-called " parallelism," or iteration of thought and phrase, which forms the distinctive feature of the poetry of the Hebrews, is in reality a form of rhyme. The thought instead of the sound is repeated. Thus rhyme of some sort seems essential to poetry. We indeed speak of "Prose-Poets," such as Jeremy Taylor, Thomas Taylor, the Platonist, Sir Thomas Browne, the author of "Urn-Burial," and Jean Paul Richter; and Moore says, " If Burke and Bacon were not poets (measured lines not being necessary to create one), I do not know what poetry means." But, after all, the fact that we denominate such men "Prose-Poets" shows that we still hold metre to be an essential attribute of poetry; and that we call these men poets only by courtesy, as it were. Not a little of Emerson's prose is poetic in thought; but, if he had written no verse, he would hardly be counted among the poets.

The calm, almost somber essay on "Greatness" stands last but one in these productions of Emerson. A citation or two from this will close what we have to say of his prose writings :

GREATNESS.

" There is a prize which we are all aiming at, and the more power and goodness we have, so much more the energy of that aim. Every human being has a right to it, and in the pursuit we do not stand in each other's way. For it has a long scale of degrees, a wide variety of views, and every aspirant, by his success in the pursuit, does not hinder, but helps his competitors. I might call it completeness, but that is later—perhaps adjourned for ages. I prefer to call it greatness.

"It is the fulfillment of a natural tendency in each man. It is a fruitful study. It is the best tonic to the young soul. And no man is unrelated; therefore we admire eminent men, not for themselves but as representatives. It is very certain that we ought not to be, and shall not be, contented with any goal we have reached. Our aim is no less than greatness. That which invites all, belongs to us all; to which we are all sometimes untrue, cowardly, faithless; but of which we never quite despair; and which, in every sane moment, we resolve to make our own. It is also the only platform on which all men can meet. What anecdotes of any man do we wish to hear or read? Only the best. Certainly not those in which he was degraded to the level of dullness or vice; but those in which he rose above all competitors by obeying a light that shone in him alone. This is the worthiest history of the world."

KINDS OF GREATNESS.

"Greatness!—what is it? Is there not some injury to us, some insult in the word? What we commonly call greatness is only such in our barbarous or infant experience. It is not Alexander, or Bonaparte, or Count Moltke, surely, who represent the highest *force* of mankind. Not the strong hand, but wisdom and civility; the creation of laws, institutions, letters, and art. These we call, by distinction, *the humanities*. These, and not the strong arm and brave heart, which are also indispensable to their defense. For the scholars represent the intellect, by which man is man—the intellect and the moral sentiment, which in the last analysis cannot be separated. Who can doubt the potency of the individual mind, who sees the shock given to torpid races—torpid for ages—by Mohammed; a vibration propagated over Asia and Africa? What of Menu? what of Buddha? of Shakespeare? of Newton? of Franklin?"

He then goes on to point out some of the forms under which greatness is manifested, such as self-respect, manliness, veracity, sincerity; and of all these, self-respect is the greatest. He says:

SELF-RESPECT.

"If we should ask ourselves, 'What is this self-respect?' it would carry us to the highest problems. It is our practical perception of the deity in man. It has its foundation deep in religion. If you have ever known a good mind among the Quakers, you will have found *that* is the element of their faith. As they express it, it might be thus: I do not pretend to any commandment or large

revelation, but if at any time I form some plan, propose
a journey, or course of conduct, I perhaps find a silent
obstacle in my mind that I cannot account for. Very
well, I let it lie, thinking it may pass away; but if it
does not pass away, I yield to and obey it. You ask me
to describe it. I cannot describe it. It is not an oracle,
nor an angel, nor a dream, nor a law. It is too simple
to be described, but is but a grain of mustard-seed; but,
such as it is, it is something which the contradiction of
all mankind could not shake, and which the consent of
all mankind could not confirm."

Germane to this are some valuable hints and
suggestions, among which are the following :

THE PATHS TO REAL GREATNESS.

"You are rightly fond of certain books or men that
you have found to excite your reverence and emulation.
But none of these can compare with the greatness of
that counsel which is open to you in happy solitude. I
mean that there is for you the following of an inward
leader: a slow discrimination that there is for each a
best counsel which enjoins the fit word and the fit action
for every moment; and the path of each pursued leads
to greatness. How grateful to find in man or woman a
new emphasis of their own!

"But, if the first rule is to obey your native bias—to
accept that work for which you were inwardly formed—
the second rule is concentration, which doubles its force.
Thus, if you are a scholar, be *that*. The same laws hold
for you as for the laborer. The good shoemaker makes
a good shoe because he makes nothing else. Let the
student mind his own charge, sedulously waiting every

morning for the news concerning the structure of the world which the spirit will give him."

And again, this :

SCINTILLATIONS OF GREATNESS.

"Scintillations of greatness appear here and there in men of unequal character, and are by no means confined to the cultivated and so-called moral class. It is easy to draw traits from Napoleon, who was not generous nor just, but was intellectual, and knew the law of things. Napoleon commands our respect by his enormous self-trust—the habit of seeing with his own eyes, never the surface, but to the heart of the matter—whether it was a cannon, a character, an officer, or a king; and by the speed and security of his action in the premises, always new. He has left us a library of manuscripts, a multitude of sayings, every one of widest application. I find it easy to translate all of his technics into all of mine; and his official advices are to me more literary and philosophical than the *Mémoires* of the Academy. His advice to his brother, King Joseph of Spain, was: 'I have only one counsel for you—*Be master.*'"

And, again, this by way of limitation and explanation of much that has been said before :

RARITY OF PURE GREATNESS.

"It is difficult to find greatness pure. Well, I please myself with its diffusion—to find a spark of true fire amid much corruption. It is some guarantee, I hope, for the health of the soul which has this generous blood. How many men, detested in contemporary hostile history, of whom, now that the mists have rolled away, we have learned to correct our old estimates, and to see them as upon the whole instruments of great benefits."

And still again, by way of further comment upon imperfect greatness :

THE GREATNESS OF MERE FORCE.

"Meanwhile we hate snivelling. We like the natural greatness of health and wild power. I confess that I am as much taken by it in boys, and sometimes in people not normal, nor educated, nor presentable—even in persons open to the suspicion of irregular and immoral living—as in more orderly examples. We must have some charity for the sense of the people which admires natural power, and will elect it over virtuous men who have less. It has this excuse, that natural is really allied to moral power, and may be always expected to approach it by its own instincts. Intellect at least is not stupid, and will see the force of morals over men, if it does not itself obey. Henry the Seventh of England was a wise king. When Gerald, Earl of Kildare, who was in rebellion against him, was brought to London, and examined before the Privy Council, one said : 'All Ireland cannot govern this earl.' The king replied, 'Then let this earl govern all Ireland.'"

And again, and lastly, by way of summation of the whole matter of greatness :

THE ULTIMATE GREATNESS.

"Men are ennobled by morals and by intellect; but these two elements know each other, and always beckon

to each other, until at last they meet in the man, if he
is to be truly great. The man who sells you a lamp
shows you that the flame of oil, which contented you
before, casts a strong shade in the path of the petroleum
which he lights behind it; and this again casts a shadow in the path of the electric light. So does intellect—
when brought into the presence of character. Character puts out that light.

"We are thus forced to express our instinct of the
truth, by exposing the failure of experience. The man
whom we have not seen, in whom no regard of self
degraded the adorer of the laws—who by governing himself governed others; sportive in manner, but inexorable
in act; who sees longevity in his cause; whose aim is
always distinct to him; who carries fate in his eye—he
it is whom we seek, encouraged in every good hour that
here or hereafter he shall be found."

XIV.

THE PHILOSOPHY OF EMERSON.

THE philosophical teachings of Emerson naturally group themselves into two great divisions :
First, the philosophy of the Infinite—that is, of
life itself and the absolute laws of life, or, as he
sometimes phrases it, of *existence ;* and second,
the philosophy of the Finite—that is, in its special
relation to humanity : the law or laws of the conduct of life.

Of this second division we may admit that his views are sound in the main, notwithstanding that they are often expressed in terms apparently contradictory of each other. This seeming contradiction is, after all, more apparent than real, arising from the natural tendency in his mind to present the one aspect of things which was uppermost in his thoughts at the moment in the strongest light, leaving out of view all the other aspects which, when they happen to present themselves, or to be called up by him, are in turn no less strongly expressed.

It is the first of these divisions of Emerson's philosophy which is now to be considered. Putting what we regard as a fair statement of it in concise terms, it resolves itself into three propositions : (1.) "Mind and matter are totally distinct phenomena ; and mind is supreme over matter." (2.) "There is only one Infinite Mind in the universe, which includes in itself all finite minds." It is more than half suggested that there may be a like unity even in matter ; so that it may ultimately be found that all which our natural philosophy regards as distinct elements are only modifications of this one matter ; so that there may be no real difference between hydrogen, oxygen, and nitrogen ; between carbon, gold, and iron ; but that all is one, and one is all. (3.) "That all laws are the product and emanation of the Infinite Mind, and are really but one law ;"

so that, as he phrases it, " The law of gravitation is identical with purity of thought."

Passing over the first two of these propositions, and all that follows from them, we shall here consider only the third, which, in our judgment, involves such a lax use of the essential word " Law " as to vitiate the entire scheme.

There are the *mathematical laws*, which are expressed by numbers, forms, and dimensions, and with which arithmetic and geometry have to do. We can not conceive these to be in any true sense the emanation or product of the Infinite Mind. We can not imagine that they could be other than they are ; or that the Infinite Mind could conceive them to be otherwise. For example : We hold that the Infinite Mind could not conceive of any number which, multiplied into itself, would produce three or five, or any other " surd number " ; of a triangle, any two sides of which should not be greater than the third, or one in which the sum of the three angles should be either more or less than two right-angles ; of any right-angled triangle, in which the sum of the squares of the base and perpendicular should not be equal to the square of the hypothenuse ; or of any circle, all the radii of which should not be equal. And so on of all the laws of trigonometry, fluxions, and the integral calculus. Some of them the finite mind perceives without any conscious effort ; some of them it perceives only by laborious effort ; the Infinite Mind perceives them at a glance. But, perceived or unperceived, they are, always will be, and always have been ; and so, from their very nature, must be eternal and increate ; as really and necessarily as the Infinite Mind is infinite and increate.

Then, again, there are the *moral laws*, those which we briefly sum up as the law of "right and wrong." These we hold to be alike eternal, immutable, and uncreated. They are as binding upon the Infinite Majesty of the Supreme Being as upon each and every sentient being capable of perceiving them. They bind God and man, because he and they can perceive them. If worm or dog can perceive them at all, they are binding upon it, and just so far as it can perceive them. If, without irreverence, we may conceive that there might be one Supreme Being, who should be the Ahriman and not the Ormuzd of some Eastern theosophists—infinitely malevolent instead of infinitely benevolent—this law of right and wrong would yet be binding upon him, and in violating it he would be an Infinite Malefactor. It is the glory of our faith, as it is the glory of all faiths worthy to be so called, that the Supreme Being is bound—does not bind himself—by this law of right and wrong. As Emerson has said : "There is no god dares wrong a worm." The law of right and wrong, like the laws of mathematics, is co-eternal with the Divine Being, and, therefore, like him is uncreate. It has this, and this only, in common with them, that neither can be conceived of as being other than it is. Plato has styled God the Infinite Geometer; but arithmetic and geometry have in themselves nothing to do with the moral sense.

Still, again, there are laws of a quite different class—those which we generally have in mind when we speak of the "*laws of nature*," meaning those by which we find that physical nature is governed. These are, in truth, merely our own generalizations from observed facts. The essential distinctions between these laws of nature and the mathematical and moral laws are these: Those of one class are eternal and immutable, having no relations to time and space. Those of this other class exist in time and space, and, for aught we can see, might have been altogether different from what they are; nay, there is fair reason to suppose that they have been different from what they are, and may hereafter be in many respects different from what they are or ever have been. Those who hold to the doctrine of miracles, as commonly laid down, believe that some of these laws have from time to time been set aside, not to say violated, by the Supreme Being. Is it not a law of nature that the moon is in constant real motion around the earth, and the sun in constant apparent motion around the earth? And yet did not Joshua, by divine command, say, "Sun, stand thou still upon Gibeon, and thou, moon, in the Valley of Ajalon"; and did not the "sun stand still in the midst of heaven, and hasted not to go down about a whole day"? Was not life restored to the dead body, even when far advanced in putrefaction?

But to pursue this train of thought in a direction a little different. There is no reason apparent to the intellect why very many of these observed laws should be as they are; why, for example, all matter should attract all other matter with a force inversely proportioned to the square of the distance; indeed, according to some cosmogonists, there was a period, or periods, in creation, when the particles of matter repelled instead of attracting each other; that is, when they were not governed by the law of gravitation. We can assign no special reason in the nature of things why certain gases should combine only in one, two, or three definite proportions, while other gases combine in any or all proportions; why the loadstone should magnetically attract iron and not copper, while the sandstone thus attracts neither; why gold should be so much heavier than iron, and not the reverse; why one metal should fuse at one temperature, and another at another.

We can perceive no reason why the orbit of one planet should have one degree of ellipticity, or a different degree of inclination to the ecliptic

from that of another; or why they should be
ranged in space as they are. Kepler indeed discovered a method or law governing this arrangement as it is; but, for aught we can perceive, any
other arrangement would have been just as well,
or there need not necessarily have been any such
law at all.

So far as we can now perceive, these and innumerable other laws of nature are arbitrary.
We by no means affirm that they are so in reality.
Ever and anon we learn that one or other of them
is productive of special uses for us. Thus, if
every stone were magnetic, the great human use
of the magnet would be destroyed. If the electric current could not be conducted through copper, and insulated, as by gutta-percha or glass, we
could have no electric telegraph. If water did
not become an elastic gas at a temperature easily
attainable by us, we could have no steam-engine.
If the general law in virtue of which bodies expand by heat were not, in the single case of water, arrested and reversed at or about its freezing-
point, the whole ocean would in time come to be
a mass of solid ice.

We are constantly learning new laws of nature—that is, discovering new facts and analogies, or making new generalizations of them;
and are constantly finding new uses of the long-
known laws. We are quite ready to admit, as a
matter of faith, that, could our mental vision take

in the whole of the mighty code of the laws of nature, with all its relations and inter-relations, we should perceive it to be the very best that infinite benevolence could wish, omniscience conceive, or omnipotence execute ; and that the defects which we think we perceive in it spring from our ignorance, not from our wisdom, and will disappear as we grow wiser.

But the dictum of Emerson, that all laws are only One Law, does not help us a single step toward such a conclusion. The theory is not warranted by the facts as known to us, or, as far as we can understand it, knowable by us. More, to us it seems a mere play upon words ; or, rather, upon the word " Law." To say that the law of gravitation is identical with purity of heart, is to our mind as inept as it would be to affirm that a mile is as *long* as an hour, or that a convincing argument is as *weighty* as the mass of the globe.

If a "Philosophy of the Infinite" is to be framed by man, no man has ever framed a true one. Plato attempted it, and Emerson avers that he failed in the attempt. In that direction he has carried us no further than Moses had done. Emerson has attempted it ; yet we do not see that he has gone a step further than Plato had gone.

Yet, though Emerson has, as we think, failed to do what he proposed to himself to do, we by no means set light by what he has done. He has

taught us many lessons of virtue and of wisdom.
He has done much to ennoble our thoughts, to
elevate our aspirations, to enliven our hopes.   No
man can be the worse for reading him ; few men
but will be wiser and better for it.   Of Carlyle
we have said elsewhere : " He has taught us
multa sed non multum—many things, but not
much."   Of Emerson we may say : " He has
taught us *multa et multum*—many things, and
much " ; and of these many things, perhaps not
the least valuable is the indirect teaching that no
man has ever framed, or most likely will ever
frame, a " Philosophy of the Infinite " ; and that
the most which mortal man, or all mortal men,
can do, is to furnish a few quite finite contributions thereto.

XV.

EMERSON AS A POET.

THUS far Emerson has been considered mainly
as a philosopher, now busying himself—sometimes
partly losing himself—in the loftiest themes of
speculation ; and now turning his thoughts upon
the familiar topics relating to man's conduct of
life, as an individual and a member of society.
The citations in verse have been made in order to
elucidate some aspects of his philosophy rather

than for their own sake as poetry.   In that view also should be regarded the little poem " Brâhma," which in many minds stands as the representative of Emerson's verse :

BRÂHMA.

" If the red slayer think he slays,
    Or if the slain think he is slain,
  They know not well the winding ways
    I keep, and pass, and turn again.

" Far or forgot to me is near;
    Shadow and sunlight are the same;
  The vanished gods to me appear;
    And one to me are shame and fame.

" They reckon ill who leave me out;
    When me they fly, I am the wings;
  I am the doubter and the doubt,
    And I the hymn the Brahmin sings.

" The strong gods pine for my abode,
    And pine in vain the sacred seven;
  But thou, meek lover of the good,
    Find me, and turn thy back on heaven."

When this poem first appeared in the " Atlantic Monthly," it was the occasion of much shedding of ink on the part of the criticasters whose vocation is to furnish to the periodical press such wisdom as they have in regard to literary matters. To most of them it was utter nonsense ; a fit object of ridicule.   A volume might be made up of

the parodies upon it which appeared. It is, in
fact, an exposition of one of the profoundest of
all human faiths—the pure Buddhist theosophy,
freed from later increments of transmigration
and the like. Bráhma, "the Adorable" and in-
comprehensible, represents himself as the All in
All; as at once cause and effect—the subject and
the object of every action—at the same time the
doer and the thing done. The "strong gods,"
who appear to have come into being, and who are
themselves only illusionary apparitions of Bráhma, are by a bold stretch of imagination represented as pining to attain the knowledge of him;
the "sacred seven," by whom we understand the
seven wise men of antiquity, as representatives of
all intellectual wisdom, also pine in vain for the
knowledge which is reserved only for the "meek
lovers of the good"; and this knowledge is the
Nirvana—the complete and beatific absorption of
all individual being and consciousness into the
Infinite Being; and this involves the renunciation
of all that can be conceived of under the name of
"heaven." This idea, more or less developed,
has been a favorite one with speculative men in
all ages. We find it almost as fully expressed by
Boëthius in that poem so nobly translated by
Samuel Johnson, which finds place in some of
our hymn-books:

"From thee, great God, we sprung, to thee we tend:
  Path, motive, guide, original, and end."

We have styled Emerson "philosopher and poet." It remains to consider him specially in this latter capacity. Mr. Frothingham has said that it is only certain defects of rhythm and rhyme which prevent him from being the greatest of American poets. Emerson makes a like remark concerning Plato. However just this may be in regard to Plato, it is only partially just in regard to Emerson. That very many of his lines, and even whole poems, have defects of rhyme and rhythm, of metre and melody, must be admitted. But in most cases a very slight change of a word now and then, or the addition of a line here and there, would remove the defect. Yet there are among his poems many which in respect to mere external form are as complete and finished as any of those of Bryant or Longfellow or Whittier.

The longer pieces belong mainly to the class of descriptive poetry, which is often little more than measured or rhymed prose—always, indeed, unless it be interfused with spiritual and human analogies, linking the material to the immaterial thing, and shone upon by

> "A light which never was on sea or land—
> Imagination and the poet's dream."

"The Adirondacks," in unrhymed decasyllables, is on the face of it a mere narrative of a visit to that wild region of mountain and forest, river

and lake.   Preserving the metrical form, yet
omitting a few touches, and the residue would be
merely measured prose, none the better for being
cut up into measured lines, each having just so
many syllables and beats.   Changing a word here
and there, or the order of the words, so as to do
away with the metre, and the result would still
be "prose poetry."   Standing as it is, it is real
poetry, not indeed of the very highest class, but
very high in its class, deserving to rank with the
best of the like class in Wordsworth, and above
anything in Thomson.   We substantiate this by
somewhat extended quotations from the poem :

THE ADIRONDACKS.

"We crossed Champlain to Keesville with our friends,
  There, in strong country carts, rode up the forks
  Of the Ausable stream, intent to reach
  The Adirondack lakes.   At Martin's beach
  We chose our boat; each man a boat and guide—
  Ten men, ten guides, our company all told.
  Next morn we swept with oars the Saranac,
  With skies of benediction, to Round Lake,
  Where all the sacred mountains drew around us,
  Taháwus, Seaward, MacIntyre, Baldhead,
  And other Titans without muse or name.

"Pleased with these grand companions, we glide on,
  Instead of flowers crowned with a wreath of hills,
  And made our distance wider, boat from boat,
  As each would hear the oracle alone.

By the bright morn the gay flotilla slid
Through files that gleamed like bayonets,
Through goldmoth-haunted beds of pickerel flower,
Through scented banks of lilies, white and gold,
Where the deer feed at night, the teal by day,
On through the Upper Saranac, and up
Père Raquette stream to a small tortuous pass.
Winding through grassy shadows in and out,
Two creeping miles of rushes, pads, and sponge,
To Follansbee Water and the Lake of Loons.
Northward the length of Follansbee we rowed,
Under low mountains, whose unbroken ridge
Ponderous with beechen forest sloped the shore.
A pause and council: then, when near the head
On the east, a bay makes inward to the land
Between two rocky arms, we climb the bank,
And in the twilight of the forest noon
Wield the first axe these echoes ever heard.

"The wood was sovran with centennial trees—
Oak, cedar, maple, poplar, beech and fir,
Linden and spruce.   In strict society
Three conifers, white, pitch, and Norway pine,
Five-leaved, three-leaved, and two-leaved, grew there-
        by.
Our patron pine was fifteen feet in girth,
The maple eight, beneath its shapely tower.
'Welcome!' the wood-god murmured through the
        leaves—
Welcome, though late, unknowing, yet known to me.
Evening drew on: stars peeped through maple-boughs,
Which o'erhung, like a cloud, our camping-fire.
Decayed millennial trunks, like moonlight flecks,
Lit with phosphoric crumbs the forest-floor."

In "May-Day" the merely descriptive is admirable, but it is almost lost in the imaginative. The metrical construction, changing at frequent intervals, is almost faultless, and in perfect harmony with the change of thought:

MAY-DAY.

"Daughter of heaven and earth, coy Spring,
  With sudden passion languishing,
  Maketh all things softly smile,
  Painteth pictures mile on mile;
  Holds a cup with cowslip wreaths,
  Whence a smokeless incense breathes. . . .
  The air is full of whistlings bland;
    What was that I heard
  Out of the hazy land?
    Harp of the wind, or song of bird,
  Or clapping of the shepherd's hands,
    Or vagrant booming of the air,
  Voice of a meteor lost in day?
    Such tidings of the starry sphere
  Can this elastic air convey. . . .

"April, cold with dropping rain,
  Willows and lilacs brings again,
  The whistle of returning birds
  And the trumpet-lowing of the herds.
  The scarlet maple-keys betray
  What potent blood hath modest May;
  What fiery force the earth renews,
  The wealth of forms, the flush of hues;
  Joy, shed in rosy waves abroad,
  Flows from the heart of Love, the Lord. . . .

" Hither rolls the storm of Heat;
  I feel its finer billows beat
  Like a sea which me infolds;
  Heat, with viewless fingers, moulds,
  Swells and mellows, and matures,
  Paints and flavors, and allures;
  Bird and brier inly warms,
  Still enriches and transforms;
  Gives the reed and lily length,
  Adds to oak and oxen strength;
  Burns the world in tepid lakes,
  Burns the world, yet burnt remakes.
  Enveloping Heat, enchanted robe,
  Makes the daisy and the globe,
  Transforming what it doth infold—
  Life out of death, new out of old;
  Painting fawns' and leopards' fells,
  Seethes the gulf-encrimsoning shells;
  Fires gardens with a joyful blaze
  Of tulips in the morning's rays.
  The dead log touched bursts into leaf,
  The wheat-blade whispers of the sheaf.
  What god is this imperial Heat,
  Earth's prime secret, sculpture's seat?
  Doth it bear hidden in its heart
  Water-line patterns of all art?
  Is it Dædalus? is it Love?
  Or walks in mask almighty Jove,
  And drops from Power's redundant horn
  All seeds of beauty to be born? . . .

" Wreaths for the May! for happy Spring
  To-day shall all her dowry bring—

The love of kind, the joy, the grace,
Hymen of element and race—
Knowing well to celebrate
With song and hue, and star and state,
With tender light and youthful cheer,
The sponsals of the new-born year.
Lo, Love's inundation poured
Over space and race abroad ! . . .

"For thou, O Spring, canst renovate
All that high God did first create.
Be still his arm and architect,
Rebuild the ruin, mend defect;
Chemist to vamp old worlds with new,
Coat sea and sky with heavenlier blue;
New tint the plumage of the birds,
And slough decay from grazing herds;
Sweep ruins from the scarpèd mountain,
Cleanse the torrent at the fountain,
Purge Alpine air by towns defiled, .
Bring to fair mother fairer child;
Not less renew the heart and brain,
Scatter the sloth, wash out the stain;
Make the agèd eye sun-clear,
To parting soul bring grandeur near.

" Under gentle types, my Spring
Marks the might of Nature's king;
An energy that searches thorough,
From chaos to the dawning morrow;
Into all our human plight—
The soul's pilgrimage and flight.
In city or in solitude,
Step by step, lifts bad to good,

Without halting, without rest,
Lifting better up to best;
Planting seeds of knowledge pure,
Through earth to ripen, through heaven endure."

In the "Snow-storm" the same spiritual predominance is manifested. It opens with a few lines, telling how the snow arrives, "announced by all the trumpets of the sky," hiding hills, woods, rivers, and human habitations, wherein the inmates sit around the radiant fireplace, "inclosed in a tumultuous privacy of storm." Thence, in the keen, bright morning air, imagination goes out to "see the North-wind's masonry":

THE SNOW-STORM.

"Out of an unseen quarry, evermore
Furnished with file, the fierce artificer
Carves his white bastions, with projected roof,
Round every windward stake or tree or door,
Speeding, the myriad-handed, his wild work,
So fanciful, so savage. Nought cares he
For numbers or proportion. Mockingly,
On coop or kennel he hangs Parian wreaths;
A swan-like form invests the hidden thorn;
Fills up the farmer's lane from wall to wall,
Maugre the farmer's sighs; and at the gate
A tapering turret overtops the work.
And when his hours are numbered, and the world
Is all his own, retiring as he were not,
Leaves, when the Sun appears, astonished Art,
To mimic in slow structures, stone by stone,
Built in an age, the wind's night-work,
The frolic architecture of the snow."

It need not be said that the charm of this description is owing mainly not to the mere description of the snow-masonry, but to the investing of the viewless architect with thought, purpose, and will, making the unseen north-wind a type of that invisible spirit, who works in matter and mind, and is only known through his works. "The Rhodora" lines, written on being asked, "Whence is the Rhodora?" have deservedly found a place among our household poems.

Among what may be styled "Poems of the Affections," rather than "Poems of Love," it would not be easy to find one more delicate in thought, or more delicately expressed, than this:

TO EVA.

"O fair and stately maid, whose eyes
  Were kindled in the upper skies,
    At the same torch that lighted mine;
  For so I must interpret still
  Thy sweet dominion o'er my will—
    A sympathy divine.

"Ah! let me blameless gaze upon
  Features that seem at heart my own;
    Nor fear those watchful sentinels,
  Who charm the more their glance forbids,
Chaste-glowing underneath their lids
    With fire that draws while it repels."

Pitched to a higher key, and far more deeply touching the deepest chords of the human heart, is the long "Threnody," a lament for one of those "whom the gods love," who died young. We give only a small part of this:

THRENODY.

" The South-wind brings
   Life, sunshine, and desire,
And on every mount and meadow
   Breathes aromatic fire:
But over the dead he has no power;
The lost, the lost, he cannot restore;
And, looking over the hills, I mourn
The darling who shall not return.

" I see my empty house;
   I see my trees repair their boughs;
And he, the wondrous child,
Whose silver warble wild
Outvalued every passing sound
Within the air's cerulean round—
The hyacinthine boy, for whom
Morn might break and April bloom—
The gracious boy, who did adorn
The world whereinto he was born,
And by his countenance repay
The favor of the loving Day—
Has disappeared from the Day's eye;
Far and wide she cannot find him;
My hopes pursue, they cannot bind him.
Returned this day, the South-wind searches,
And finds young pines and budding birches,
   But finds not the budding man.

Nature, who lost him, cannot remake him;
Fate let him fall, Fate can't retake him;
　　Nature, Fate, men, him seek in vain.

"O child of Paradise!
Boy who made dear his father's home,
　　In whose deep eyes
Men read the welfare of the times to come!
I am too much bereft.
The world dishonored thou hast left.
Oh, Truth's and Nature's costly lie!
Oh, richest fortune sourly crossed!
Born for the future, to the future lost!"

Thus far, and through many more stanzas, the "Threnody" breathes the mournful tone of the Greek Moschus, who, in his elegy upon Bion, the idyllic poet, after lamenting over all the once green herbs now lying withered in autumn, bursts out:

"These live again at last, and in another year
　　Spring forth.　But we, the great, the mighty, and the
　　　　wise
Of men, when once we die, unhearing in the ground,
We sleep the long, unending, unawakening sleep."

All this is touching, and true so far as the common conception of the Greeks went; for, according to this, death was an unawakening sleep to all save a few of the human race. In Elysium there was no place except for the greatly good; in Tartarus, for none except the greatly bad; none in either for the child early cut off. But in the close of the "Threnody" Emerson rises to a loftier vision—a vision springing from the universal harmonies of Nature. To his mournful plaint—

> "The deep Heart answered: Weepest thou?
> Worthier cause for passion wild
> If I had *not* taken the child.
> And deemest thou as those who pore,
> With agèd eyes, short way before—
> Think'st Beauty vanished from the coast
> Of matter, and thy darling lost?—
> Taught he not thee—the man of eld,
> Whose eyes within his eyes beheld
> Heaven's numerous hierarchy span
> The mystic gulf from God to man?
> To be alone, wilt thou begin,
> When worlds of lovers hem thee in?—
> To-morrow, when the masks shall fall,
> That dizzen Nature's carnival,
> The pure shall see by their own will,
> Which overflowing Love shall fill,
> 'Tis not within the force of Fate,
> The Fate-conjoined to separate. . . .

> " Wilt thou not ope thy heart to know
> What rainbows teach, and sunsets show?
> Verdict which accumulates
> From lengthening scroll of human fates;
> Voice of earth to earth returned;
> Prayers of saints that only burned—
> Saying: *What is excellent,*
> *As God lives, is permanent;*

21

Hearts are dust, hearts' loves remain;
Heart's loves will meet with thee again. . . .
Silent rushes the swift Lord
Through ruined systems still restored;
Broad-sowing, bleak and void to bless,
Plants with worlds the wilderness;
Waters with tears of ancient sorrow
Apples of Eden, ripe to-morrow.
House and tenant go to ground,
Lost in God, in Godhead found."

In poetry, as well as in prose, Emerson's range of themes is not a very wide one. Only rarely has he written anything inspired by the current events of the day. Of the few poems of this sort which he has written, it can only be said that they are about as good as the mass of those of the sort. The best of these is the hymn for the celebration of the inauguration of the Concord Monument, April 19, 1836, the last two lines of the first stanza of which have a clear and sharp ring:

THE CONCORD HYMN.

"By the rude bridge that arched the flood,
  Their flag to April breeze unfurled,
Here once the embattled farmer stood,
  And fired the shot heard round the world.

"The foe long since in silence slept;
  Alike the conqueror silent sleeps;
And Time the ruined bridge has swept
  Down the dark stream which seaward creeps.

"On this green bank, by this soft stream,
  We set to-day a votive stone ;
That memory may their deed redeem,
  When, like our sires, our sons are gone.

"Spirit that made these heroes dare
  To die, and leave their children free,
Bid Time and Nature gently spare
  The shaft we raise to them and thee."

Mere humor rarely has place in the poems of
Emerson ; but the following "fable" is worthy
of Æsop or La Fontaine :

THE MOUNTAIN AND THE SQUIRREL.

"The mountain and the squirrel
  Had a quarrel ;
And the former called the latter 'Little Prig.'
  Bun replied :
You are doubtless very big ;
  But all sorts of things and weather
  Must be taken in together
    To make up a year
    And a sphere,
  And I think it no disgrace
    To occupy my place.
  If I'm not so large as you,
    You are not so small as I,
    And not half so spry.
  I'll not deny you make
  A very pretty squirrel track ;
Talents differ ; all is well and wisely put ;
  If I cannot carry forests on my back,
Neither can you crack a nut."

There are a number of quatrains which are real epigrams, such as these :

BORROWING TROUBLE.

"Some of your hurts you have cured,
   And the sharpest you have still survived;
But what torments of grief you endured
   From evils which never arrived!"

HOROSCOPE.

"Ere he was born, the stars of fate
   Plotted to make him rich and great;
When from the womb the babe was loosed,
   The gates of gifts behind him closed."

YESTERDAY, TO-MORROW, TO-DAY.

"Shines the last age, the next with hope is seen,
   To-day slinks poorly off, unmarked between:
Future or Past, no richer secret folds,
   O friendless Present! than thy bosom holds."

SACRIFICE.

"Though love repine and reason chafe,
   There came a voice without reply :
'Tis man's perdition to be safe,
   When for the truth he ought to die."

The general idea of the irreversible past, so often expressed, has never been more characteristically set forth than in the following poem :

THE PAST.

"The debt is paid,
　The verdict said,
　The Furies laid,
　The plague is stayed,
　All fortunes made.
Turn the key and bolt the door,
Sweet is death forevermore.
Nor haughty Hope, nor swart Chagrin,
Nor murdering Hate can enter in.
All is now secure and fast;
Not the gods can shake the Past;
Flies-to the adamantine door,
Bolted down forevermore.
　None can reënter there.
No thief so politic,
No Satan with his royal trick,
　Steal in by window, chink, or hole,
To bind or unbind, add what lacked,
　Insert a leaf or forge a name,
New-face or finish what is packed,
Alter or mend eternal Fact."

In the "Song of Nature," poetry and the
Emersonian philosophy are blended. Only about
half of the stanzas are here cited :

THE SONG OF NATURE.

" Mine are the night and morning,
　The pits of air, the gulf of space,
The sportive sun, the gibbous moon,
　The innumerable days.

"I wrote the past in characters
 Of rock and fire the scroll—
The building in the coral sea,
 The planting of the coal.

"Time and Thought were my surveyors;
 They laid their courses well;
They boiled the sea and baked the layers
 Of granite, marl, and shell.

"But he, the Man-child glorious—
 Where tarries he the while?
The rainbow shines his harbinger,
 The sunset gleams his smile.

"I travail in pain for him,
 My creatures travail and wait;
His couriers come by squadrons,
 He comes not to the gate.

"Twice have I moulded an image,
 And thrice outstretched my hand:
Made one of clay, and one of night,
 And one of the salt sea-sand.

"One in a Judæan manger, ·
 And one by Avon stream,
One over against the mouths of Nile,
 And one in Académe.

"I moulded kings and saviours,
 And bards o'er kings to rule:
But fell the starry influence short,
 The cup was never full.

" Yet whirl the glowing wheels once more,
   And mix the bowl again ;
Seethe, Fate ! the ancient elements,
   Heat, cold, wet, dry, and peace, and pain.

" Let war and trade and creeds and song
   Blend, ripen race on race—
The sunburnt world a man shall breed
   Of all the zones, and countless days."

Here we conclude what we had to say by way
of setting forth and elucidating Emerson's right
to be ranked among the true poets of this country and of all countries, of this age and of many
ages to come. We think it indisputable. Most
likely his audience at any one time will be comparatively small. In a single half-generation the
platitudes of a Tupper found more admirers than
Emerson will have found for ages. But be his
auditors many or few, they will surely be " fit."
If voters were to be weighed, not counted, his
would be a heavy vote. And, in the long result,
it will be weight, not numbers, which will decide
the final issue.

THE END.